A TOWN CALLED HARMONY

Delightful tales that capture the heart of a small Kansas town—and a simple time when love was a gift to cherish . . .

KEEPING FAITH
by Kathleen Kane

TAKING CHANCES
by Rebecca Hagan Lee

CHASING RAINBOWS
by Linda Shertzer

PASSING FANCY
by Lydia Browne

PLAYING CUPID
by Donna Fletcher

COMING HOME
by Kathleen Kane

GETTING HITCHED
by Ann Justice

HOLDING HANDS
by Jo Anne Cassity
[FEBRUARY 1995]

AMAZING GRACE
by Deborah James
[MARCH 1995]

Available from Diamond Books

Dear Reader . . .

There's a place where life moves a little slower, where a neighborly smile and a friendly hello can still be heard. Where news of a wedding or a baby on the way is a reason to celebrate—and gossip travels faster than a telegraph! Where hope lives in the heart, and love's promises last a lifetime.

The year is 1874, and the place is Harmony, Kansas . . .

A TOWN CALLED HARMONY

GETTING HITCHED

Instead of forever daydreaming about her ideal man, Mary Taylor decided to find him—by advertising for a mail-order husband.

Exploring the West kept him roaming for five years. But lately Matthew Hubbard had the urge to settle down—and he came to Harmony in response to Mary's ad.

Still unwed at twenty-one, Mary spent her nights sewing with the gossipy ladies in town—and was perilously close to becoming an old maid. Then this breathtakingly handsome man entered her life, and it was like a dream come true—they were instantly attracted to each other, they seemed to get along fine, and planned to be married right away. But that was before their first argument . . . Shaken by a misunderstanding on the day before their wedding, Mary handed Matthew a list of conditions, a guarantee that her husband-to-be would never hurt her or let her down. Outraged, Matthew makes plans to hightail it out of Harmony—and Mary begins to see that she's never learned the first thing about loving a real man, with all his imperfections. In a very unusual courtship, she must woo Matthew back before they tie the knot, as they discover that true love means trusting each other— from this day forward . . .

Welcome to
A TOWN CALLED HARMONY . . .

MAISIE HASTINGS & MINNIE PARKER, *proprietors of the boarding house . . .* These lively ladies, twins who are both widowed, are competitive to a fault—who bakes the lightest biscuits? Whose husband was worse? Who can say the most eloquent and (to their boarders' chagrin) the longest grace? And who is the better matchmaker? They'll do almost anything to outdo each other—and absolutely everything to bring loving hearts together!

JAKE SUTHERLAND, *the blacksmith . . .* Amidst the workings of his livery stable, he feels right at home. But when it comes to talking to a lady, Jake is awkward, tongue-tied . . . and positively timid!

JANE CARSON, *the dressmaker . . .* She wanted to be a doctor like her grandfather. But the eccentric old man decided that wasn't a ladylike career—and bought her a dress shop. Jane named it in his honor: You Sew And Sew. She can sew anything, but she'd rather stitch a wound than a hem.

ALEXANDER EVANS, *the newspaperman . . .* He runs *The Harmony Sentinel* with his daughter, Samantha. It took an accident at his press to show Alexander that even a solitary newsman needs love and caring—and he found it in the arms of his lovely bride, Jane Carson.

JAMES AND LILLIAN TAYLOR, *owners of the mercantile and post office* . . . With their six children, they're Harmony's wealthiest and most prolific family. Their daughter Libby got herself married to the town sheriff. But none of the local bachelors are of interest to their girl Mary—so she takes a chance on a mail-order husband!

"LUSCIOUS" LOTTIE McGEE, *owner of "The First Resort"* . . . Lottie's girls sing and dance and even entertain upstairs . . . but Lottie herself is the main attraction at her enticing saloon. And when it comes to taking care of her own cousin, this enticing madam is all maternal instinct.

CORD SPENCER, *owner of "The Last Resort"* . . . Things sometimes get out of hand at Spencer's rowdy tavern, but he's mostly a good-natured scoundrel who doesn't mean any harm. And when push comes to shove, he'd be the first to put his life on the line for a friend.

SHERIFF TRAVIS MILLER, *the lawman* . . . The townsfolk don't always like the way he bends the law a bit when the saloons need a little straightening up. But Travis Miller listens to only one thing when it comes to deciding on the law: his conscience.

ZEKE GALLAGHER, *the barber and the dentist* . . . When he doesn't have his nose in a dime western, the white-whiskered, blue-eyed Zeke is probably making up stories of his own—*or* flirting with the ladies. But not all his tales are just talk—once he really *was* a notorious gunfighter . . .

A TOWN CALLED HARMONY

GETTING HITCHED

Ann Justice

DIAMOND BOOKS, NEW YORK

This book is a Diamond original edition, and has never been previously published.

GETTING HITCHED

A Diamond Book / published by arrangement with the author

PRINTING HISTORY
Diamond edition / January 1995

All rights reserved.
Copyright © 1995 by Charter Communications, Inc.
This book may not be reproduced in whole or in part, by mimeograph or any other means, without permission.
For information address: The Berkley Publishing Group, 200 Madison Avenue, New York, NY 10016.

ISBN: 0-7865-0067-0

Diamond Books are published by The Berkley Publishing Group, 200 Madison Avenue, New York, NY 10016.
DIAMOND and the "D" design are trademarks belonging to Charter Communications, Inc.

PRINTED IN THE UNITED STATES OF AMERICA

10 9 8 7 6 5 4 3 2 1

GETTING HITCHED

CHAPTER

1

He stepped off the train and for an instant was lost to her in the swirling fog and smoke. It was night, and he had come as he had promised. Her heart pounded as she watched him stride the length of the platform, his eyes searching the crowd for a glimpse of her. His worn saddlebags were slung over one powerful shoulder. The black hat that was as uniquely his as a signature was pushed back on his head, and the lamplight from the station caught the features of his handsome face, accentuating the rugged and weathered beauty of his skin and the eyes shielded by long lashes.

When he spotted her at last, he paused for an instant and then shrugged off the heavy saddlebags, allowing them to fall to the ground. He ran the last yards to sweep her high into his powerful arms as if she were no heavier than a butterfly . . . in fact, that's what he called her as his mouth descended to hers. "My little butterfly . . ." The rest was lost in the passion and hunger of the kiss.

*   *   *

"Mary Taylor!"

Mary blinked and whirled in the direction of the sound of her name. Maisie Hastings frowned down at her from across the counter of Taylor's Mercantile. Maisie was older and taller by quite a few years and inches. Mary felt a little like a delinquent schoolgirl under the woman's stern gaze.

"I'm sorry, Miz Hastings," Mary said as she turned her attention back to measuring the flour Maisie had come into the store to buy. "Was there something else?"

Maisie pursed her lips and tucked one single strand of gray hair back under her bonnet. "Heavens, no. As slow as you are today, I'd be a sight better off raising my own wheat, milling it, and making my own flour. What are you lollygagging about for, Mary?"

"I just didn't hear you," Mary answered, wondering what the devil Maisie had been yelling about if there was nothing else she wanted.

"You didn't hear the four-oh-eight eastbound train coming through, either. Lord, child, you wouldn't have heard a tornado coming right down Main Street. Now, hurry up with that, or Minnie is bound to find some excuse to make that glop she calls corn bread before I can get some descent biscuit dough stirred up for supper."

Maisie and her twin sister, Minnie, ran the local boarding-house, and if ever there was a more incongruous place for the two sisters to live than Harmony, Kansas, Mary could not imagine it. Harmony was the last thing that reigned whenever Minnie and Maisie were in a room together. They competed in everything, contradicted each other on every issue, and gener-ally kept the townspeople supplied with plenty to talk about with their latest antics.

"Sister, dear, I thought you said a moment only." Minnie Parker stood at the double doors of the general store silhouetted against the strong, late September sun.

Maisie frowned and raised her eyebrows at Mary as if to say, *See what you've done now.*

"It's my fault, Miz Parker," Mary called as she hurried to

finish filling the flour order. Had Maisie wanted one pound or two?

"That's too much," Maisie whispered impatiently as Mary doubled her efforts to scoop the white powder into the sack.

"It's on the house," Mary replied. "Tell Miz Parker you got a bargain." She closed the sack and plopped it on the counter. Flour dust exploded in all directions and settled on Maisie's navy bonnet and Mary's black hair. Minnie pulled her lace handkerchief from the sleeve of her dress and coughed into it delicately.

"Will there be anything else, ladies?" Mary asked sweetly.

"No, Mary. Thank you." Maisie picked up her purchase and headed for the door. "Don't dawdle, dear," she said to her sister as she swept grandly past her and out to the boardwalk. "We have a great deal to do before supper."

When they were gone and the store was quiet once more, Mary took her time wiping the flour from the counter, hoping to escape once more into the fantasy of her daydreams. She liked having the store all to herself. Weekday afternoons in the fall were always slow. Most folks were occupied with the harvest. Her father, the store's owner, was busy with the mill the family also owned, and her mother Lillian was off at one of her political or social meetings . . . Mary could not keep up with which one Lillie Taylor had announced would be held this afternoon. Mary sincerely hoped that the meeting was her mother's book discussion group or garden club.

Lillie Taylor was given to causes and projects, grandiose schemes she saw as a means to put Harmony on the map and to bring its citizens the cultural and moral lifestyle she deemed necessary for happiness. Unfortunately Lillie's schemes usually involved everyone . . . especially Mary.

Thanks to her older sister, Libby, Mary had been designated as the "good" daughter. Lillie had made it her mission to show the people of Harmony that at least this daughter was responsible and properly raised. It was bad enough that Libby had moved back to town following the death of her husband and started the Temperance Union, getting the entire town up in arms before she was finished. On top of that, she and the town's sheriff, Travis Miller, had practically made love on Main Street before they were even formally engaged, much less married.

Oh, Lillie had made the best of that by hustling the two of them down the aisle and pretending the whole thing was incredibly romantic . . . which in Mary's eyes, it was. But the truth was Mary's mother had been hell-bent to restore the Taylor name to its former dignity and respectability ever since, and Mary had been selected as the means to do that.

As the oldest child at home, Mary was expected to manage the store when her parents were busy elsewhere. Once she married she supposed the job would fall to her younger sister Sissy. After all, before her older sister Libby had gotten married the first time and her brother Joseph had taken the job as stationmaster at the train station, they had been the ones to manage the store.

Certainly once Mary got married . . . if she ever got married . . .

"Mary, Mary! Thank goodness you're here. Everyone else seems to have disappeared for the afternoon. I just have to share this with someone or I'll burst!" Samantha Spencer rushed into the store and down the center aisle to the counter waving the latest edition of the town newspaper. "The *Sentinel* has come into the modern age at last," Samantha announced as she spread open the paper on the counter. She quickly thumbed to the back of the paper and with a triumphant smile pointed to a single column. "Classifieds," she said proudly.

Samantha and her father ran the newspaper. Samantha wrote and edited a great deal of the content, and with her Eastern education was always anxious to have her paper measure up to what she thought the city dailies out East might contain.

"Classifieds," Mary repeated, smiling and nodding as she bent to get a closer look at the column.

"You know . . . for instance, if your mother and father needed to hire extra help for the store or the mill, they could place a help-wanted notice . . . a classified advertisement."

"Oh." Mary hoped she sounded properly impressed. She didn't want to mention that in the past if extra help was needed, word of mouth was adequate to have someone on the job within a day, if not sooner.

"Harmony is growing," Samantha continued. "We're not some little wide place in the road anymore. The paper needs to come along with the times . . . mirror that growth . . ."

Mary had stopped listening. One ad's headline had captured her attention: WIFE WANTED.

"What? Which one are you reading?" Samantha peered down at the column to where Mary had placed her finger, marking her place as she read the ad.

WIFE WANTED

Must be willing to cook, clean, and raise 3 orphaned children. Must be good Christian woman, not too young or old, willing to work hard in exchange for place on farm between Ellsworth and Salina.

The information was followed by a box number. There were two other ads seeking mail-order brides, and Mary noticed that not one of them said anything about what the woman might expect from the situation other than hard work and a roof over her head.

"I don't believe it," Mary said as she scanned each ad. "Do women actually answer these . . . actually do this?"

"Of course," Samantha said breezily. "Mail-order brides are quite common." She winked and leaned closer. "I guess the men get a little lonesome living out there in the middle of nowhere for months on end. After a bit they need some . . . uh, companionship of the female sort." Then she frowned. "As a matter of fact, Abby Lee Sutherland was a mail-order bride."

Mary tried to imagine the quiet, shy blacksmith placing an ad for a woman. "Jake would never—"

"Oh, heavens no, not Jake." Samantha giggled at the

preposterous idea. "No, it was her first husband . . . the one who was killed in some sort of fracas out in Wyoming?"

Like everyone else in Harmony, Mary had heard the stories and rumors. Abby Lee had been found huddled on the doorstep of the First Resort saloon, pregnant and badly beaten. Jake had helped deliver the child, Dinah. Abby Lee had stayed on in Harmony, earning her living by playing piano at the saloon. She and Jake had fallen in love and married and were now raising Dinah together.

"Actually I think Abby Lee is the best thing that ever happened to Jake Sutherland. Why, the man positively beams, and he's become so . . . loquacious," Samantha prattled on. "And Abby Lee—why, heavens, have you ever seen a more darling and talented girl? Why, that rose garden of hers is the envy of everyone. She still has roses in full bloom, and we're almost to October. Must be all that loving—in *and* out of the house, if you know what I mean." She gave a hoot of laughter.

Since Samantha had married the raucous and devilish Cord Spencer, she had definitely changed. Once she'd been quite prim and oh-so-proper, but loving Cord had changed all that. These days Samantha was as open and honest about what she felt to be the wonders of love and marriage as she had once been horrified by the goings-on at Cord's Last Resort saloon.

"Maybe you should answer one, Mary," Samantha suggested slyly, nodding toward the ads seeking mail-order brides.

"Absolutely not." Mary practically leaped away from the open paper. "I'm not that desperate," she added primly. Not yet, anyway, she thought ruefully.

Samantha laughed gaily. "I'm just kidding, though heaven knows we could use a bit of fresh blood in this town. Since Faith married Kincaid, there just doesn't seem to be anyone left . . . I mean, not that I'm looking for myself, but there's you and . . ." She faltered slightly and frowned.

"Yes, there's me," Mary said softly, knowing that Samantha had stopped because she was hard-pressed to come up with any other eligible young women in town who weren't married yet, or at least promised.

"Well, it isn't as if you haven't had opportunities," Samantha said as she briskly folded the newspaper and laid it on the edge of the counter. She perused the selection of hard candy in the jars that lined the top of the divider between where Mary stood and the postal station. "I mean, heavens, the Lind boy was clearly head over heels for you. And then there was that stagecoach worker . . . Danny, wasn't it?" She selected three horehound sticks and half a dozen licorice whips and placed them in front of Mary.

Mary wrapped the candy and accepted the coins Samantha handed her, noticing the beautiful and obviously new silk reticule Samantha opened to deposit her change. Samantha was always dressed in the height of fashion. "Yes, there have been opportunities," Mary agreed.

"And good for you for not settling," Samantha said firmly, her eyes riveted on Mary's face. "You're quite lovely, and one day soon I just know some handsome stranger is going to show up here, ready to make a life in Harmony, and just literally sweep you off your feet, Mary Taylor."

Mary smiled. "Anything's possible," she agreed.

"Now then, will you be going to Bea Arnold's for the Quilt Circle tonight?" Samantha's change of tone told Mary the newspaper editor had an assignment for her.

"I might," she hedged.

"Oh, you must. I understand Faith Hutton may be pregnant. If anyone knows, those women will. It must be something that comes with age, but it seems every woman has a sixth sense about such things once she passes forty. Anyway, you'll let me know first thing tomorrow?"

"I'll see what I can find out," Mary said.

"Wonderful. Well, I'm off. Cord promised to be home for supper tonight, and if I play my cards right, maybe I can get him to forget about going back to work for once." She smiled mischievously, picked up the package of candy, and left the store.

"Your paper," Mary called, but Samantha was already halfway across the street by the time Mary reached the door.

She watched her friend navigate the rutted street, lifting her fashionable skirts to keep them as safe as possible from the dust clouds raised by a passing wagon.

Mary saw Cord Spencer watching his wife move toward him, his eyes shadowed by the brim of his hat. Mary might not be able to see the man's eyes, but everything about his posture and the set of his mouth revealed that he was watching the woman he wanted more than any other . . . the woman he loved. It was exactly the way the man in Mary's fantasy had looked at her when he stepped off the train, and he'd been far handsomer than Cord Spencer or any other man in Harmony.

Cord offered his hand to his wife to help her step onto the boardwalk. But when she was safely there, he did not release her hand. Instead the two of them stood looking at each other, and the undisguised desire in that look made Mary turn away. What she saw between Cord and Samantha, and more recently between Libby and Travis, was so incredibly private that Mary felt like an intruder. Would she ever look at a man that way, oblivious to the rest of the world? More to the point, would a man ever look at Mary Taylor as if the only thing on his mind was to take her in his arms and the rest of the world and propriety be damned?

"Quite frankly, I think Faith Hutton has quite enough to do without being pregnant on top of everything else." Mary's mother, Lillian, adjusted the thimble on her finger and bent to examine her handiwork.

Bea Arnold jabbed her needle through the quilt patch she was appliquéing and frowned. "It seems to me that all our young women are more interested in running businesses than they are in doing what God gave them to do." She glanced over the tops of her glasses at Mary.

"Faith and Kincaid are doing a wonderful job with the hotel and restaurant," Mary said quietly.

Bea raised her eyebrows and continued her sewing. "Well, it just seems to me that if you young women insist on taking over the men's jobs, you're gonna find yourselves alone and lonely in your later years. In my day——"

"Oh, honestly, Bea," Minnie Parker interrupted, "you talk as if you're eighty-five instead of fifty. Times are changing."

"But I do believe our Bea makes a valid point, Sister dear," Maisie argued. "Take Mary, for example. Lately she's forever behind the counter of that store of yours, Lillie. How do you expect her to meet an appropriate suitor?"

"I expect that one day Mary will look up and straight into the eyes of some extremely appropriate suitor, that she'll probably not recognize him as her future husband, but that he will nevertheless persevere. By the time we next have this conversation, it will be Mary's pregnancy we will be debating." Lillie winked at her daughter and laid her handwork aside, a clear signal that she was about to change the subject. "Now, ladies, shall we discuss the Harvest Festival?"

The Harvest Festival was her mother's latest plan for Harmony's social scene. It was to be an annual event, featuring food and games and dancing for the whole town and surrounding rural community. In her usual manner, Lillie simply assumed the women in the sewing circle would be as enchanted with the idea as she was.

Mary allowed the discussion to whirl around her while she considered what her mother had said. She knew that in Lillie's mind the young suitor who would magically appear across the counter one day was someone already known to Mary and her family. But Mary could not think of one eligible man in the whole region with whom she would consider spending the rest of her life.

She knew what she wanted in a husband and a marriage, and as wonderful as things were for Faith Hutton and Abby Sutherland and her own sister, Libby, Mary wanted something . . . different. When she thought of a man in her life, it was someone who had seen places she had only dreamed of . . . who might take her to those places. Oh, she'd always want to come home to Harmony, but to travel and meet other people—other kinds of people—that was her dream.

No, her mother was wrong. The man who would win Mary Taylor's hand would never do so by standing docilely on the other side of the counter at the Taylor Mercantile. He might emerge from the fog of the night or come galloping up to her on his huge stallion or step off the train one day, thinking he would only pause for a bit in Harmony, Kansas, unaware that he was about to meet the love of his life there.

"Mary!"

Mary glanced at the forgotten handwork on her lap and turned toward Maisie Hastings, who was looking at her curiously. "I swear, Lillie," Maisie announced as she spoke to Mary's mother but kept her clear blue eyes focused directly on Mary, "I think the child may be developing a hearing problem."

"I'm sorry," Mary stammered, trying to remember the thread of the conversation. "I was thinking of something else."

"Something? Or someone?" Minnie said softly and then smiled knowingly.

"Well, all I can say, Mary Taylor," Bea announced grandly as she bit off a new thread and knotted it, "is whoever that young man on your mind is, you'd best consider the idea of spending less time managing that store and more time looking in the mirror. You could do with a bit of color in those cheeks, and that dress is—"

"May I serve the lemonade and cookies now, Bea?" Lillie Taylor stood and moved toward the table set with refreshments in Bea's small parlor.

The other ladies in the sewing circle glanced at one another uncomfortably. Everyone knew that Lillie Taylor would gossip with the best of the townspeople, but if someone started on one of her children, the subject would be changed or closed.

"Let me help you, Mother," Mary said, laying her own handwork aside and moving closer to the warmth of her mother's smile.

Later that night Mary lay awake long after the busy Taylor household had grown quiet. She found herself mulling over the conversation at Bea Arnold's. What was she doing spending her evenings sitting and sewing with these women, most of whom were old enough to be her mother?

Lillie had insisted Mary attend the sessions after Libby married. It was as if she wanted to keep her eye on Mary every moment. When Mary had protested spending so much time with the older women of the town, Lillie had dismissed her objections.

"You sew beautifully, dear, and I need your eyes and ears there so that I'll know if there are any problems. I'd hate to have the circle fall apart."

Mary did enjoy sewing, and she was extremely good at it. Besides, the gossip and reminiscing the older ladies did was fascinating. They talked of the old days when Harmony had first been settled. They talked of parents who had come cross-country by covered wagon. They talked of Indians and places back East she'd only read about. They talked of people who had come and gone and left their mark on the town and its history. It was all so incredibly romantic to Mary.

But the fact was she was twenty-one years old, and instead of spending her evenings buggy-riding with some eligible bachelor, she had spent another evening sitting in Bea Arnold's parlor, sewing and gossiping and making judgments on other people's lives. Lord, she was becoming an old maid.

Mary pushed back the covers and padded barefoot to the dresser. She lit the lamp and studied her reflection in the mirror. Bea had said she needed color. Mary had always thought her smooth pale skin in contrast to the midnight of her hair was one of her best features. Even the unexpected sprinkling of freckles across her nose didn't bother her. Her eyes were large and dark, and her mouth . . . well, her mouth was a bit on the full side, it was true. But she wasn't so bad looking. She didn't have the voluptuous curves of Faith Hutton, but . . .

She stepped back and pressed her muslin gown tight around her small body and sighed. There was no *but*. She was skinny and flat-chested and short. And the fact of the matter was that there wasn't a man in Harmony of marriageable age who didn't think of her as Joe's kid sister. Furthermore, the chance of some handsome stranger stepping off the train and choosing her seemed remote from several angles. One, the last eligible man who'd stepped off the train had turned out to be a con man and been run out of town by her brother-in-law, Sheriff Travis Miller. And two, if some romantic hero did come riding into town, in all likelihood his ideal woman would *not* be barely five feet tall, weigh less than a hundred pounds, and have trouble making even a ripple in the shape of a nightgown.

Mary sighed and looked out the window. The town was quiet except for the faint sound of the music and laughter coming from Cord Spencer's saloon. She sighed again and sank down on the edge of her bed. The truth was, the only way Mary Taylor was going to have any say at all in the man she married was to make sure somehow that before he ever met her he had already agreed to her terms and expectations for what the marriage would be. She knew from her experience with Danny Vega of the stagecoach line that men just thought she was being cute when she talked of all the ways she wanted her married life to be different.

Why, as recently as last month Danny had laughed at her when she'd begun to outline her ideas to him. "Darling," he said, "you are so funny—I like that about you. When we're married, I hope our kids have that same funny side you have."

And when Mary had insisted she was serious in her expectations, he'd looked down at her and frowned. "I think we'd best have an understanding, Mary Taylor. If we marry, things will be the way I say. I'll take care of you, but I don't need some woman telling me what to do."

"Then you don't want me," Mary had answered and walked into her parents' house and run up the stairs to the family living quarters over the store, without so much as a backward look.

Mary sighed and punched the pillow. How come everybody else seemed to get exactly the man they hoped for, exactly the life they hoped for? Well, she could have that, too. She just had to stop waiting for something to happen by itself and make a plan. Mary had that much of her mother's nature in her. If things weren't going along the way you thought they should, then you simply needed to make a plan that would change the course of events.

She moved to her writing table and pulled out a notebook and pen. Carrying them to her dresser where she'd lit the lamp, Mary pushed aside the paraphernalia that cluttered the surface and began to write.

Several minutes later she looked at the finished product and drew in a sharp breath. The paper had a number of scratched-out lines. She had begun a column entitled *Physical Description* and jotted down a range of ages from *22–35*, then scratched it out. There followed the words *handsome, tall, well muscled* . . . all scratched out. And then the words:

HUSBAND WANTED

Age and looks not important. Intelligent, modern woman seeks companion to share travel and adventure, yet willing to settle down in Kansas community to work and start family. Only men who are openminded need apply.

Good Lord, she had written an ad for a mail-order husband.

CHAPTER

2

Matthew Hubbard sat next to his campfire, listening to the sounds of the night. He deliberately stirred the fire so that it would crack and spark. Once it settled, he was again surrounded by a vast silence. He leaned against his saddle and sighed. Matt would give his right arm for somebody to talk to right now, and that didn't even come close to saying what he'd give to have a good hot bath and sleep in a soft bed, preferably with a soft woman next to him.

With nothing else to do, he carried the thought one step further and wondered what he might be willing to give up if that woman had half a brain and could carry on a decent conversation while rubbing his aching back. To say Matt Hubbard was lonely was possibly the greatest understatement of 1874.

Just then his horse, Traveler II, snorted as if ridiculing the folly of his master's thought. Matthew smiled. "Just go to sleep," he muttered aloud in the general direction of the animal. Matt got up and rearranged his blanket preparatory to getting some sleep himself. He lay down with his hands behind his head and stared up at the stars.

Funny how when he'd been lying in camp back in Virginia during the war, the stars had looked the same as they did out here in the wilderness of Colorado. But those nights he'd been surrounded by other men—boys mostly, waiting to do battle with the Yanks come daybreak . . . scared, exhausted, brave, and often doomed kids.

Hubbard's company had been there at Appomattox when Lee and Grant met . . . when Lee had surrendered. He'd seen the general take that last long ride past his troops, and Matt had felt glad it was over and proud to have served under such an incredible man as Robert E. Lee.

The next day Matt had headed home to Tennessee with a fresh horse his commanding officer had given him and which Matt had named Traveler II in honor of the General Lee's horse, Traveler. Every horse Matt had owned since had been named the same thing. There was something about that day he never wanted to forget . . . something about the futility of war . . . how little all the lost lives and destruction had really meant in the long run.

Increasingly on these long lonely nights out under the stars, Matt thought about those days, going over and over them in his mind, trying to find the key to what he might have done differently . . . how things might have turned out better. He remembered his homecoming, how proud and relieved his father had been. He remembered the months of struggle to put everything back together for his father and himself. He remembered . . .

Matt's mother had died the summer he enlisted. He had heard the news as he marched east toward Richmond. Now as he stood beside her grave, he was glad she hadn't had to suffer the years of the war, didn't have to witness the devastation all around them. How his mother would have hated what the war had done to the people and places she cherished. For Tess Hubbard had been a loving and giving woman. She had cared for the people around her without regard for their station in life. A slave was the same as family to her.

Matt recalled one time when his father had been gone, and Tess had observed the new overseer chastising and then whipping one of the young Negroes who worked the fields of the Hubbard tobacco plantation. Matt had only been eight or nine at the time, but the image of his mother in that moment was one he'd carried with him all his life.

Tess Hubbard had observed the action for less than a moment, then walked into the house and reappeared with one of Jack's hunting rifles. From the veranda she had taken aim and fired, and the whip had gone flying out of the overseer's upraised hand.

"Mr. Bennett," she had called as she had calmly lowered the rifle, "I wonder if I might have a moment of your time." She had not stirred one step from the veranda.

The house servants had gathered just inside the front hallway to watch. "Tilda?" Matt's mother had said the cook's name softly as she kept her eyes on the overseer walking slowly from the yard to the house. "Please see to the young man."

Matt had continued to sit cross-legged on the porch where he'd been playing with his toy soldiers and stared wide-eyed up at his mother. The overseer had reached the house now and stood with one booted foot on the lowest step, scowling up at Matt's mother.

"You damn near killed me," he snarled, and Matt noticed for the first time that he was cradling the hand that had held the whip.

"No, Mr. Bennett. Make no mistake about this: Had I intended to kill you, you would be dead. Now, then, please collect your things and leave my property."

The overseer's eyes had widened in surprise. "You can't fire me, missus. You got no right . . ."

Tess had lifted the gun a fraction of an inch. "I believe I asked you to leave, Mr. Bennett. I am sorry our arrangement has not worked out, but apparently you were not listening when my husband explained the way we work our people."

"We'll just wait and see what the mister has to say about this." Bennett had smirked and turned to saunter off toward the yard.

Tess had lifted the rifle once more and fired it straight into the air. When Bennett dived for cover, Matt had laughed out loud.

He smiled now at the memory. His mother's voice had never been raised above the genteel tones she used at a formal dinner, but Mr. Bennett had gotten the message. By noon he'd been gone.

As he stood by her grave, Matt thought of how his mother had looked that day, holding a gun that was almost as tall as she was. Even with the overseer standing several steps below her, he'd seemed huge compared to Tess's small thin frame. Matt recalled that his mother had been both the smallest and the strongest-willed woman he'd ever known. One day he hoped he'd be so lucky as to find a woman like her for himself.

Throughout the long years of the war, Jack Hubbard had had the good business sense to diversify and to cooperate when there was no other choice. So, in those months following the war Jack and Matt were able to steadily build on that. Five years later the Hubbard enterprises encompassed a thriving lumber business and sawmill in Memphis, as well as the huge tobacco plantation where Matt had grown up.

Then Matt's father remarried. Louisa was younger than Matt, and almost everyone agreed that she wanted only one thing from the union: Jack Hubbard's estate. She was the youngest daughter of a prominent family who had lost everything in the war. Louisa was not used to the life she'd been forced to live for the past several years, and she was willing to marry a much older man as long as he came with a fortune she might spend now and inherit later.

Of course, Matt's father couldn't see beyond the cut of Louisa's neckline, revealing the flesh of her full bosom straining against the fabric, or the sway of her hips as she moved across the room. He squired her all over the countryside, proudly showing her off. And he lavished gifts on her . . . clothes, jewelry, a new horse, and two fine carriages.

Matt tried to understand his father's need for someone as young and vibrant as Louisa in his life. The war had been hard on everyone, and no one could blame a man who'd watched his first wife die and then lived through a terrible war if he wanted a little fun . . . a little beauty in his life.

So Matt tried to ignore the way Louisa flirted with the men who came to do business with his father. He tried to ignore the way she always seemed to find ways to brush against them as she served them lemonade on the veranda or moved through a gathering in the large parlor. He tried to ignore the innuendo of her conversations. His father found her charming and delightful, secure in the hold he had on her by virtue of what he could give her and happy to be able to bring pleasure to someone so lively and beautiful.

Most of all Matt tried to avoid Louisa's increasingly blatant sexual advances toward himself. For his father's sake he attempted to humor her and to laugh off her excesses. And the interesting part of the whole business was that his struggle wasn't to resist her. His struggle was simply to avoid her. The truth was he was not the least bit attracted to Louisa.

After several months Louisa became downright brazen in her chase. She sought Matt out when he was doing chores in the barn or fields. She left notes for him, inviting him to meet her. And when that didn't work, she pouted.

One evening Jack asked Matt to entertain Louisa. "I'll be busy with our guests for at least an hour, son." New investors were pouring into the county from the North. They sought Jack's advice and they were eager to do business with someone who had managed not only to survive the war, but also to thrive.

"Louisa is the sort of woman who has no head for business, Matt," Jack said with a smile. "She's bored by all this talk of deals and contracts. Do me a favor and take her for a walk in the gardens while I finish this meeting. I can give you the details in the morning."

In the garden Louisa played the child, racing ahead, inviting Matt to play along in her game of hide-and-seek when they reached the boxwood maze Matt's mother had planted when he was a child.

Because this was preferable to her constantly throwing herself at him, Matt agreed. All he wanted was to kill the hour. Then

Louisa could go back to the house and his father, and Matt could take his nightly walk alone through the woods at the edge of the fields.

Suddenly Louisa shrieked in pain. Matt rushed to her side. He knew the maze well and found her easily. She had tripped and fallen. "I think it may be broken," she whimpered as she gingerly touched her exposed ankle.

In fact, a great deal of her was exposed. For the dinner she had chosen a gown cut almost indecently low, baring much of her ample breasts and all of her flawless shoulders. Her red hair now fell over those shoulders, and she tossed it back impatiently as she watched Matt come toward her.

He knelt to examine her ankle, trying hard not to stare at the way her skirts had remained pushed up to reveal much more than a lady should allow.

"Can you put weight on it?" Matt asked and helped her to her knees preparatory to helping her to stand.

"Matt," she whimpered once more, her hand tightening on his shoulder.

He glanced at her. Their faces were close, and in the shadows he could not read her expression. "I can carry you," he said firmly and started to stand, but her hand snaked to the back of his neck and she urged his face to hers.

"Louisa," he warned.

Then her mouth was on his, hot, open. With both hands she pulled him toward her as she lowered herself back to the ground. Her tongue swept the inside of his mouth.

The little vixen knew exactly what to do to get the response she wanted. Her hands were everywhere at once, tugging at his shirt, urging him to straddle her.

He decided to teach her a lesson. Perhaps if he called her bluff and actually started to take her, she would realize the dangerous game she was playing and keep her distance.

He stopped trying to resist her and instead took command of the kiss. With his tongue he searched the depths of her mouth. With one hand he imprisoned both her hands high over her head, while with the other he plundered the cleavage of her gown until one breast had nearly fallen free of its boundary. With his hips he ground his lower body against hers. His intent was to scare the bejesus out of her.

But he had underestimated Louisa. Instead of a shriek of protest, what she uttered was a moan of triumph. Working one hand loose from his grip, she pulled the neckline of her gown lower until she was fully exposed, her breast filling his hand as her tongue laved his ear. "Matt," she moaned, pressing his mouth toward her exposed nipple. "Suckle me, Matt," she urged.

Matt rolled off her and stood, his breath coming in hard spasms as he stared down at her. "How can you do this?" he demanded. "My father loves you, and you throw yourself at everything in pants."

"I only want you, Matt," she entreated.

"I thought you were simply innocent . . . naive. It was my intention to give you a scare . . . to . . ."

She smiled. "To teach me a lesson, Matt?" Calmly she redressed herself. "I want very much to learn the lessons you want to teach me. I thought I was quite a quick study a few minutes ago." She swept the masses of hair to the top of her head and anchored them with pins she removed from her pocket.

In that moment Matt saw how she had planned the whole thing. "You play a dangerous game, Louisa," he warned. "One day someone far less scrupulous than I will take you seriously, and believe me, you will not like the consequences."

She stood up and rearranged her skirts, brushing the grass and debris from the smooth silk of her gown. Then she moved close to him and ran her fingers lightly over his stomach and down to his thigh. "I'm a married woman, Matt. I already know the consequences . . . and I like them . . . a lot."

Once again Matt caught her wrist and forcibly restrained her. "My father loves you," he rasped.

"Your father worships me," she corrected, "and he denies me nothing." With that parting shot she resumed their walk through the garden back toward the house as if nothing had happened at all.

For several days Louisa treated Matt as if he were her brother, teasing him at mealtime and making no attempt to follow him or tryst with him behind his father's back. Matt had just about decided that she had been more frightened than she let on by what had happened in the garden. He was sure Louisa had learned her lesson. He began to relax.

One sultry summer night as Matt lay awake near midnight, however, Louisa opened the door to his room and slipped inside. She was wearing nothing but a thin batiste nightgown, which she removed as she walked silently toward his bed.

Matt made no attempt to protect her modesty as he got up and pulled his pants over his naked body. Without a word he strode out of the room and straight downstairs to his father's library.

"We have to talk about Louisa," he began when his father glanced up at his sudden entrance.

"Son, cover yourself in case Louisa—"

"Louisa is not—"

But before he could say more, Louisa herself came rushing into the room, sobbing as she threw herself into Jack's arms and cowered under Matt's furious gaze. "Darling Jack, do not be upset," she whimpered. "It's my fault. I'm sure I led Matt to believe . . . that is . . . well, he's a man now, and it's only natural . . ."

Jack Hubbard stared first at his son and then at his wife. He set her a little away from him and saw at the same time Matt did that the gown was now torn from one shoulder. A pulse throbbed in the veins of Jack's neck as he turned toward his son, his eyes taking in the bare chest, the half-buttoned pants. "You!" he roared.

"No!" Louisa screamed and reached to restrain the older man. "It's my fault, truly. Oh, darling Jack, don't you see? I was naive and never thought about how Matt might interpret my innocent flirting and sisterly teasing. Please, Jack . . ." She clung to her husband, but her eyes were on Matt, mocking him.

"Dad," he began, "can't you see—"

"Get out," Jack ordered in a raspy voice. His face was mottled and red, and his hands shook as he allowed Louisa to restrain him. "Get out of my house."

"No," Louisa whispered. "Please. I couldn't stand it if I were the cause of strife between a father and son, not after so many families have been torn apart by the war already. I'll leave."

It was a hell of a performance and one Jack Hubbard bought. His arms gathered Louisa to his breast as he glared at his son. His choice of her over his only son was clear. "I'll be gone in the morning," Matt said and left the room.

He did not even wait for dawn. He packed one small bag, saddled Traveler, and headed west. It seemed the most likely spot . . . raw, untamed, vast. A man could map out his own life out there. To someone like Matt who had grown up with only one identity, that of Jack Hubbard's son, the idea of finding himself was irresistible.

Matt couldn't imagine why all of this was coming back to him in such graphic and painful reality tonight. He hadn't allowed himself to think about the details of that night for a long time, though he had thought often of his father.

After several months had passed, Matt had started writing to Jack, telling him where he was, what he was doing, about the things he saw. He never mentioned Louisa or that night. He also never got an answer, but he kept sending the letters. He thought one day his father might finally see Louisa for what she was and need his son. And Matt intended to answer that need.

Maybe that's what the last few years had been about— marking time until Jack Hubbard needed him again. Matt stared up at the vast star-studded sky. What kind of life was this for a thirty-two-year-old man? Matt had gotten what he wanted out of this part of his journey: time to quench the wanderlust born of too many months as a soldier and too many years walking in his father's shadow. But he'd also had time to think, time to get himself figured out. What he knew was that family was important. A man without a family was only half a man. When he'd figured that out, he'd started to write those letters, wanting to reach out to his father but too stubborn to make the journey home.

Maybe tomorrow when he got back to town, he'd check on the train headed east.

"You got mail, Hubbard." Sam, the bartender, sailed an envelope across the room so it landed at Matt's feet as he started up the stairs.

He'd used a rented room above the small saloon as his base of operation for the last year. It was a comfortable setup. When he was in town he helped out in the bar, provided a little extra muscle when the cowhands came through on the cattle drives, and kept pretty much to himself the rest of the time.

When he left to take a job as a scout or a guide, the owner of the saloon was willing to handle an occasional letter or telegram as long as it didn't get to be a habit. Since this was the first mail Matt had gotten, he assumed the imposition wasn't too much.

"Thanks." He picked up the envelope and continued climbing the stairs.

"Looks official," Sam said as he returned to his newspaper.

"Could be," Matt answered and kept walking down the hall.

The envelope did look official. In fact, the return address was for a law firm in Memphis. He dropped his saddlebags just inside the door and stood half in and half out of his room as he read the single page:

We regret to inform you of the passing of your father, Jackson Hubbard. Mr. Hubbard died last Thursday in a riding accident on his estate.

As you may know, you have been named as his sole heir. You may not be aware, however, that your father added a provision to that inheritance. Simply stated, it was his desire that you marry prior to receiving the estate. If you are not already married, you have three months to fulfill the requirements of the provision, or the estate will revert in its entirety to his widow, Louisa Annabelle Walworth Hubbard. Under the terms of the will, you and Mrs. Hubbard may not marry one another.

GETTING HITCHED

While there are, of course, more details involved to the provision, these are the relevant points. We extend our personal condolences for your loss and will await your response.

Emotion washed over Matt in waves that stunned him with their power. He had known he loved his father, but the news coming like this . . . Matt felt the lump that had started to form in his throat the moment he'd started reading the letter. He tried to swallow around it. He glanced down and saw that even as he gripped the letter, his hand shook.

He looked into the room . . . barren with nothing to say it was his other than the saddlebags he'd just left there. The last thing he needed was to hole up in that room. He considered his options. He was standing in the upstairs hall of the only saloon in a cow town. There was the saloon and what passed for a general store and livery. When Matt had ridden through town fifteen minutes ago, there hadn't been a soul around.

He walked downstairs, still clutching the letter, and looked around. The newspaper was still spread out across the bar, and Sam was reading it intently. There were no customers in the saloon.

Matt pulled out a chair and sat at a table closest to the bar. He reread the letter once and then again.

"Bad news?" Sam asked.

"Yeah."

The newspaper rustled as Sam folded back a page.

"Can I get you something?"

"My father died." Matt said, testing the words out loud for the first time.

There was a pause and then the sound of bottle against glass and liquid transferring. Sam came out from behind the bar and delivered the drink. "Sorry to hear it," he said with sincerity and headed back to his position.

"Funny, just last night I was thinking about maybe . . ." Matt let the thought trail off and drained the whiskey, closing his eyes as the heat of it raced the length of his body without easing one ounce of the pain.

Another shot glass appeared in front of him. "When's the funeral?" Sam asked, and this time he pulled out a chair and sat down opposite Matt.

Matt glanced at the letter and saw that it was dated early September. It was now the first of October. "I missed it," he said and frowned as he reread the contents of the letter once more.

"Well, now, it's always been my opinion that we put way too much stock in ceremonies like funerals, if you get my meaning. Seems to me . . ."

Matt leaned forward and read the letter once again more intently. "Jesus," he swore.

"Now look, son, if you—"

"The bitch is going to get it all."

Sam looked worried. "I'm not following you, son," he said.

Matt glanced up, realizing that Sam had been talking to him. The man was trying to console him, but now he looked confused. And because the thing Matt Hubbard needed most in the world right now was a friend, he decided to tell Sam— whose last name he had never known—the whole story.

"So, you need yourself a wife in short order," Sam said when Matt had finished.

For the first time since opening the envelope, Matt smiled. "Yeah, that's the way it looks. You got one stashed behind the bar there?"

"Maybe I got one *on* the bar," Sam said and got up to get the newspaper. "I just might have the answer to your prayers, son." He thumbed through the paper and finally folded it back and laid it in front of Matt. With one grubby finger he pointed to a small ad in the classifieds. "Read that," he ordered. "I'll tell you it sure caught my eye."

Matt read the ad, glanced up at a grinning Sam, and then read it again. "What kind of woman orders a husband through the mail?" he asked.

Sam chuckled and took up his post once again behind the

bar. "Beats me, but she sounds like a feisty one. Still, beggars can't exactly be choosy, if you get my meaning."

"She must be in trouble or uglier than an armadillo, or both," Matt said. "And she's got a nerve . . . what's all this 'open-minded' crap?"

"On the other hand, let's suppose for a minute she is in some kind of trouble," Sam said slowly. "Let's suppose she's looking to get out of some little hick town for some reason like maybe somebody got her in the family way, and the scandal and all . . . Seems to me a bargain could be struck."

"Hmmm." Matt was only half listening as he once again studied the terms of his father's will. The way things were stated, he had about eight weeks tops to show up married and take his father's inheritance right out of Louisa's eager little fingers.

"I mean," Sam mused on, "let's say neither you nor the little lady really wanted to be married. Let's say both of you needed to be married as a sort of convenience. Seems to me she might be willing to pretend to marry or even to marry and then kind of disappear . . . taking her bastard baby with her, of course . . . for the right payment."

Some of what Sam had said began to penetrate. Matt reread the ad. There was one chance in a million this might work, and since it was the only chance he had, Matt tore the ad from the paper.

"If I was you, I'd send a letter right away," Sam said as he watched Matt head for his room. "Stage is due here yet this afternoon. Could get a letter sent when he pulls out."

Matt only nodded and started taking the stairs two at a time. His mind raced with ideas. How to phrase the letter in just such a way that this woman would answer. Maybe if he mentioned the inheritance . . . yeah, that would get her, and if it did he would know exactly the kind of woman he was dealing with—a woman like Louisa.

He sat down and pulled a fresh piece of paper and pen out of the drawer of the small table. He dipped the pen in the inkwell and started to write—and as quickly as the words appeared, he scratched them out. He reread the ad and started again.

Dear Miss,
It was your quest for adventure that first attracted my notice. I have recently received news that I am to come into a large sum of money.

Matt paused and looked out the window. What kind of woman ran an ad for a mail-order husband? What did she want . . . really? He tried to imagine circumstances that would drive any self-respecting woman to take such drastic measures.

He wasn't any closer to figuring it out when he heard the stagecoach pull up to the saloon.

CHAPTER
3

When the reality hit that she had actually not only written an advertisement for a husband, but also placed it in three major newspapers, Mary was stunned. At first it had been a lark, relief from the nagging worry of whether or not she might end up a spinster; and the whole business had not been without the element of adventure.

Once she had written the first draft of the ad, she'd spent another two hours refining it, ultimately mentioning the possibility of a vocation in her father's mill, land, and a house as part of the dowry. By that time it had been nearly dawn, and Mary's mind had raced with the details of what must be accomplished in order to actually place the ad.

Opening the front door of the mercantile the following morning, she was pleased to see Samantha Spencer hurrying toward the newspaper office.

"Samantha, good morning," she had greeted her friend. "I was just thinking about you and your classified-advertisement section. The more I consider the idea, the more I think it is just what Harmony needs."

Samantha had beamed with delight. Aside from her love for Cord, there was nothing Samantha would rather talk about than her newspaper. "I agree," she said as the two young women walked along the boardwalk. "Will your parents be running an ad soon?"

"I'm not sure they will grasp the potential. They are, after all, rather old-fashioned . . . especially Father."

Samantha had nodded sympathetically, and her bright spirits had been noticeably dampened.

"On the other hand . . ." Mary had mused, and deliberately stopped.

"Yes?"

"Well, perhaps if you could allow me to borrow some of the larger papers in the state and show Father how the ads are used to advantage for business in other cities, then he might see the wisdom of the idea."

"Of course. Wait right here, and I'll get you copies." Samantha had hurried to unlock the newspaper-office door. She rushed inside to the back of the shop, emerging a moment later clutching three of the larger papers from Kansas and Nebraska. "Show him these."

"I will," Mary promised. "Well, I'd better get the store open. See you later, Samantha, and thank you."

"Thank *you*," Samantha had called after Mary, and never noticed the triumphant smile on Mary's face.

Without raising one bit of suspicion, Mary had gotten exactly the information she needed: the names and addresses of the most likely places for her to run her own advertisement. As she hurried back to the mercantile, Mary felt exhilarated. Her plan was going so well.

With each step in the process Mary experienced a fresh burst of triumph. Within two days she had sent the ads to a paper in Wichita, one in Salina, and one in Goodland on the Colorado border. She accomplished this by making excuses to bring the mail to the train station and then slipping her own three envelopes in with the rest of the contents.

Joseph handed the mail to the conductor as the train sat snorting like an impatient horse at the starting line. She had not been able to resist watching the train pull away, knowing it possibly carried her own future among its other cargo.

"What are you grinning at?" Joseph had asked as she watched the train until it was just a speck on the horizon.

"Nothing," she answered, but the momentum of her adventure could not be stilled, and she winked at her brother as she passed him on her way back to the store.

It was nearly a week later when the enormity of what she had done hit her. Good Lord, what if someone actually *saw* the ad? Worse still, what if someone *answered*? Keeping her escapade a secret had been a cakewalk to date, but what if a letter arrived answering the ad?

In a panic Mary made it her business to become sole manager of the postal station housed in the back of the family store. Anything that came by stage or train would have to pass through her hands first.

"Mother," Sissy whined one afternoon when Mary practically pushed her aside to get to the mailbag the stage had just left.

"The mail must get through." Mary tried to sound lighthearted and dedicated at the same time.

"Well, I don't see why you have to always be the one to sort through the bag. I enjoy seeing what comes the same as you, you know."

"Now, darlings," Lillie had interrupted, "don't quarrel. Mary is very good at this sort of thing, Sissy. Managing the mail is something that Mary's organized nature was made for. You, on the other hand, have a much better eye for fashion. Now, come help me select a bonnet for Mrs. Hutton."

Appeased by the compliment, Sissy easily gave up the fight. But Mary did not miss the curious glance her mother sent her way as she followed Sissy back to where Faith Hutton waited.

Hurriedly Mary shuffled through the pile of envelopes. A

great many of them were for her father . . . orders, bills, and other business correspondence. There was a letter from Charleston for Abby Lee Sutherland. Her family lived in South Carolina, and there was a letter for Abby Lee nearly every week.

Mary heard the jangle of the cash register and knew her mother was finishing the sale to Faith Hutton. She sifted through the stack with greater speed.

And there it was. A reply. It was addressed to her, and the return address was that of the Wichita paper. The envelope was fat, and Mary imagined dozens of replies to her ad as she hurried to get to the contents. Her heart pounded, and her mouth went dry as she carefully removed the folded stack of papers.

"What's that?"

Mary had been so intent on her work that she hadn't heard Sissy's approach. As a result she nearly jumped out of her skin and stifled the urge to snap at her younger sister.

"Oh, just some stuff for Papa," she answered breezily. "I'll take it over to the mill for him in case it's important or something. I mean, maybe he'll need to get a reply out with the next stage or send a telegram. . . ." She continued to babble on as she quickly stuffed the papers in her hand in with the stack of real mail she had set aside for her father. She tied on her bonnet and headed for the back door. "Tell Mama I'll be back in just a little bit, Sissy," she called, intentionally not giving her sister a chance to respond.

"I thought sorting all the mail was so all-fired important," Sissy called after her as she rode away.

To reach her father's gristmill, Mary had to cross the Smoky Hill River. In the evenings the bridge was a favorite spooning place for young lovers. It was said that a young man could demand a toll in the form of a kiss for taking the young lady safely across the bridge. Mary had played the game herself, but she hadn't yet found even one man she would deliberately set out to cross the bridge with so she could pay the toll. Truth was, she didn't quite see what all the fuss was about kissing, though her friends certainly gossiped about it enough.

She reined in the horse just on the other side of the bridge in the shade of a huge old cottonwood tree along the banks of the river. The horse was delighted with this unexpected opportunity to graze. Mary dismounted and found a smooth rock near the river to sit on as she searched through the stack of mail and pulled out the sheaf of papers. Before unrolling them to read, she closed her eyes tightly for one second.

"Please, God," she said aloud, "don't let this be terrible." With that she opened the papers.

It was one letter . . . one very long letter, written in large print in pencil. It was from a farmer named Elmer in a place called Elmo.

Elmer from Elmo. Mary tried not to prejudge.

He wrote that his wife had died the previous winter leaving him and his seven "boys" to fend for themselves. He admitted that he was not a young man and then reminded her that she had indicated age was not important. *I do have all my own teeth,* he added.

Mary sighed.

He rambled on about his land and the *gosh darn* drought that had nearly wiped them out the year before. He talked about his "boys" . . . Edgar, the oldest at thirty-two, had had a terrible fall as a youngster and *hasn't been quite right-headed since.* They all missed their mother something terrible and hoped the young miss who ran the ad might be the answer to all their prayers.

Then Elmer talked about his departed wife. In glowing terms he described a woman who cooked, cleaned, toiled in the fields, minded the livestock, took in laundry from townsfolk, and served as a midwife for families all over the county until her death. *If it's adventure you're wantin', you'll find it here,* he promised.

Mary could not help but notice that he had completely missed the point that she expected the husband to move to Harmony. Although perhaps that was unfair. He did mention that his middle son, Elias, would be happy to take the promised job in her papa's mill and his youngest, Eleazer, would be getting the dowry land she'd promised.

By the time she reached the end of the letter, Mary was so enraged she could barely keep herself from ripping the thing into a thousand shreds and scattering them in the river. What was it about men that made them think they could take the words of a woman and twist them around to suit their own purpose? She'd been most specific in her ad: adventure, open-mindedness, modern woman. Heavens, how much more could she spell it out?

She stuffed the letter inside her bonnet and rode on to her father's gristmill, muttering to the horse as she went. "I just won't get married if this is any example of what I can expect." Then, "Oh, there just has to be a young man out there somewhere who's right for me. Everyone else has someone. Why not me?"

Followed by, "It's only one letter. Wait till the rest come. There are bound to be bad ones as well as good ones. I'm just fortunate to have had the worst first."

Mary reined in at the mill, tied the horse, and went in search of her father. Most towns had to advertise in large cities for millers, but Harmony had not had to look beyond Mary's grandfather.

Back in Europe, Abel Taylor had been trained as a miller. Once he reached America, he and dozens of other immigrants had headed west and stopped when they reached the green and fertile plains that were central Kansas. Together they had farmed the land and eventually built the mill, which her grandfather had quit farming to operate.

He'd been a very popular man and very successful as farmers traveled from all over the area, sometimes for weeks, to bring him their grain to mill. Mary's father James had learned the trade from his father and now owned not only the mill and the store, but served as Harmony's mayor as well. But with all that, he was as shy and reserved as Mary's mother was outgoing and opinionated.

Mary watched her father lift and carry the large heavy bag of grain a farmer had just delivered for milling. James Taylor was in top physical condition, strong and solidly built. Mary wanted someone like that for a husband. Looks were important in that way, she realized.

James plopped the heavy sack onto the stack other farmers had brought to be processed. The farmer said something to him, and whatever her father responded made the farmer laugh. James Taylor was well liked, a fair and respected man throughout the region. Those were also important qualities for a husband, Mary realized.

As he walked the farmer back to his wagon, James spotted Mary. His delight at seeing her so unexpectedly in the middle of the day was clear. Mary waved and headed across the footbridge that traversed the dam as the farmer tipped his hat and drove away.

"Mary, what brings you out here?"

James Taylor was an optimist. Others might assume tragedy at an unexpected visit, but he assumed only pleasure.

"I brought your mail," Mary answered. "I thought there might be something important," she added as she handed him the stack.

James Taylor cocked one bushy black eyebrow at his daughter. "That's all?"

Mary shrugged. "That's all," she assured him.

"Hmmm." He shifted through the envelopes. "Your mother tells me you've been acting a bit . . . keyed up lately." He kept looking through the mail.

Mary shifted from one foot to the other. "Really? I can't imagine—"

"Your mother thinks it may be because of some young man," he added and gave her a sidelong glance to judge the effect of his words.

"Really?" Mary should have known better than to assume her little adventure had escaped the notice of Lillie Taylor. The woman knew most of the town news before the subjects of that news were fully aware of it. What on earth made Mary think her mother wouldn't have honed in on something monumental involving her own daughter? "You know, Papa, I think the wheel sounds a little rough today."

James immediately turned his full attention to his machinery's repetitions. As Mary had expected, he was so attuned to the inner workings of his business that any hint of trouble had his immediate and full attention.

"You could be right," he said absently as he headed to the lower floor of the three-story mill to have a closer listen to the gears.

Mary followed. Once there she watched as her father walked around the mechanism inspecting the gears. She felt a bit guilty for having raised the question. There was probably nothing at all wrong, and she had worried her father unnecessarily.

"Perhaps I was mistaken!" she shouted above the creak and grown of the machinery.

Her father held up a finger to silence her and listened intently, then he smiled. "Good ears, darling Mary." He reached for the bucket of liquid fat he kept handy and smeared some on one particular part of the gears. "There," he said as he replaced the bucket and smiled down at her. "All fixed."

Together they walked up to the main floor, past the men who helped her father grind the wheat into flour and meal, and into James Taylor's office. He dropped the stack of mail on his desk and indicated that Mary should take a seat.

"So, is your mother right? Is there a young man?"

"There's no young man," Mary protested. "Truly."

"I'm sorry to hear that. I am not getting any younger, and my children are not exactly rushing to inherit the businesses I've so carefully built for them. If I have to wait for your brother Harry to be old enough to take over here, I may not make it."

"Oh, Papa, you're still a young man," Mary argued.

"A tired man," James corrected. "Now, don't you think you could do this tired old man a favor and find a husband who would like to step right into a ready-made business opportunity? I could train him myself."

Mary blushed and knew her father thought it was because he

was teasing her. Actually she was blushing because it occurred to her that her father had just made a whole truth out of the promise she'd made of a job for her mail-order husband.

"You know, Mary, you are the best prospect I have. You manage the store so well, and with your quick head for figures you could help your husband with the record-keeping here."

"All I need is the husband," Mary replied before thinking.

"You'll find the right young man some day, darling," her father said softly. "I know you will."

Mary felt moved almost to tears at her father's open tenderness. "I'd better get back, or Sissy will accuse me of playing hooky."

James laughed at that. "If anyone is prone to hooky-playing, it's that sister of yours. Her mind is in the clouds most of the time." He hugged her. "Your mother and I sometimes wish Sissy were more like you . . . responsible and level-headed."

The following week brought two more answers to Mary's ad, another from Wichita and one from the town near the Colorado border. Mary opened the one from Wichita first, already having decided that running the ad in the Goodland paper was a mistake. Any man who had traveled west like that surely was looking for land of his own and not at all likely to want to move to Kansas. Mary hoped the letter from Wichita would hold more promise.

Dear Young Woman,

In regards to your advertisement in the classified section of the morning's paper, I must say that I am appalled and shocked. If this is the state to which our young womenkind have descended, then woe be to all of us. I have wrestled with whether or not to respond to your scandalous advertisement for a husband and have decided that God is leading me to do so that I may save your wretched soul from further sacrifice to the demons of so-called modernism and feminist caprice. My dear child,

*you must get down on your knees at once and beg
forgiveness. Then you must write to me, and I will set you
back on the path of God's own way. Please desist from
any further solicitation of men . . . especially by means
of respectable family newspapers. I have also written the
editor of this paper and demanded that he cease accepting
such ads as yours at once. If you persist in this disgraceful
behavior, I pity your soul, for you shall surely burn in hell
for your folly.*

> *Yours in God's Love,*
> *Reverend Milhouse Agnew*

Suddenly Elmer from Elmo seemed quite charming.

"Might as well get it over with," Mary muttered to herself as
she edged her fingernail under the flap of the letter from
Goodland.

Mary scanned the contents quickly, her mind ready for either
recrimination or total distortion of her original request. Distortion seemed most likely as she read the opening line: *It was
your quest for adventure that caught my attention.*

Mary swallowed and closed her eyes, resting her head for a
moment on the wall behind her. Lord, wasn't there one man left
out there who wasn't looking for a servant to manage his
sodhouse and orphaned children? She sighed and read on.

> *What I have to offer is a bit unusual but, I assure you,
> absolutely legitimate and aboveboard. It is difficult to
> fully address the matter in a letter, but suffice it to say that
> I have just received news of a large inheritance from my
> recently departed father in Memphis—*

Memphis . . . a Southerner . . . well-mannered . . .
traveled . . . used to the finer things in life.

> *If a wedding trip to Tennessee would have any
> appeal—*

Mary reread the line and then read it again. Was he serious? She'd never in her life been away from home overnight. Think of the things she might see on a trip from Kansas to Memphis! She frowned and read on. There had to be a catch.

> *I will trust that age and looks are not of importance.*

Ah-ha.

> *I am 32. I have not been married. I am a veteran of the recent conflict and have spent the past several years seeking my own adventures here in the West.*

Her heart softened as she felt something of a kindred spirit pass from the letter to herself.

> *Oh, but it is so hard to know what to say. Will you reply? Perhaps if we exchange letters for a time or two we can better gauge the suitability of our mutual—*

And here he had scratched the word *need* and then the word *plan* and finally added in a hasty scribble:

> *I fear you have caught me speechless, and the stage is coming that will carry this to you. Please write. I promise you it will not be in vain. Knowing my circumstances and judging from yours as expressed in your advertisment, I think we can perhaps—*

There was a line and then the words: *Please write. Most respectfully yours, Matthew Hubbard.*

On the back of the single sheet was a hastily scribbled address.

By the time she was dressed for bed that night, Mary had already read the letter so many times that the folds of the paper were deeply creased and becoming fragile. With each reading, Matthew Hubbard became a little more real to her. She found a map of Colorado and tried to locate the town he'd used as his address, but to no avail. Then she looked at the map of Tennessee and saw how close it appeared to be to the ocean. Might she actually see the Atlantic?

Her heart went out to him that he had been so very far away when his father died. What would she ever do if Papa died and she couldn't be there to say good-bye?

In her dreams that night she conjured up the familiar romantic image of the stranger stepping off the train. But this time the stranger had a name, and when he swept her into his arms, she called him Matthew.

By morning she had imagined the life they would share . . . the trip east to Tennessee . . . the house he would build her here in Harmony . . . the way he would work with her father at the mill, learning the craft and eventually assuming the role of miller for the whole valley while she ran the mercantile. There would be children, of course, and he would be a gifted and tender father. They would use the money he inherited to travel. They might even go to Europe—

"Mary!"

Mary's head snapped up, and she stared straight up and into the eyes of Maisie Hastings. Next to Maisie stood her sister Minnie, and next to her stood Mary's mother. All three were looking at her curiously.

"I swear, Lillie, I thought Sissy was the dreamer in your brood," Maisie said.

"Maisie and Minnie would like to see some of our lovely calico, Mary," Lillie instructed as if speaking to a not-so-bright child.

"Yes, ma'am," Mary replied and hastened to take down the bolts of fabric.

It was late afternoon before Mary had even a moment to begin her reply.

GETTING HITCHED

Dear Matthew Hubbard,

I am in receipt of your letter and quite agree that perhaps an exchange of letters might be wise. I will endeavor to tell you a bit about myself and my circumstances, and perhaps you could respond with more information about your own situation. Let me start with age and marital status as you did: I am 21 and also have never been married. I come from a large family. My father is a miller, and my mother and I run the other family business, a general store here in Harmony. I have a married sister and another younger sister and three brothers. I am most grieved to hear of the loss of your father, since I cannot imagine the pain of losing even one member of my own family. Please accept my condolences. You did not say, but if your mother survives your father, I do hope you know the condolences extend to her as well.

Mary read what she had written and frowned. She had said too much about the loss of his father, been too emotional. But just as she started to begin again, she heard the train whistle. *Not yet,* she thought and bent again over her words.

I do so much want to get this out in the next mail, and the westbound train will arrive any minute. We only have one a week. What do you want to know? As for me I have dozens of questions, and they fill my head. Do you understand that you would need to settle here in Harmony, and is that a problem for you? I truly believe that it is here that we have the greatest hope of making a success of this. Please reply at your earliest convenience . . . even if you have changed your mind.

Sincerely,
Mary Taylor

CHAPTER

4

It was the part about only one westbound train a week that had lit a fire under Matt and made him forsake his plan of exchanging letters. Time was of the essence, and if he were to make it to Memphis in time to save his family's heritage, he needed to move this marriage along. The day Mary's letter arrived, he checked the schedule and bought a one-way ticket to Harmony, Kansas. Then he wired Mary of his impending arrival.

PLANS CHANGED STOP ARRIVING ON FRIDAY 4:08 STOP

For some reason he didn't sign it, an action Mary indicated had been wise in her return message:

FAMILY DOES NOT KNOW STOP WILL WEAR WHITE ROSE STOP
PLEASE WAIT FOR SIGNAL STOP

"Please wait for signal?" Matt muttered aloud as he scanned the contents of the telegram. What the hell did that mean? What the hell was he getting himself into here? The family had sounded nice in her one letter. What was she hiding? What did he need with more aggravation?

Before he could change his mind, he packed his belongings in his saddlebags, bought freight passage for Traveler II, and boarded the train. Maybe there would be a stop along the way where he could buy a decent suit of clothes and get cleaned up a bit. The train would be hot and dusty; the jeans, shirt, and vest he normally wore on the trail would do for the ride.

Mary paced the perimeter of her room. On the pretense of an upset stomach, she had left the store just after lunch and come upstairs. She'd been dressed for an hour already and waiting. She alternately watched the horizon for signs of the approaching train and the garden of Abby Sutherland below where the single white rose still clung to its branch.

The problem was Abby had picked today to work in her garden in the afternoon. Normally she was there early in the morning or just at dusk, but today she was there at two and still there at three.

Mary needed that rose. It was going to be hard enough making it to the train station in broad daylight without being seen. She had no idea what she was going to do once Matthew stepped off the train. Why on earth had she begun this? And why had he insisted on speeding things along? She had counted on time, the promised exchange of letters, and all the while she would perhaps figure out a way to tell her family about Matthew . . . make up some plausible story.

But no. Just like every other man, this one had taken matters into his own hands. *He* had decided they needed to talk in person. *He* had been the one who first thought writing was a good idea. Honestly. And men thought women were fickle.

She scanned the horizon—the flat plains that surrounded the town, the dazzling blue of the late-afternoon sky. In the distance were the buildings that made up the Lind farm and the Double B. Maybe Matthew Hubbard would prefer farming to working the mill. Well, she could be reasonable . . . she could compromise on some things.

A wisp of smoke. The train.

Mary glanced down. No sign of Abby. It was now or never. She eased her way down the back stairway, taking care to walk only on the outsides of the steps where the nails held the boards securely and lessened the chance of telltale squeaks.

She heard her mother and Sissy talking. They were in the storeroom. Good. She tiptoed out the door and scuttled around the side of the building. The town was quiet. Thank heaven for harvest time. People were always busier this time of year. There was so much to be done before winter set in.

Abby's rosebushes lined the fence, their fragrance a sweet contrast to the manure Jake supplied as fertilizer. Mary focused her attention on the single white blossom. She had watched it for a week, starting the day she'd sent the telegram, and the blossom had been only a tight bud. Carefully she'd calculated its opening. It was late in the season, and even Abby's spectacular roses were becoming sparse.

She reached for the blossom, fully open now with petals like white velvet and a yellow center.

"Isn't it lovely?"

Mary snatched her hand away from the blossom at the sound of Abby's voice just on the other side of the fence. "Take it, please. It won't last another day anyway." Abby reached out and clipped the rose with her snippers, handing it to Mary with a shy smile.

"I . . . that is, I . . ."

Abby smiled. "It will be lovely with your bonnet. Here, let me tuck it into the band."

She broke off two thorns and clipped the stem short, then stood on tiptoe as she slid the stem into the band of Mary's hat. "There."

Mary was speechless with guilt and embarrassment. "Thank you," she mumbled. "It's lovely."

The train whistle pierced the air, and Mary could not resist an anxious glance toward the station.

"You seem to be expecting someone, Mary," Abby said knowingly, and smiled. "Hurry along, then. Mustn't keep him waiting."

"I . . ." Mary started a protest, but Abby was already headed back toward the shady spot where little Dinah played with her doll.

Mary hurried on to the station. She peeped through the window and saw that the place was blessedly empty. No townspeople there to meet the train today. Just her brother Joe, and he was busy checking the freight and mail to be loaded on when the train stopped. She took up her position at the corner of the station, chosen for its clear view of the train and any passengers who might get off, as well as for its easy escape back to the store.

The train wheezed to a stop. Joe went into action, greeting the crew who worked on the train, directing the unloading of freight. A magnificent horse was first off . . . gleaming black and spitting saliva after the confining ride. For a moment the splendid beast held Mary's full attention.

And then she saw him . . . tall, his long muscular legs encased in well-worn jeans, his shirt stained with sweat, the sleeves rolled back to reveal forearms that were tanned and strong. He wore a wide-brimmed hat tipped slightly back so that she could see the lower half of his face, as tan and weathered as his arms, but chiseled and shaped, the jaw strong and determined, yet the mouth was . . . softer.

He was carrying saddlebags slung over one broad shoulder, and for a moment he scanned the platform looking for someone . . . her. Then he started walking, striding along as the man in her fantasy did . . . heading straight for her. Mary gulped and moved three steps back around the side of the building. He couldn't have seen her. He couldn't possibly . . .

"Help you, mister?"

Joe.

The determined booted feet stopped.

"I . . . ah . . . this is Harmony, right?"

Lord, his voice was wonderful—deep and confident. With sweat pouring down her spine from the hot October sun and her own nervousness, Mary shivered at the sound of that voice.

"Yep. I'm Joseph Taylor, stationmaster."

Mary knew Joe had offered his hand. She risked a glance around the edge of the station.

"Matthew Hubbard," he replied and took Joe's hand in a firm handshake. Papa had always said one measure of a man was the way he shook hands. "A man who's got something to hide just can't seem to put any weight behind it," Papa had observed. Judging from Joe's reaction, there was no strength missing in Matthew Hubbard's handshake. Mary experienced an unexplainable burst of pride.

"You staying in town?" Joe asked.

"Well, I think I might be." Matt glanced at the brightly painted buildings fanned out to either side of the station. "Maybe you could suggest a place to stay?"

"Sure. You got two choices: the hotel back over there or the boardinghouse. If you're watching your money you might want the boardinghouse. If privacy is a concern—" Joe paused and then grinned. "Better get back on the train. You won't make it till sundown before everybody in Harmony knows you're here, why you came, and how long you plan on staying."

Matthew laughed, and that sound, too, was wonderful . . . deep, rumbling, rising from way down inside him and spilling out.

So, Matt wondered, was this Mary's brother? He'd caught the name Taylor immediately and tried hard not to show any reaction. He glanced around the platform again. When he'd first stepped off the train, he'd been certain he'd seen her, but only for a second, and then the platform had been as vacant as the endless Colorado range country he'd left behind.

"Why don't you come on in the station here," Taylor offered as he returned from checking some freight and saw Matt still

47

waiting. "I've got some lemonade if you're thirsty. 'Course, if you've got a stronger thirst, there's a couple of saloons just down the street there."

"Lemonade sounds good," Matthew answered and followed the tall young man in to the cooler but still close air of the train station.

Joseph Taylor seemed like a nice enough fellow, and if he was indicative of the whole family, Matt didn't understand why Mary might be worried. He accepted the tin cup of lemonade and drained it.

"Hot on the train, huh?" Taylor said as he refilled the cup.

Matt smiled. "Yeah. Thanks." As he drank the refill of lemonade, he glanced around the station. It was small. A few benches for waiting passengers, Taylor's small office behind the ticket window. The telegraph was in there. Had Joseph sent the wire?

He caught a glimpse of navy and white just outside the window and edged closer. "Have you lived here in Harmony long, Mr. Taylor?"

"All my life. My pa owns the gristmill as well as the mercantile. It's that yellow building yonder." Joseph pointed out the window and returned to sorting the bills of lading from the freight.

Matt glanced out the window. He could just see the top of what might be a lady's bonnet if one were hiding beneath the window listening. "Colorful little town," he observed as he moved directly to the window.

Joseph chuckled. "That's my ma's handiwork. A year or so ago she got it in her head to paint the town—everything had to be a different color. Raised quite a ruckus at the time, but now everybody's kind of used to it. Actually most folks like it."

Matt was at the window now. He was sure someone was out there, so he just waited.

Mary couldn't stand it anymore. What was happening? She had to see. Things had gotten much too quiet. Maybe he'd gone out the other way and any minute might come around the building. Why was Joseph doing all the talking?

She inched her way along the side of the depot to the window. Glancing out over the town to make sure no one was observing her curious actions, she turned slowly to the window.

He was standing right there, looking straight at her. Lord help her, he was absolutely gorgeous, with eyes of pale blue that seemed to see right inside her. On top of that he was smiling . . . a lazy sort of smile that did strange things to her heart. Without a word he tipped his hat and nodded.

Mary gulped, gathered her skirts, and raced across the yard to the mercantile.

So, this was Mary Taylor, Matt thought as he watched her go. The first thing he'd noticed when she'd come to the window were her eyes . . . huge and wide and as brown as his mother's molasses used to be. And then there was the mouth, red full lips . . . the lady had added a bit of color for the occasion. For some reason that made Matt smile. And her skin . . . white . . . alabaster . . . with a sprinkle of freckles across her nose and cheeks that made her seem younger than he knew she was.

He'd only had a second to take in her features before that mouth had formed a startled exclamation, and she'd gathered her navy skirts and hurried across the yard toward the general store. Matt saw the single white rose fall unnoticed in the dust as she ran.

"Now, what the devil's gotten into that girl?" Joseph asked as he watched his sister.

Matt had been so absorbed in watching Mary that he hadn't even heard Joseph come up next to him. "You know her?"

"She's my sister . . . one of 'em. Unusual for her to be all got up like that. Well, maybe she's late for one of my mother's meetings."

Matt considered his options. How long was he going to play this game? Time was passing, and he didn't have a lot to spare.

Might as well throw the fat in the fire and see what popped out. "Is that Mary Taylor?" he asked as he shouldered his saddle-bags and reset his hat.

Joseph Taylor's mouth dropped open. "How'd you know that?" he asked suspiciously.

"I came to marry her," Matt answered as he strode out the double station doors and headed for the mercantile. He paused once to pick up the single white rose but otherwise never broke stride.

"You what? Hey, mister, wait up!" Joseph Taylor hurried along behind him.

Mary's breath came in audible heaves as she collapsed on her bed and tried to sort through the myriad emotions and questions racing through her mind. What on earth had she been thinking to run the silly ad, to answer the letter he'd sent, to actually approve his coming here? She could have wired that she'd changed her mind, anything to keep him from showing up, but no. Now he was here, talking to her brother and looking at her with a knowing grin that made her feel as if he was already thinking about their marriage bed.

Now, where the devil had *that* come from? Not a word had passed between them. The man had smiled and tipped his hat. Men did that to Mary every day of her life, and she'd never read such a scandalous interpretation into the gesture. Maybe she was the one thinking about the marriage bed. Lord knows from the moment she'd first watched those long legs moving toward her and those broad shoulders hefting the saddlebags and that face, tanned and rugged and smiling down at her, her mind had been filled with all the same fantasies she'd entertained for months.

"Mary?"

It was her mother calling. She sounded puzzled but insistent. "Mary? Are you up there?"

Then she could hear Joseph talking, and his tone was stern and big-brotherly. Next, Sissy got her two cents' worth in.

GETTING HITCHED

"Mary Eloise Taylor, you get down here right now." That would be Mama.

Like a prisoner going to the gallows, Mary sighed and moved down the stairs. "Coming, Mama," she said quietly. She nervously smoothed her skirts and checked that her hair was presentably pulled back at her nape with the navy bow that matched her skirt. The hat had been discarded the moment she'd arrived safely in her room.

The scene that greeted her as she rounded the landing and headed down the last few steps into the store was worse than she'd imagined. Joseph was standing there glaring at the stranger. Sissy was looking him over as if he were a giant stick of peppermint candy. Mama was clutching the counter in preparation for swooning should the occasion warrant it, and to either side of her stood Maisie and Minnie, their sharp eyes missing nothing as the drama played on. In the midst of everyone stood Matthew Hubbard, perfectly at ease, his hat in one hand, his eyes riveted on Mary. As she descended the last two steps. He moved forward and offered her his arm and the single white rose.

"I believe you dropped this," he said softly.

Before Mary could answer, Joseph was in front of her. "Do you know this man, Mary Taylor? Because he seems to know you . . . well enough to announce he's marrying you. Now, how is it that a stranger—a man nobody in these parts has ever laid eyes on before—comes into town on the train and announces just like that that he's come to marry my sister?"

Lillie Taylor heaved a great sigh, and Minnie and Maisie moved a step closer to her. "Now, Lillie, wait for the explanation so we don't have to be filling you in later," Minnie admonished.

"I'm sure everything will be answered to your complete satisfaction, folks, but first, if Miss Mary and I could just have a moment." Matthew kept Mary's hand firmly tucked in the crook of his elbow.

She should have been thinking about the trouble she was in. She should have been thinking about how this was going to be all over town by suppertime. She should have been thinking about what Papa was going to say. She thought about how Matthew made her feel protected and special just in the completely proper gesture of offering her his arm and standing next to her.

"You and *Miss Mary* aren't going to spend one second alone until we have some answers here!" Joseph roared. "Sissy, go get Papa, and while you're at it, bring Travis."

Matt glanced down at Mary, his eyebrows raised in question.

"Travis is the sheriff and my brother-in-law," she said softly.

Matt nodded. "Good idea. Let's gather the whole family, and meanwhile Miss Mary and I will just step out here . . ."

Joseph moved quickly to block the doorway. "Get your hands off my sister, or I'll have you on your backside faster than you can—"

"Oh, honestly, Joseph," Mary said as she released Matthew's arm and stepped between him and her brother, "it's broad daylight, and the man wants to step out onto Main Street to talk to me. I'm hardly in any danger, and I'll thank you to let me handle my own affairs."

There was a communal sucking in of breath at the word *affairs*. Mary glanced over her shoulder to see Maisie and Minnie fanning her mother and looking as if they'd both swallowed the contents of the barrel of sour pickles where her mother rested.

"What's going on here?" James Taylor entered the store from the back, huffing and wiping the sweat from his forehead.

"Oh, James, it's the most disastrous moment of my life," Lillie moaned. "After Libby, I thought . . . I always counted on Mary's . . . uh . . . discretion . . . but this . . . this . . . cowboy says he's come to marry her."

James glanced at Lillie and then turned his full attention to Matthew. "Is that a fact?"

"Now, Papa—" Mary began, but her father silenced her with a look.

"Suppose you explain yourself, young man."

Matthew sighed and reached into his vest pocket where he

removed a single piece of newspaper. "Perhaps you should read this," he said and gave Mary an apologetic half-smile as he handed the paper to her father.

James read to himself, his eyebrows lifting higher with each line. By the time he'd finished, Samantha Spencer and Travis Miller were pushing their way through the door.

"You ordered a husband through the newspaper, Mary?" her father said disbelievingly.

Samantha smiled; Joseph made a move toward Matthew that was blocked by Travis; Maisie and Minnie clucked; and Lillie passed out cold on the floor.

"Perhaps someone should attend to Mrs. Taylor?" Matthew observed.

"Mrs. Taylor will be fine," James answered quietly, his full attention still riveted on his daughter. "Mary?"

Mary felt cornered, and her defenses went on alert. "Will everyone please just calm down and listen?" she said and started to pace the aisle of the store along the counter and past the potbellied stove. Joseph moved to stand in her way, questions and demands sputtering from his lips.

"Joseph, I said sit down and listen," she ordered and firmly pushed her big brother into the nearest chair. "I am twenty-one years old, and it's time I found a husband and started my own family. I have tried to find a suitable mate here in Harmony, but to no avail. Even Mama will agree that my choices—such as Danny Vega—have less than measured up to her standards." This last was delivered by leaning across the counter and speaking directly to her mother, who was now sitting up, albeit on the floor, and listening intently.

"When Samantha showed me some classified advertisements for mail-order brides, it occurred to me that what was good for the goose was good for the gander. The men who order brides are no more specific than I was in what I was seeking in a husband."

"I knew there was something going on," Samantha chimed in with delight.

"You and your Eastern ideas," Joseph muttered.

"Hush up and let her finish," Maisie ordered.

"Well, if you ask me—" Minnie began.

"No one did," Maisie interrupted.

"Mary?" This from her father who had remained silent and was still holding the small piece of newspaper.

"So I wrote an ad, ran it in several reputable papers, and received a number of responses that I have been carefully screening for the past several weeks. Mr. Hubbard seemed a potential candidate. We exchanged letters, and he convinced me of his integrity and honesty. He is a gentleman of Southern heritage. His family owns a great deal of property in the Memphis area."

"That's true," Matthew said as he stepped to Mary's side. "If everything works out for Mary and me, we'll be traveling to Memphis for our wedding trip to make arrangements for an inheritance I have recently received."

"He's a distinguished veteran of the last war, and he's got the ribbons to prove it. On top of that he's—" Mary faltered as she ran out of words. After all, she barely knew the man. He could be the blackest of outlaws for all she really knew.

"I assume I could verify all this if I took a notion to, Mr. Hubbard?" Travis had remained in the background since entering the store, but now he turned his full attention to the stranger.

"Absolutely," Matthew answered and moved one step closer to Mary. "For my part, I could not have been more charmed by Mary's wonderful letters. They were filled with her love of family and her home here in Harmony. And though she wants very much to travel, she has made it equally plain that her home and roots are here. As a Southerner whose own roots were badly disposed of during the war, I respect that more than you could ever imagine."

"So, if everyone has gotten over the shock, would you mind if Mr. Hubbard and I stepped outside for a moment?" Mary asked.

"Mr. Hubbard may come to supper tonight," Lillie announced. Fully recovered now, she moved around the side of the counter and faced this stranger who had come to claim her daughter. "Until that time, there will be no assignation alone with my daughter. Do I make myself clear, Mr. Hubbard?"

"Crystal clear, Mrs. Taylor. I admire your principles and would not think of disobeying them."

Mary watched her mother's eyes narrow and then soften with delight. "Very well. It'll be nice having a gentleman to supper," she said with a glance toward Travis. "Some people in this town might want to take a lesson or two. Travis, why don't you and Libby come, too?"

It was no secret that Lillie Taylor had nearly had heart failure over the goings-on of her eldest daughter Libby and Sheriff Travis Miller. Once Libby had come back to town, Travis had made it his mission to woo and win her, and he didn't seem to give a whole lot of thought to proprieties in the process. In the process he had kissed her in the middle of Main Street and made love to her in the town jail. Of course, the result of all that had been that Mary's own opportunities for courtship had been sharply chaperoned to the point where most young men had simply given up calling.

"You'll be needing a place to stay," Maisie suggested as she too sized up Matthew Hubbard. "I suppose Sister and I could find a place for you over at the boardinghouse."

"Heck, Miz Hastings, you got lots of room," interjected Mary's youngest brother, Harry. No one had paid any attention to the nine-year-old standing just inside the entrance and taking in the entire scene with wide-eyed interest.

When all eyes turned on him, Harry moved half a step toward the door. "Well, she does," he protested. "The boardinghouse is durn near empty since Travis left . . . not to mention . . . uh . . ." His voice trailed off under Minnie's glassy stare.

"That would be very nice, ma'am. I'd appreciate the opportunity to enjoy your hospitality," Matthew answered with an ingratiating grin. "However, since my stay will hopefully be a short one, I wouldn't think of tying up a room you could rent to a more permanent customer. I thought I would just stay at the hotel."

Neither Minnie nor Maisie could think of an answer to that, especially since they'd been reluctant to take the man in the first place. And there was something about the way he phrased his explanation that left them feeling as if somehow he'd done them a huge favor by not taking the room.

Mary let out the first full breath she'd taken since first rounding the stair landing. For the moment disaster had been averted. There was supper to be gotten through, of course, but for now she could take a breath.

"How come, if you're from out East, you arrived on the train from Colorado?" Joseph asked quietly, and the room froze.

Mary sighed in exasperation. "Joseph Taylor, just stop it. Mr. Hubbard has come calling in response to a legitimate advertisement I placed in a legitimate newspaper. We may or may not get married, but whether we do or don't is none of your business. Now, will you be at supper tonight or not?"

"I'll be there," Joseph answered as he got up from his chair to tower over his sister. "You'll be wanting to board your horse over at the livery. I got no room for him over at the station," he said to Matthew, then stalked out the back door of the store and across the yard to the depot.

Having relaxed once, Mary was not about to allow herself to be surprised again. "Any other questions?" She challenged as she glanced around the room.

Matthew ducked his head to hide a smile. The woman was not only the best-looking female he'd laid eyes on in months, but she also had spunk. He liked that. Life was hard out here on the frontier, even in a town as close-knit as this one obviously was. It took guts to make a success of life out here. He already knew Mary Taylor had courage. She was also smart as a whip. He'd been mightily impressed at the quick way her mind had worked to come up with information about him based on their single exchange of letters. She'd made it sound as if they'd been writing for months.

But it was her person that drew him the strongest. She was

slight, coming just under his chin. When he kissed her, she would have to stand on tiptoe, or he would have to lift her. He imagined his large hands spanning her tiny waist, her arms around his neck. And when she'd stepped between him and her brother, he'd had a momentary desire to pull her against his chest, his arms folded protectively across her breasts, the scent of her beautiful thick hair filling his senses.

"Mr. Hubbard?" She was standing there looking up at him, those deep brown eyes wide and searching.

"Miss Mary," he acknowledged with a smile.

"I . . . that is . . . you probably would like to . . . freshen up. . . ." The words brought a charming blush to her cheeks, and Matt wondered if she were imagining him shirtless as he washed. He stopped smiling as the thought of her washing entered his own mind.

"That . . . uh . . . that would be nice," he answered and tired not to in any way reveal the fact that in that moment he had started to imagine unbuttoning the shirtwaist, releasing the ribbons on her chemise . . . He glanced down to avoid her wide-eyed stare and saw the rise and fall of her chest . . . the press of her breasts against the fabric. "I'll go," he said in a husky whisper.

"Yes," she whispered back.

"Hrmmp," Lillie Taylor interrupted. "Mary, you have work to do. Mr. Hubbard, we will see you promptly at six."

"Yes, ma'am," Matthew answered and backed toward the door. Since his eyes were still fastened on Mary, he tripped over the threshold and had to steady himself with one hand on the door frame.

Lillie rolled her eyes heavenward, then glanced at her husband. "And just what are you smiling about, James Taylor?" she demanded, but did not wait for an answer as she brushed grandly past him and headed to the living quarters upstairs.

CHAPTER
5

The preparation of the evening meal was an unusually silent affair, making the clatter of pans and dishes seem uncommonly loud.

"What are you doing to those biscuits, Mary?" her mother asked testily as she took the glass Mary had been using to cut the dough and began grinding out perfect circles of dough herself. "I don't know how you can even be thinking about getting married, young lady. I can see that I have sadly neglected your training in the domestic skills . . . not that such a thing would matter to a man who would answer a newspaper ad in search of a wife."

She held up two samples: one Mary's mangled attempt to get the circle free of the rolled dough and next to it her own perfectly cut biscuit. Mary opened her mouth to compliment her mother, but got only one word out before Lillie Taylor continued.

"Heaven knows, he may have been a so-called Southern gentleman once, but no self-respecting gentleman—Northerner or Southerner—would take advantage of an innocent young woman's folly the way this man has. Now, you listen to me, young lady—"

"How's supper coming?" Harry asked as he strolled into the room and snatched a piece of raw potato to nibble on.

"Fine," Mary and Lillie barked in unison.

"Now, scram," Mary added.

Harry did not have to be asked twice.

"Mother, I—" Mary began as soon as Harry was out the door.

"You're not talking here, missy, I am. You are listening. Do we have this straight?"

"Yes, ma'am." Mary sat down to finish snapping the beans.

"I'll admit the man is handsome . . . perhaps a bit too much so. Not that a good-looking man hurts the marriage . . . not that there's going to be a marriage, mind you." She shook one finger at Mary sternly. "I have not agreed to this."

"Yes, Mama." Mary continued stringing and snapping beans.

"Now, what I want to know is this business about money . . . an inheritance. You know, Abby Sutherland's first husband gave her the very same song and dance—yes, he did, and if you think your father and I are going to allow a daughter of ours to—"

"Now, Lillie, calm down." James Taylor entered the kitchen and patted his wife's arm. "He's just a young man coming for supper."

"I'll set the table," Mary said, handing the bowl of beans to her father. "I can see you and Papa need to talk." She gave her father a pleading look as she backed her way into the dining room.

"Now, Jimmy Taylor, don't be thinking you're going to sweet-talk me into agreeing to anything here," Lillie began. "Of all our children, Mary is the one who's got you wrapped right around her little finger."

"Ah, Lillie," Mary heard her father reply. She resisted the urge to stay and eavesdrop. Matthew would be here any minute, and she was a mess. She hurried to set the table, grabbing a stack of plates from the china cabinet.

"Mary Taylor," her mother's voice boomed from the kitchen. "If you break one dish, young lady—"

"Now, Lillie," James said.

The answer was an unnecessarily loud rattling of metal pans against iron stove parts.

As quietly and quickly as possible, Mary finished setting the table. With each setting her heart dropped a bit. Her parents were bad enough, but there would be Joseph and Harry and Sissy, not to mention Libby and Travis. Her fourteen-year-old brother Billy would be there as well. Normally Billy could be counted on to ignore the usual family uproar because he was completely absorbed in his dream of heading west to be a "real" cowboy.

Matthew Hubbard was a real cowboy. Billy was going to have the vapors when he met Matthew, which would make Lillie all the more upset. Oh, Lord, the evening was going to be a disaster. Perhaps she should wear black for the occasion.

"Mrs. Taylor, I hope you don't mind. When I boarded my horse with Jake Sutherland, he introduced me to his wife Abigail, and she insisted on cutting me a bouquet for your table."

Matthew had shot to his feet the moment Lillie Taylor entered the room, and held out the magnificent display of roses Abby had cut for him to bring as a peace offering.

Lillie accepted the bouquet with a narrowed glance and a nod.

"And if I'm not being too forward, ma'am, may I add that that's a very becoming color on you?"

Lillie's eyes widened at the compliment, and she could not resist the urge to preen just a bit. "Thank you, Mr. Hubbard. It's quite an old gown actually, but then, we have little occasion for entertaining here on the prairie."

Matthew nodded sympathetically. "Not through any lack of effort on your part. Miz Hutton over at the hotel was telling me that you've spearheaded any number of civic projects in this community. I find that quite admirable in view of your other obligations . . . the store and raising such a wonderful family."

Lillie Taylor capitulated and smiled. "Why, thank you for noticing, Mr. Hubbard. We are just in the planning stages of our first annual Harvest Festival for the town. Perhaps you might have some ideas to contribute, being from Memphis and all. I imagine you've seen your share of cultural functions growing up in such a place."

Matthew chuckled. "Well, Memphis does like to throw a party now and then, ma'am. We call them balls."

"A harvest *ball*." Lillie tried out the sound of it. "It's perfect. Ah, Sissy, what on earth is keeping your sister? Here, put these in the crystal vase while I see how our dinner is coming." She pronounced vase with a broad *a* and drew out the sound of it dramatically.

"Can I be of any help?" Matthew offered.

"Oh, heavens, no, Mr. Hubbard. You are our guest. Please sit down here and make yourself comfortable." As soon as she was satisfied that Matthew was comfortably settled in the best chair, she left the room, giving James silent instruction via one arched eyebrow that he should talk to the young man.

"Well, you've made it over the first hurdle," James Taylor noted in his quiet calm way, once his wife had left the room.

"I'm glad we have this opportunity to talk before Mary comes in, Mr. Taylor. I imagine there are questions you must have."

"One or two," James agreed and took his time lighting his pipe.

Matthew waited for the older man to continue. When he didn't, Matthew picked up the conversation. "Mary tells me you own the gristmill in town."

"Yep. Store . . . gristmill . . . some land west of town. You interested?" James Taylor studied Matthew through the veil of pipe smoke.

"I'm interested in Mary," Matthew answered, which was the

truth as far as it went. Mary was the key to his getting his father's inheritance away from Louisa.

"And if you get Mary, what do you intend to do about it?" James asked, still in that same calm, steady tone. They might have been discussing the weather.

"'Do,' sir?"

"Mary has some strong ideas about how her life should go, young man. Perhaps you caught a hint of that when you realized a female had actually run an ad for a husband in the newspaper."

Matthew smiled. "It did seem a bit—"

"Headstrong?" James answered his own question with a curt nod. "The women in this family are that, Mr. Hubbard. They come by it honest . . . straight from their mother. Don't be thinking you'll change all that once you're married."

Matthew waited a beat to digest the whole sentence. "Are you giving me your permission, sir, to marry your daughter?"

James Taylor let loose a hoot of laughter and slapped the arm of his chair. "Son," he said when he had caught his breath, "if my daughter decides you're the one, there won't be a damned thing you or I can do about it." Then he tapped out the ashes of his pipe and stood up. "Lillie, when are we gonna get some food around here?" he shouted in the general direction of the kitchen.

"Coming, dear," Lillie sang out from somewhere in the recesses of the house. Then Matthew heard frantic whispering and the sound of a door opening and closing.

A moment later Mary stood at the entrance to the parlor, looking scrubbed and flushed and absolutely stunning in a skirt the color of a pine forest, topped by a blouse of mint trimmed in white lace.

Matthew shot to his feet and tried to think of something to say. "Hello," he finally managed, but the word came out a whisper. Had her hair been that shiny this afternoon? Had her skin been that perfect, her lips that full, her lashes that long?

"Hello," she whispered back.

James Taylor rolled his eyes heavenward and left the room. "Lillie, let's eat. What are we waiting for?"

They were alone . . . at least for the moment. Not that there wasn't family in practically every nook and cranny of the house, but at this particular moment she and Matthew Hubbard had some time for themselves. She risked a glance and sucked in her breath.

He was dressed in brand-new jeans and a shirt that she recognized as coming from the stock of their own store. His boots had been freshly polished, and his hair was slicked back in an attempt to tame the natural waviness of it. His skin had been scrubbed until his tanned cheekbones had taken on ruddy highlights, and she resisted the urge to take a more thorough inventory of his eyes and mouth.

"Your brother Harry was nice enough to help me get some new clothes," he said. "He's been very helpful getting me settled in and all."

"You look nice." *Nice?* He looked positively incredible. No one could have ever told Mary Taylor that anybody would make the clothes sold in her family's mercantile look the way they did on this man.

"I was hoping to maybe find a suit for the wedding, but Harry says there's nothing in my size in the store right now."

"We don't get a lot of calls for suits," Mary said as her brain tried desperately to come to grips with the rest of that statement . . . *for the wedding?* The man actually intended to marry her.

"Well, we'll think of something."

They stood opposite each other in silence. The room was not that large, and what room there was, was pretty well occupied with furnishings and knickknacks. If Matthew wanted to, he could reach out his hand and touch her, and he wanted to very much.

"You are very lovely, Mary Taylor," he said as he arranged the place where her collar did not quite lay flat. "And I'm glad

I came," he said huskily as his fingers left the collar and skimmed the line of her jaw.

Mary tilted her head back to look up at him. Lord, he was tall, and his eyes reminded her of the Kansas sky on a July day. His fingers lightly touched her skin and made goose bumps race all over her body—and if he wanted to kiss her right this minute, she didn't think she'd have the strength to do one thing about it.

"Ma says you should come on and eat," Joe barked from the doorway.

Caught in the web of Matthew Hubbard's spell, Mary had not heard her brother approach. She rocked unsteadily on her feet and was glad of Matthew's hand on her waist to steady her. "Nice to see you again, Joseph," Matt said and extended his free hand.

Joe ignored it and led the way to the dining room.

When they entered the room, all faces turned toward them. James was standing at the head of the table and indicated the chair to his right for Matthew. Mary took her place near her mother at the opposite end, shooting Matthew an apologetic look as he sat down across from Joseph and next to Sissy. Billy and Harry fought for the chair next to Joseph so they could be close to their guest and hear whatever he might say, but Libby outmaneuvered both of them, so they had to be content to take their places down at the end of the table where Lillie sat. Travis quietly held Mary's chair for her, then took his place next to her.

"Mr. Hubbard, perhaps you would like to say grace for us," Lillie suggested.

"It would be my honor, ma'am," Matthew replied with a devastating smile in Lillie's direction.

During the next half hour Mary was aware that grace was said, meat was carved, Harry's hands were slapped as he grabbed the biscuits, dishes were passed, forks hit china, and people talked . . . about what, she could not have said, but somehow the meal progressed.

"Won't you have another biscuit, Mr. Hubbard?" Lillie offered, then added, "Mary made them herself."

Libby stifled a smile, and Sissy actually snickered.

Matthew looked at Mary and smiled. "They are quite delicious," he said and caught a bit of melting butter with his tongue.

"Oh, our Mary is quite good at so many things," Lillie continued, ignoring the strange looks the rest of the family gave her.

Everyone knew that Mary's domestic skills left a great deal to be desired. She was a wizard at arithmetic and running the store, but things like doing laundry and canning peaches and waxing floors did not exactly come to mind when one thought of Mary's talents.

"Mary and I have discussed—through our correspondence, that is—her thoughts on many subjects. I believe that she may have the idea that it is a man's responsibility to at least help with some of the domestic chores. And I must say I quite agree, particularly when Mary herself has such a good head for business and could be such a help to me in that way."

Mary blushed with pleasure that he had actually picked up on the part of her ad that had stated that she was a modern young woman with modern ideas. Furthermore, he actually agreed with her.

"What is your business, Mr. Hubbard?" Joe asked suspiciously.

"Since the war I've been serving as a scout and pathfinder in the Colorado territories."

"What about your vast business holdings in Tennessee?" Joe persisted. His voice remained level, but the tenseness of his posture told the real story behind his questions.

"Those holdings were my father's," Matthew answered equally calmly, his entire attention now focused on Joseph, forcing the other man to meet him eye-to-eye. "My father passed away last month, and word has just reached me."

"You didn't get to say good-bye?" Libby asked sympathetically.

"No, but I have an opportunity to make that up to him. You see, he had written a somewhat unusual will, leaving his estate to me if I claimed it as a married man, and to his widow if I did not. Since his widow is someone I know to have betrayed my father, you may understand why I am anxious to make certain that my father's good name does not fall into her hands."

"And that's why you answered my daughter's advertisement for a husband?" James Taylor was the only person at the table who was continuing to eat after this shocking revelation from Matthew."

"Yes, sir."

"Did you know this, Mary?" Papa picked up the platter of beef and offered it to Matthew.

"Yes," she lied.

"Mary knew a part of it. I had come here to tell her the rest." Matt looked directly at Mary. "For whatever reason, fate made me read that ad and has brought me here. I never had any intention of deceiving Mary. This afternoon I wanted the opportunity to tell her the full circumstances of my coming in private. And if Mary chooses not to accept me, I'll be gone tomorrow."

There was a long silence as each person at the table looked at Mary.

"If I may say one thing more," Matt continued quietly.

All eyes swung back to him.

"I have told you my motive for coming here. What I have not told you is that even before receiving the news of my father's death I had begun to long for the kind of family ties I had always known and which tragically had been severed, first by the war and then through my own stubbornness and pride."

Matthew stood up and walked to where Mary sat. He stood behind her chair and placed his hands lightly on her shoulders. "Mr. Taylor, I would ask your permission to call on your daughter for the next few days. I regret that time is a factor here, but I believe that if Mary and I are allowed to have the opportunity to get to know each other—"

"There will be no getting to know one another without an

engagement, young man." Lillie's tone left no room for debate. "There will be an engagement, a formal date set for the wedding, and *then* the two of you can get to know each other. I will not have this family's name scandalized yet again." Her eyes riveted on Travis Miller.

"Would two weeks be enough time?" James asked.

Matthew's fingers tightened on Mary's shoulders, and she reached up and placed her hand over one of his. "Yes, Papa, two weeks is quite enough time," she said.

"Two weeks!" Lillie shrieked. "You expect me to plan a proper wedding in two weeks? Really, James . . . that's exactly the time we've set for the Harvest Festival! How can I possibly—"

"Papa, do we have a bargain?" Mary persisted, afraid of losing the advantage just gained.

James studied Matthew. "Mr. Hubbard, do you understand that if my daughter agrees to have you and the two of you marry, I will tolerate no mistreatment of her?"

"Yes, sir."

"Let's just put that in terms a cowboy might be a little better at understanding," Joe added. "If you do anything to hurt my baby sister here before or after the wedding, I'll come after you myself."

Matthew nodded. "I hope one day you'll be proud to call me your brother, Joseph."

When the meal was finally over, Matthew insisted that he and Mary would clear the table and wash the dishes. "You put in a full day at the store, Miz Taylor, then came home to prepare this wonderful meal. No, you rest yourself. Mary and I can do this in short order."

The man was a charmer. Lillie made the weakest of objections before giving in.

"I'll help too," Sissy announced, casting adoring glances at the tall handsome stranger who had traveled hundreds of miles just to meet her sister.

"You and your brothers will attend to your studies, young lady," James Taylor instructed.

There was a chorus of "Oh, Papa" from the three youngest Taylors, but they all trudged off to their rooms.

Matthew said his good nights to Libby and Travis. "It seems the two of you might give me some pointers when it comes to getting on the good side of Miz Taylor," he said softly to Travis as the two men stood at the door waiting for Libby to bid her parents good night.

Travis grinned. "Well, I sure could tell you what *not* to do."

Libby came through the kitchen, trailed by her parents. "I'll come by the store tomorrow, Mama, and maybe you and Mary and I can discuss plans for the wedding." Then she stopped by the dry sink where Mary was stacking the dishes and gave her sister a quick hug. "I like him, Mary," she whispered.

Mary blushed and smiled and fought down a panic that had been growing ever since the date had been set—a date for a wedding—her wedding. She glanced at Matthew as he stood at the door to the back stairway, smiling and waving to the departing Libby and Travis. Good Lord, this man was a total stranger . . . good-looking and charming as all get-out . . . but a stranger nonetheless. Could she actually take vows to love, honor, and obey this man? And could she actually do that in two weeks?

Mama busied herself with wiping the large table in the center of the kitchen, pretending not to be finding things to do to stay in the kitchen.

"Lillie, let's go and sit for a spell and give these young people a chance to get to know each other," James said as he gently took the rag from his wife and handed it to Mary.

"We'll be right in the next room," Lillie warned.

"Yes, Mama," Mary said quietly.

"Come along, Lil," James urged, and led her from the room.

Mary and Matthew worked in silence for several minutes.

"My family used to call me Matt," he said finally.

Mary nodded and gave her full energy and attention to scrubbing a pot. Suddenly it was enormously important that she make a good impression on him with her skills at getting that pot to sparkle.

"You could call me Matt or Matthew."

Again, Mary nodded and kept scrubbing.

"I like the name Mary. It suits you."

"It's very . . . ordinary." Mary ventured a glance and then immediately concentrated once again on her scrubbing.

"You're not ordinary," he answered, and gently removed the pot from her hands and rinsed it in the pan of water next to her. "Did I scare you in there when I told your family why it's so important that I marry soon?"

Mary examined her feelings at the moment he'd made that announcement. "No. I'm a little . . . confused, I suppose, but not scared. I'm rarely scared about anything, Matthew."

He grinned and, having wiped the pan dry, waited for her to give him the next dish. "I gathered that."

"I do have a question or two," she said, gaining confidence.

"I would imagine you do," he said wryly. "Fire away."

"Well, your father—I mean his wife—you said she betrayed him, but how do you know that if you've been gone and haven't had contact all this time?"

"Her betrayal of him was the reason I left. I assume that it continued after I was gone."

There was a sadness in his tone that touched Mary. What must it have been like to have left his father and had no word all this time? "But if you knew she was betraying him, why didn't you tell him?"

"I did. He didn't believe me."

"But later . . ."

"May I tell you the whole story, Mary? I want you to know exactly what has happened to bring me here to you." He had stopped drying the dishes and stood very close to her, staring down at her. His expression reflected many emotions . . . grief, regret, and mostly profound sadness.

"Please tell me, Matthew."

"It isn't a pretty story," he warned, "and I am no hero in it."

"I outgrew fairy tales some years ago," she answered softly, and touched his hand. What was it about this man that made her want to touch him, to hold him, to be held by him without even really knowing him?

"Is everything all right in there?" Lillie called from the parlor.

Matthew smiled and covered Mary's hand with his own, then clunked a heavy metal skillet against the top of the cookstove. "Yes, ma'am, right as rain. We shouldn't be much longer here."

He picked up three glasses Mary had already washed and put them back into the soapy water, clinking them together and swishing the water with one hand to create appropriate noises.

Mary smiled and followed his lead, taking a stack of already washed and dried plates and depositing them in the soapy water as well.

As they rewashed the dishes, Matt told Mary the story of his leaving his father's home. He left nothing out, and she made no comment during the telling of it. The part about Louisa's brazen behavior made her stiffen and even blush a bit, but she endured it without comment.

"Was she very beautiful?" she asked when he had finished.

He shrugged. "She was missing some of the key ingredients."

"Such as?"

"Kindness . . . loyalty . . . a kind of generous spirit."

They worked in silence for a few minutes.

"What was your mother like?" Mary asked.

He smiled immediately. "Now, there was a beauty. She was one of the most decent people I've ever known. Everyone loved her—everyone. On the other hand, when she set her mind to something she could be as stubborn as any mule you ever met."

"She sounds like a wonderful woman."

Matt looked down at her. "She would have liked you, Mary Taylor. She would have seen the way you stood up to Joseph this afternoon and taken to you at once . . . just as I have."

His voice had gotten very low and soft, and he was standing

very close to her. Mary had to tip her head back to look up at him, and she was very aware of the breadth of him. He curled a wisp of her hair around one of his long fingers as he watched her.

"Matt," she whispered and felt her body moving closer to his.

"Can we make this work, Mary?" he asked huskily as he released the strand of hair and allowed his finger to trace a path down her cheek and across her parted lips.

"Perhaps," she answered and resisted the insane urge to take his finger between her lips, nip it with her teeth, tease it with her tongue.

"Shall we make a bargain, then?" He cupped her chin with his large hand and tilted her head to one side as his face came nearer.

Unable to speak, Mary nodded.

When he kissed her, Mary forgot all about the last plate she'd been about to hand him for drying. It dangled precariously from her wet soapy fingers as his mouth met hers.

Holy Moses.

In her whole life Mary Taylor had never been kissed in such a way . . . gentle, but not the least bit tentative. No, he was being fairly clear about his intentions here. With his fingers on her chin he was guiding her to accept his kiss, and he wasn't about to offer some quick little peck and break off. No, this was a kiss that could go on forever if she was lucky.

His tongue slid across her lips, and Mary gasped and reached for him to steady herself or pull him closer . . . she wasn't sure which. But in that moment the plate clattered noisily to the floor and shattered.

"What in the name of sweet . . ."

Lillie Taylor could be heard moving heavily down the short hallway.

Matt broke the kiss and steadied Mary before kneeling and starting to gather the shards of the plate.

"I am sorry, Miz Taylor. I'll make it up to you, I promise. It just slipped. I feel like such a clumsy oaf, ma'am. Can you forgive me?"

By focusing all of Lillie's attention on the broken dish and his distress, he gave Mary the moment she needed to get hold of herself.

"It's just a plate, Mama," she said, bending to help gather up the chips and pieces. "Actually it was my fault. We were talking, and I just wasn't paying attention and—"

"I had turned away for a moment, and Mary thought I was still standing there and—"

"All *right*," Lillie interrupted their chatter with an exasperated sigh. She reached behind the door and produced a broom. "Just make sure you get all the pieces up."

"Yes, ma'am," Matthew said sheepishly.

"After that I'd suggest it's about time you went back to the hotel, Mr. Hubbard," Lillie continued. "Mary has a full day at the store tomorrow."

"Perhaps I could help out, ma'am," Matt suggested as he swept the floor with gusto.

Lillie gave him a suspicious glance, then looked at her daughter who was still kneeling and picking up nonexistent chips of glass. "We'll see."

CHAPTER
6

By morning everyone in town knew of the arrival of Matthew Hubbard. He had been waiting outside the store when Lillie snapped the shades open. With a cheery greeting, he had relieved her of the broom she carried and began sweeping the boardwalk. When he'd finished that he'd begun restocking shelves. By eight o'clock Lillie was ordering him around as if he'd been working for her for years. The store did a brisk and steady business that morning, as just about everyone in town found some urgent need to purchase something so they could get a look at the tall, handsome stranger. Few of them were subtle about it. Some, like Zeke Gallagher from the barbershop, walked into the store and right up to Matt.

"You'll do," he announced as he looked Matt over from head to toe. "Yes, I think you'll do just fine."

"So happy to have your approval, Zeke," Lillie huffed. "Was there something you needed?"

"No. That'll do it," Zeke answered. "Just wanted to see what all the fuss was about."

"Nice meeting you," Matt called after the older man with the full white beard and the twinkling blue eyes.

Zeke was barely out the door before Fred Winchester arrived. "Lillian, my dear, what can you be thinking? A wedding on the weekend of our festival?" He bustled into the store, straight past Mary and Matt, then stopped and turned his full attention to Matthew. "Oh, is this the bridegroom?"

Frederick Winchester and his nephew Edward had arrived in Harmony from England the previous year. In keeping with the stereotype most of the people of Harmony had about the English, Edward proved to be aloof and standoffish. A bit too proud for his own good, some folks thought . . . at least, until he had met Zan Bailey.

Fred, on the other hand, had seemed to take to the life he found in Harmony like the proverbial duck to water. Since he had arrived, Lillie had found a soul mate for all her various projects. If enthusiasm for her latest civic improvement waned among the citizenry of Harmony, Lillie could always count on Fred's support and involvement.

"Mr. Winchester, I'd like you to meet Matthew Hubbard, my . . ." Mary paused. She had been about to introduce Matt as her fiancé, but the word simply would not come.

"Your betrothed, of course. So pleased to make your acquaintance, Mr. Hubbard." Fred was short and stocky, and he had to look up almost as far as Mary did in order to meet Matt's eyes.

Matt accepted the man's handshake and smiled. "The pleasure is mine," he replied.

"Ah, a Southern gentleman!" Fred exclaimed. "The accent, you know . . . borders on the proper British, some say, though I can't quite agree. Still, it is distinctive, isn't it?"

Matt sifted through the comments looking for a compliment, and wasn't sure one was to be found. "I suspect my accent has faded a bit. It's been several years since I left Tennessee."

"Ah, Memphis. My nephew and I stopped there to visit some distant cousins before heading west. Quite lovely in its own way." Without waiting for a response, he turned his full attention back to Lillie. "Well, my dear, we do have a bit of a dilemma here, do we not? I mean the festival and the wedding all in one weekend. Unless . . ." He stroked his chin and paced the area in front of the candy display.

"Nothing is really finalized yet, Mr. Winchester," Mary said, risking a quick look at Matt to see how he was reacting to all this talk of a wedding. Would the reality of what they were planning finally hit him and give him cold feet? It was a thought she had been wrestling with all morning as her mother and Libby and practically every woman in the town of Harmony had discussed colors and flowers and music and attire for the wedding without seeming to pay one bit of attention to either Mary or Matt.

"I believe Mary and I would be happy with something quite small and simple, Mr. Winchester," Matt offered as he continued to sort and shelve the small hardware pieces that had arrived on the train with him.

"Oh, my good man, no. Harmony does not do small and simple weddings, do we, Lillie? Each joining is an occasion . . . a celebration of the growth of the community. No, we'll have to . . . I have it . . . just the thing." He snapped his fingers and turned on one heel to face them.

Two men who'd been loafing around the unlit stove all morning pretending to play checkers while they actually picked up the gossip about the new man in town gave Fred their full attention. Jane Evans turned from the bolt of fabric she'd been considering, and Faith Hutton, who'd just entered the store, paused just inside the doorway.

When Fred was certain he had the attention of all in the room, he outlined his grand plan. "The wedding will be held at the festival. It will, in fact, be the highlight of the festival. We've been casting about for some suitable afternoon and evening's entertainment—this is it."

"I don't think—" Mary began.

"Shhh," Lillie warned, and pulled out pencil and paper to make notes. "Let me think."

Mary gave Matt an apologetic smile and moved closer to her

mother. "Mother," she whispered, "perhaps Matthew and I could—"

"Shhh!" Lillie answered with more authority as she continued to scribble notes.

Mary rolled her eyes and waited, as did everyone else in the store, except Matt, who calmly continued sorting nails and screws and hinges into their proper bins.

"I have it," Lillie crowed triumphantly after several moments of muttering to herself, scratching out notes, and starting over with new lists. She hurried around the edge of the counter and showed the paper to Fred. "We'll have the ceremony on Friday morning, serve a bountiful lunch, and offer dancing and entertainment through the afternoon, and the happy couple can leave on the four-oh-eight for their wedding trip to Memphis that very afternoon."

"It's perfect," Fred agreed.

"I—" Mary began.

"A wedding on a Friday morning?" Jane Evans dropped all pretense of studying the bolt of fabric and moved to participate more directly in the conversation. "That's a bit unconventional, isn't it?"

"There ain't a powerful lot of *convention* to any of this business," muttered one of the men at the checkerboard to his partner.

Jane ignored the men and continued. "I mean, wouldn't it make more sense to hold the ceremony on Sunday morning during services, or even Saturday afternoon?"

"But then they'd have to wait a whole week longer to head for Memphis," Faith Hutton said as she abandoned her position near the door and joined the rest of the group.

"I must say that all the rush is a bit beyond me. What is the reason for your haste, Lillie?" Fred asked.

"They must get to Memphis in time," Faith answered for Lillie. "I mean, they could lose everything if they don't get there as soon as possible. Matthew's entire fortune is at stake here."

"I—" Mary tried again.

"Oh, how perfectly awful," Fred said without giving the slightest indication he was aware that Mary was even in the same room, much less trying to speak.

"Excuse me," she said more forcibly as she edged her way to the center of the group. "Will everyone please stop making plans for Matthew and me as if we didn't have any say in all this?"

"Of course, dear," Lillie replied as she frowned and studied her notes yet again. "What was it you wanted to say?"

"Well, maybe Matthew would rather . . . that is, we . . . that is . . ."

"I think what my beautiful bride-to-be is trying to say is that all this planning is a bit overwhelming. After all, Mary and I have barely had time to say more than hello, much less explore what sort of wedding ceremony we might like. Perhaps, Mrs. Taylor, you wouldn't mind if Mary and I took a picnic just across the river there near the mill and spent an hour talking?"

Lillie frowned. "Well . . ."

"We'd be in plain sight of half the town, Mother, not to mention the mill where Papa might look out at any moment and observe us."

"I suppose . . ."

"Wonderful!" Matthew exclaimed. "Mary, why don't you go up and get your bonnet and a blanket while Mrs. Hutton and I go over to the hotel restaurant and pack a lunch." He moved to take Faith Hutton's elbow and started for the door.

Mary could not help smiling. How neatly he had turned the tables on them all. Just minutes before, her mother and the others were making all the plans. But now Matthew was firmly in charge. Lillie could do little more than nod and smile as Matt led Faith back to the restaurant and Mary hurried upstairs to collect her bonnet and a blanket.

"I'll meet you at the livery, Mary," Matt called. "Perhaps Jake would permit me to rent a small surrey for the afternoon."

"I'd like that," Mary replied, and gave him her brightest smile. When she looked back at the others, they were all smiling too . . . even her mother. Young love got to people every time.

"Colorful little town you've got here, Mary," Matt observed as he leaned against a tree after they had finished eating the cheese, apples, and bread Faith had packed for them. "It was the first thing I noticed as the train pulled in. I could see the colors for some distance, and it looked so . . . I don't know, like a rainbow or circus or something."

"That was Mama's idea. She wanted the town to stand out so people would remember it and also because for so many years it was like every other little town in Kansas . . . kind of dull and barren."

"I like your mother. She has a lot of spunk."

Mary smiled. "Some people might call it something else."

Matt laughed. "Well, I'll call it spunk until she gives me cause to call it something else. I expect in the course of our lives your mother and I may clash a time or two."

For the third time since they'd left the store, he made a comment indicating that he and Mary would indeed be spending many long years together. On the ride past the mill, he'd asked about the milling business and wondered if he had what it took to help her father. "I suppose with time I can learn," he'd said.

When she set out the food, he had said that after they were settled in their own home he hoped they would always take time for picnics and outings like this.

"Mary?" Matt was looking at her with a slight frown clouding those blue eyes of his.

She had been lost in thought, and clearly Matt had been talking to her.

"I'm sorry. My mind wandered off there." She tried giving him a big smile, but his expression remained serious and concerned.

"Why did you run the ad, Mary? I can't imagine that the young men of Harmony, Kansas, aren't standing in line to marry you."

Mary laughed. "Well, they aren't."

"Do you mean to tell me there hasn't been one serious beau?"

"There have been . . . suitors, but . . ."

"But what? I've told you my story, Mary. Now it's your turn."

"Well, the boys here . . . the men who might be suitable husbands for me are so . . . conventional. They all think that once a woman marries, her life is given over to them and the children and the housework and heaven only knows what else."

"You mean that's not the way it is?" Matt asked in a shocked tone.

Mary shot him a look of surprise. "Surely you understood from the advertisement that I wanted—" But then she saw that he was teasing her and gave him a poke in the arm. "You're just teasing me, aren't you?"

"Pretty successfully, I might add," he said.

She hit him once again. "Don't be so cocky, Matt Hubbard."

"All right, go on with your story. Do you mean to tell me there wasn't one modern man in the bunch? What about Danny Vega?"

"How do you know about Danny?"

"Little Amanda dropped by while I was shaving this morning. She and her dog plopped themselves onto my bed and filled me in. Danny sounded like a serious contender."

Mary made a mental note to talk to Faith's daughter Amanda about the problems of gossiping. "Danny and I saw a quite a lot of each other."

"Lucky Danny," Matt muttered and then grinned and wiggled his eyebrows at her to show that he'd caught the double entendre of her words and was making the most of it.

She poked him again. "Do you want to hear this or not?"

"I don't know. Tell me how it turns out. Are you still in love with him?"

"I never said I was in love with him or any other man," Mary protested.

"You must have been in love," Matt challenged.

"You mean a woman of my advanced years," Mary huffed.

"I didn't say that. It's just that—"

"Have you been in love, and how did that end? You certainly haven't told me that."

"I've never met a woman I felt that way about," he protested.

"Oh, really. A man of your advanced years and never even been close."

"It's different for a man," Matt argued. "Besides, you're deliberately avoiding the issue. What about Vega?"

"Well, I'm certain this will come as a major surprise to you, but the truth is that I broke it off."

"You?"

"Good heavens, Matt, you're just like all the others. It just never occurs to any of you that a woman might actually have her own ideas, her own needs, her own dreams, that do not rise and set in some man." Which technically wasn't one hundred percent true, since a great many of Mary's fantasies and dreams revolved around her ideal man, who had in the last twenty-four hours taken on the personage of Matthew Hubbard.

"So tell me your dreams, Mary." Matt reclined on one elbow and pulled a long piece of prairie grass to chew on as he studied her.

"I'd like to travel some, but also come home here to Harmony. You know, as much as I want to see different places, I'll always want to come back here. I can't imagine what it would be like to be miles away from my family." She looked out across the field toward the mill. "Did you know that when my grandfather came here from Europe, he never saw his parents or brothers and sisters again? Ever! I don't think I could bear that."

"It's tough, all right," Matt said quietly and followed her gaze out toward the mill.

"Oh, Matt, I'm sorry. You must be thinking of your father and how you left, and now he's gone and . . . Oh, how insensitive of me. I'm so very sorry."

He smiled. "It's all right, Mary. But I know what you mean. As I told your family last night, even before I got the news of

my father's death I had begun to long for family connec-
tions . . . roots."

"Do you have siblings?"

"My two brothers died in the war."

"And your mother died then as well. Oh, Matthew, how
horrible for you."

He shrugged. "What I said last night about family wasn't
some scam. I meant every word of it. Do you want children?"

"Yes."

Her prompt response seemed to give him pleasure. "How
many?"

"However many come," she said, suddenly uncomfortable
with the image she was attaching to the process of conceiving
and having babies.

He grinned broadly. "Me, too. Let's make sure there are a lot
of them, okay?"

There it was again, that assumption that they would in fact
spend years and years together as a result of a newspaper ad
and an old man's will. Mary gave him a tentative smile and
busied herself with clearing the scraps of their picnic.

"You don't have to go through with this, you know," Matt
said after several minutes in which she could feel his eyes
watching her face. "We can end it any time. I would just
appreciate sooner rather than later, since it's very important that
I fulfill the terms of my father's will."

Mary's heart fell. For the briefest of moments she had
allowed herself to imagine he might truly care for her. But of
course theirs was an arranged marriage, not a love match.
Perhaps in time he would grow fond of her, but for now they
had a business arrangement, nothing more.

Last night, alone in her room, she had allowed herself to
relive his kiss again and again, and by morning she had
convinced herself that in that brief moment of contact they had
moved beyond the unusual circumstances that had brought
them together. Of course, that was all part of her fantasy life.
Mary was finding out that with Matt here, keeping her real life
and her dreams separate was becoming increasingly difficult.

"Mary?" Matt sat up and reached to still her hand from its busywork. "Are you having second thoughts about marrying me?" His voice was soft and much too close.

"No," she murmured, not daring to look at him, not daring to risk showing him how much she had already come to care for him. "Are you having second thoughts?"

He tipped her face up to his and smiled at her. "Not a single one."

"Good," she answered, but it came out a whisper as she realized how close his lips were to her own and how very much she'd like him to kiss her again. "Perhaps we should get back."

"No. We still have Faith's chocolate cake to eat, and I still have to kiss you, Mary Taylor." His voice was low and mesmerizing. He still cupped her face in one of his large hands. Their lips were only a whisper apart.

"I think you're right . . . I mean, about the cake . . . Faith would be very hurt if . . ."

"And what about the kiss, Mary?"

Mary swallowed. "Well . . . that would be . . ." She fumbled for an appropriate word other than the one that sprang to mind, which was *heavenly*.

"That would be what, Mary?" His lips grazed her cheek and nuzzled her earlobe.

Her pulse raced, and her heart threatened to pound its way out of the tight confines of her blouse. "That would be all right," she whispered and allowed herself the luxury of touching his hair where it curled a bit just at the nape of his neck.

"Just all right?" he argued quietly as he moved to kiss the very spot where her pulse pounded in her throat.

Her fingers clenched, grasping a whole handful of his soft thick hair, and the action brought him closer. "It would be quite . . ."

"Wonderful? Disastrous? What, Mary?" He continued to question her, punctuating each question with a fresh kiss on her neck, her cheeks, her eyelids.

"Quite heavenly," she whispered, and wasn't certain if she had said the words aloud.

"I agree," Matt whispered back just before his lips covered hers.

The kiss was every bit as wonderful as the one of the night before. Only it was far too short. His lips met hers, pressed, moved away. The tip of his tongue touched her lips. Then he opened his mouth and tugged at her lower lips with his lips and teeth. When she gave a whimper of frustration at being so inexperienced and not knowing what to do to give him pleasure, he pulled away.

"It's okay," he said to soothe her, stroking her hair.

"Where did you learn to kiss like that?" She blurted the first thing that came to mind. Danny's kisses had been wet, slobbery ones, and he seemed intent on devouring her. The Bailey boy's kisses had been dry and sterile.

Matt smiled. "I could teach you if you like."

"Teach me?" Was this normal? Did girls take lessons from more experienced men?

Matt nodded and readjusted his position. "Just follow my lead . . . do what I do," he said softly as once again his mouth descended to hers.

At first he once again pressed his closed lips to hers. She pressed back. They held that for a moment, and he pulled back.

"How was that?"

"Okay," she responded, her eyes still closed.

"Lesson two," he whispered. This time when his lips met hers, she could feel the tip of his tongue wetting her lips. Tentatively she edged her own tongue out and traced it along the outline of his mouth. When he shuddered against her, she felt a sense of undeniable power.

Once again he pulled back. "Very nice," he said, and his words came out raspy and husky as if he were having trouble finding his breath. "Lesson three."

This time his mouth was open when it met hers, and he began to nibble, stroke, and probe. When she worked up the courage

85

to open to him, his tongue was immediately inside, filling her with an incredible need.

She could hear their teeth meeting and feel the rush of his breath coming into her. Her response was to follow his lead. She allowed her tongue a quick foray in and out of his mouth. Then he caught it between his teeth, holding it there, and she thought he might pull back yet again. To keep him there, she snaked her arms around his back and hugged him to her.

To her delight, he did not pull away. Instead his arms surrounded her, and his hands roamed over her back, down to her hips. All the while his mouth moved over hers, open and hot and wet . . . not in the slobbery way Danny's had been, but in a way that seemed to somehow match the liquid heat that raced through her limbs.

This time when he pulled back, they were both breathing as if they had just finished some sort of race. His face was flushed, and Mary could feel the color in her own cheeks as well.

"What's lesson four?" she whispered, following the urge to snuggle against him with her face against his tanned neck.

Matthew gave an unsteady chuckle. "You must have been at the head of your class in school, Mary," he said softly, then kissed her hair, her temple.

"I was. What's lesson four?" she repeated.

"Lesson four is far too complicated for us to get into today."

Mary felt profoundly disappointed and then had another idea. She sat up so she could see his face. "In school we used to review our lessons just before a test," she said.

This time he laughed out loud, and Mary found that the sound of it filled her heart with an emotion she could not begin to identify, but one that gave her such a feeling of well-being and pleasure.

"So, shall we review?" she pressed.

Matt was tempted. Lord, the woman was going to be a regular little hellion in bed if this afternoon was any indication at all. And therein lay the problem. He'd thought he could steal a few kisses, make a little progress toward easing the speed with which they were moving toward this marriage. But the truth was, every time he even thought about kissing her, his body knotted in ways he hadn't thought possible. In addition, last night he had realized that in the span of less than a day he had made the transition from marrying Mary Taylor as a matter of convenience for both of them, to seriously considering the realities of a lifetime with this woman. He must be completely out of his mind.

"Matt?" Her face was close to his, and she was sifting his hair through her fingers. He tightened his hold on her.

"How much do you know about . . . uh, men and women, Mary?"

Mary felt the color in her flushed face change from a rosy glow to bright red. "I . . . that is . . ." Suddenly her eyes filled with tears of embarrassment. "You must think me a terrible child," she murmured.

"Shhh." He kissed her cheeks. "I want you, Mary Taylor. I want you in the same way a man wants a woman when they lie together to make their children. And kissing you makes me want you that much more. That is lesson four."

Mary sucked in her breath on a shocked sigh. He was whispering in her ear the very words she'd been thinking. When he'd asked about what she knew of men and women, the image of lying with him had immediately sprung to mind. She had found herself imagining the two of them naked, coupled . . . Lord, such thoughts!

She moved away from him and opened the picnic basket. "Perhaps it would be wise for us to have that chocolate cake now," she said primly.

"That might be a good idea," Matt agreed and thought to himself that it was going to be a month of Sundays till two weeks had gone by and he could marry this woman.

CHAPTER
7

On Sunday morning Mary and Matt got a slight reprieve from being the center of the town's attention. Just before he began his sermon, the Reverend Abraham Johnson announced that he and his wife Rachel would be moving west to California to start an orphanage there.

His news was met by a communal gasp, followed by a few seconds of stunned silence, then a low buzz of speculation as to what might be done about attracting a new minister as soon as possible. The reverend allowed a minute for reaction to die down before announcing the topic of his sermon.

"This morning I'd like us all to consider the topic of the Challenges of Life. Shall we begin with prayer?"

Every head bowed, but few citizens actually heard the words of the prayer until the minister came to the familiar congregate rendering of the Lord's Prayer. Mary's own attention was less on the good reverend and his sudden announcement and more on the man sitting next to her.

Matt had arrived at the church just as everyone was taking a seat for the service. The Taylor family had occupied the second and third pews on the left for as long as the church had been standing. As the children had grown and needed more space, the older children had been assigned the second pew, just in front of their parents. Almost everyone liked to sit a little farther back from the minister, so the first and second pews were often vacant . . . except for the Taylor children.

These days the second pew was occupied by Mary, Joe, Libby, her husband Travis, and their son from Libby's first marriage, Robert Junior. Lillie and James sat in back of them with Sissy, Billy, and an ever-squirming Harry. They had all just gotten settled when Matt came down the side aisle and slid in next to Mary.

Mary could hear the tongues of the other families wagging behind them, heard Lillie whisper something to James in a startled squeak, heard her father reply, "Now, Lil, they are engaged after all," and heard the Reverend Johnson clear his throat to indicate he was prepared to start the service as soon as everyone got settled.

When the first hymn was announced, Matt reached across Mary and took a hymnal from the rack, opening it to the song and holding it out for himself and Mary to see. His large hand spanned the back of the hymnal, holding it flat and steady. Mary's own fingers were shaking as she gingerly took hold of one corner of the book.

Matt had a wonderful voice, deep and rich, and he seemed to enjoy singing. On top of that he knew the hymn, which gave Mary some comfort; to her it indicated that he had been raised as a churchgoing man. That was important in a marriage and for raising their children properly.

Their children?! Good Lord, what was happening to her? When he had responded favorably to her ad, she hadn't really thought about a schedule of events. If she had, though, her plan probably would have covered months, not mere weeks. Actually only a few days remained—if all went as planned, by Sunday after next she would be Matt's wife!

She risked a look at him.

He had on a freshly laundered white shirt with a starched collar that made his tanned skin look more bronze than brown. A leather vest and the same stiff jeans he'd worn for supper the night before completed his outfit. His boots were polished to a high shine, and his cheeks were ruddy with a fresh shave and scrubbing. His hair was still damp and fighting his efforts to smooth it back from his forehead.

He looked down at her and smiled, then moved half a step closer as the organist launched into the final verse of the hymn. The kisses they had shared on their picnic raced through Mary's mind, and the memory brought a flame to her face. When the hymn was finished and they sat down again, Matt sat as close to her as propriety would allow, making her keenly aware of his height, his solid body, the muscles in his thighs, his . . .

Libby leaned across Travis and offered Mary one of the cardboard fans kept in the pews during the hot weather. "Are you not well?" Libby mouthed.

Mary realized her breathing was irregular, and she was quite flushed. She willed herself to calm down, refused the fan, and turned her full attention toward the pulpit.

Matt might have enjoyed Mary's predicament if he weren't having some problems of his own. The woman always smelled of springtime. . . . How did she do that? The perfumes he knew of were usually the heavy, cloying type favored by the employees of places like the First Resort. And every time he was with her he realized all over again how petite she was. It had occurred to him last night as he lay sleepless in his hotel bed that when he took her to bed he was in danger of crushing her and that he'd have to be careful not to hurt her.

Today she was dressed in blue. Was there any color she didn't look wonderful in? It was the hair, he decided, black as night and shiny as the obsidian cliffs he'd seen in Wyoming. Or maybe it was her skin, creamy and pale, with that dusting of freckles across her nose. Or maybe it was the way she filled out her clothes. For someone so petite, she had a figure that made a man look twice . . . three times. The tight bodices that were currently the fashion here in Harmony emphasized her breasts and tiny waist in a way that bordered on indecent, for all that her dresses were always buttoned to her chin.

Matt swallowed and ran one finger under his tight, stiff collar. Kincaid Hutton had brought him the shirt and collar this morning, saying it was his wife Faith's idea. He'd noted that Matt could wear the shirt or not, but Faith was sure he wanted to make an especially good impression in his first public appearance. Lord, the town was infested with matchmakers. He tried to concentrate on the sermon and ignore the fact that if he moved an inch to his right, he and Mary would be touching.

"Well, the reverend certainly had startling news," Libby said as they all stood outside the church in the bright October sunlight following the service. "You aren't by any chance a Methodist minister, are you, Matthew?"

Matt grinned. "No, ma'am. I've been a lot of things in my life, but a preacher isn't one of them."

"Too bad. I suppose we'll need to run some ads in some of the larger papers. I see Samantha over there. Perhaps she has some ideas."

"Libby's very active in the church," Mary said as she and Matt watched Libby hurry across the churchyard to catch up with Samantha.

"Your whole family seems to be quite involved in everything that goes on in this town," Matt replied. Though they were surrounded by other churchgoers, for the moment they were alone, standing a little apart from the others under the shade of a large oak tree.

"My grandfather started the mill, and the town sort of grew from that."

Matt nodded.

"I suppose you'll be wanting to see the mill," she continued. "After all, I did promise you a job."

"Does your father know that?" Matt grinned at her.

She shrugged. "You showed him the ad. He read it for himself, and it's right there in print."

Matt laughed. "Meaning he didn't know about it any more than he knew about me coming here."

Mary shifted uncomfortably and focused on an acorn just beyond her shoe. "Well, please don't feel that you are under any obligation . . ."

With one finger under her chin, he tilted her face so that she had to look up at him. He was no longer laughing. "I came to see if this would work, Mary—for both of us. The more time I spend with you, the more certain I become that from my standpoint it will indeed work out just fine. You have to decide how it looks from where you stand."

"Just like that? You've decided in little more than a day that it will work?" She jerked her chin out of his hand and walked away from him and the curious glances of the others, to the other side of the large oak.

Matt followed her. "Look, I have been completely honest with you as to why I answered this ad of yours. I'm sorry we can't take the time we need to see this thing through in a more conventional manner, but I'm willing to take a chance. What you have to decide, Mary Taylor, is whether when you ran that ad you were prepared to follow through on it, or were just playing out some silly fantasy."

She stiffened at his tone and kept her back to him.

Matt sighed and moved to stand behind her, placing his hands on her shoulders as he spoke more softly next to her ear. "I'm sorry. I don't mean to press you, Mary, but there are some pieces of this that I have no control over, and that includes my father's conditions in his will. I cannot let Louisa get her hands on his estate . . . on my heritage. I owe that much to my father. And to my children when they come. I need your help, Mary, and if for some reason it doesn't work out for us down the road, I promise you we'll find a way."

Mary knew he was right. A man as handsome and independent as Matthew Hubbard would not need to answer an ad for a mail-order husband except in the most unusual of circumstances. He had come in answer to the business arrangement she herself had proposed. In her ad she had laid out certain conditions, and Matt was prepared to meet them. Upon his arrival he had laid out his own conditions. Was she prepared to meet them? It was as simple as that. They had a business arrangement.

She could have adventure, financial security, and a good, strong, handsome man to father her children, or she could wait around for love.

"Perhaps this afternoon we could ride out to see the land I mentioned in the ad," she said softly.

He turned her around to face him. "I'd like that," he said solemnly. Then he kissed her softly on the lips. "Thank you, Mary," he whispered just before pulling her into his arms and kissing her once again.

"Mama had a fit when Travis kissed Libby right out in town," Harry announced from just behind them.

Mary and Matt leaped apart.

"How long have you been standing there?" Mary asked her youngest brother as she adjusted her bonnet and smoothed one hand over her skirt.

"Long enough to know Matt kissed you twice. Travis only did it once, and he'd known Libby since they were babies practically. You and Matt hardly know each other a bit, and he's already kissed you about a thousand times."

"Twice," Mary corrected with a nervous glance toward Matt.

"Nope. Lots more than that. Yesterday when you two went on your picnic I bet he kissed you umpty-nine times."

"You were spying!" Mary shrieked and lunged for her brother.

"Was not!" Harry yelled back as he took off down Main Street with Mary in hot pursuit.

Matt watched her go, grinning as he noticed how the very proper young woman had turned magically into a delightful girl bent on throttling her little brother.

"Mr. Hubbard," Lillie Taylor called, glancing back and forth between her two children racing through town and the young man her daughter had sent for in the newspaper.

"Good morning, Mrs. Taylor. You're looking lovely as

always." Matt swept his hat off and stood respectfully waiting as Lillie Taylor took a final look at Mary and Harry. "I can't imagine what has gotten into Mary. She's always been such a quiet sedate little thing. Well, no matter. Mr. Taylor and I would like to have you join our family for Sunday dinner."

"It would be my pleasure, ma'am."

"The minister will be there. With his startling announcement this morning, I believe we'd best get our plans made for the wedding, assuming it is going to take place?" She deliberately made the last statement a question and eyed him shrewdly to gauge his reaction.

"Oh, yes, ma'am, it most definitely is taking place. As a matter of fact, I was quite intrigued by the plans you and Mr. Frederick Winchester were discussing yesterday at the store. Including the wedding in the Harvest Festival seems such a wonderful idea. I wish I had your talent, Mrs. Taylor. You always seem to know exactly the right thing to do."

"Why, thank you, Mr. Hubbard." Lillie Taylor actually blushed with pleasure.

Matthew moved to take her arm as the two of them headed down the street toward the mercantile. "I hope you will understand when I mention that in light of the shortness of our courtship, Mary and I really will need to make a great many plans very quickly. We'll need a place to live, for example, and I will need a position of some sort so that I can support a family."

"I thought there was an inheritance," Lillie challenged, eyeing him suspiciously once again.

"And there is. But the size of it is unknown to me—enough certainly to purchase land from your husband and perhaps set up a small business. I did not come here looking for charity, ma'am, in spite of Mary's promises in her ad."

Lillie relaxed. "Each of our children has been promised a piece of land when they marry, Mr. Hubbard. Think of it as my daughter's dowry. In fact, why don't you and Mary ride out and look at the location after dinner this afternoon?"

"I think that's a wonderful idea. Perhaps young Harry could

go with us . . . just so there is no question of Mary's reputation being sullied."

Lillie beamed. "You are quite a thoughtful young man, Mr. Hubbard—and perceptive, I might add."

"You invited Harry?" Mary could not believe her ears. Had the man not been standing right there when her younger brother had made it known he'd been spying on the two of them?

"Is that a problem?" Matt asked, innocent as a newborn as he helped her into the buggy he'd rented from Jake.

"Of course it's a problem," she whispered vehemently, aware that they were still in earshot of her family. "You heard him. He saw . . . that is, he . . ." She searched for the right words. She couldn't exactly imply that if Harry was along there was not one chance in heaven that they would find a moment alone—a moment to continue their lessons.

Matt grinned. "You're blushing, Mary," he said softly and touched her cheek. "Trust me. Harry is about to become our biggest ally." Once Mary was settled, he went back into the livery and brought out his own horse, Traveler II. "Harry, I wonder if you'd do me a favor and ride ol' Traveler here. He needs the exercise, and he's not much for pulling buggies."

Harry's face was almost too small to contain the grin that spread across it. His eyes practically popped out of his head as he looked at the big horse.

"Mr. Hubbard," Lillie protested, "I'm not sure—"

"Traveler's old and gentle, ma'am. Harry will be fine."

"Well, if you're sure." Lillie looked up at the large horse skeptically.

"Ma, I can ride a horse," Harry argued.

"I know that, but—"

"Tell you what, ma'am. I'll tie Traveler to the back of the buggy here, and Harry can just sit on him as we go. How's that?"

Lillie breathed a sigh of relief. "That would be preferable, Mr. Hubbard, thank you."

Harry's face collapsed. "Ah, Ma," he argued, "that's no fun."

"Perhaps you'd rather not go at all, young man," Lillie said sympathetically. "Perhaps your brother Bill would like to go in your place."

"I'll go," Harry grunted.

"Then we're all set," Matt observed as he boosted Harry onto Traveler's back. "Let's get started."

"This is boring," Harry announced repeatedly between heavy sighs from his position behind Mary and Matt.

They had barely gotten to the edge of town and crossed the river before the litany began. "Treating me like some little kid . . . woulda stayed home . . . wish I'd gone fishing."

Mary flinched with annoyance at each fresh pronouncement. Matt just kept driving the buggy slowly out toward the prairie, humming to himself.

"I hope you're happy," Mary whispered irritably after Harry had expelled a particularly dramatic sigh.

"Just wait," Matt said, and started to sing out loud. "You know this one, Harry," he called over his shoulder after a few bars of a cowboy song. "Come on, sing along." He bellowed it out at the top of his lungs as Mary and Harry looked on in stupefied amazement.

"You're crazy," Harry announced when Matt stopped in mid-song and turned to look back at him.

Matt just grinned and snapped the reins so the horse pulling the buggy would pick up the pace. He glanced back to see Harry bouncing in the saddle, clinging to Traveler's mane to hang on.

"Fast enough?" Matt called.

Having gotten his grip and not willing to be called a coward, Harry called back, "Faster."

Matt snapped the reins once more.

"Matt," Mary said in warning as she hung on to her hat with one hand and the buggy seat with the other.

"Faster!" Harry cried with a laugh and a cowboy whoop.

"No!" Mary shouted when Matt raised the reins once more.

Matt grinned and allowed the horse to slow the pace a bit.

"Aw, Mary," Harry complained.

"We're almost there," Mary called and gave Matt directions to the piece of land she had picked out with her father. "It's just over that rise where the river turns."

"You know, Harry, ol' Traveler could do with a bit of exercise," Matt declared after they had spent several minutes walking over the land Mary's father had given her. The youngster had made no secret of his boredom as he straggled along behind the two adults. At Matt's nonchalant comment, however, his interest was instantly rekindled. On the other hand, he wasn't about to reveal that to his sister and this tall stranger.

"I reckon he had plenty of exercise comin' out here," Harry suggested.

Matt seemed to consider that. "You might have a point, but Traveler here is used to stretching his legs. Coming out here, being hooked to the back of that buggy, wasn't much more than a stroll down Main Street for him."

Harry pretended to mull this over. "Yeah, well, I reckon he could run a little out here. It's all open country. You could ride him over to that ridge yonder and back. It's pretty even, and he'd be in no danger of being hurt or throwing you."

Matt studied the indicated ridge.

Harry waited.

Mary watched the two of them and suppressed a smile.

"Well, you seem to know this country pretty well, Harry. That'll come in handy after Mary and I set up housekeeping out here." Matt strolled over to where Traveler was contentedly chewing on a patch of tall, wheatlike prairie grass. He patted the animal's forehead and picked up the loose reins. "Maybe . . . I mean, if you're careful . . . you could ride Traveler over there and back for me."

This time Harry could not disguise his astonishment. The most he'd hoped for was that Matthew might let him lead the horse around some. "You mean *ride* him?" His eyes threatened to pop right out of his freckled face.

"Well, that is, if you don't ride him hard. He does like to run, but after all, he also has to make the trip back to town. I was thinking a nice canter—not a gallop, mind you."

Harry's red head bobbed in agreement, his young face a study in concentration as Matt laid out the rules. Then he glanced at Mary. Sisters could sometimes be a problem—especially older sisters who had somehow gotten the idea that they had the right to boss a guy around when Ma and Pa weren't present.

Mary frowned and Harry's hopes plummeted.

"Well, I don't know about this," she said as she looked from Harry to Matt and back again.

Harry refused to lower himself to begging. Instead he scuffed the dirt with the toe of his boot, shoved his hands into his pockets and hunched his shoulders the way he'd seen his hero Cord Spencer do when things weren't going the way he liked them to.

"I suppose," Mary continued, "if you promised to be real careful and—"

"Oh, I'll be careful, Mary, I promise." Harry raced to Traveler's side before his sister had a chance to reconsider, but he was stopped short by the sheer size of the beast.

It was one thing to straddle the animal's back when he was tied to the back of a buggy. It was something else to be standing there, his eyes level with the horse's stirrup, trying to figure a way to mount up without looking like an idiot.

"Put your foot here," Matt said quietly as he cupped his hands and bent down. "Then grab hold of the saddle post and pull yourself up."

In one swift, fluid motion, Harry was astride the horse. Matt handed him the reins and tipped his hat. "Thanks, Harry. Traveler and I both appreciate your help."

"Don't you dare get hurt," Mary called as Harry nudged the horse into action and took off across the flat prairie.

Impatiently Harry waved at her, then gave a shout of sheer joy as he and the horse sped toward the ridge.

"He'll be fine," Matt said. "Traveler's very gentle."

Mary's attention had been so focused on Harry and her own doubts about the wisdom of allowing a small boy to ride such a large horse that she hadn't noticed Matt coming to stand just behind her. As he spoke he placed one hand lightly on her shoulder as if to reassure her, but all it accompished was to make her more aware than ever of his presence . . . and their impending marriage.

"Oh, Harry is a very good rider," she said brightly and moved deliberately a step away from Matt's closeness.

When Matt followed, she kept walking, pointing out the landmarks as she went. "That's Libby and Travis's place over there. And over this way is where Jake and Abby Lee have their farm." She lengthened her stride to try to keep a little distance between them. "I always thought I'd like my—that is, our— house here," she said, her voice still sounding forced and overly chirpy to her own ears.

Matt easily closed the distance between them and fell into step alongside her. He was carrying his hat and walking so as not to touch or brush against her in any way. "That looks like a good place," he said agreeably.

They continued to walk in uneasy silence for several more yards.

"The barn would probably be there," Mary said, finally breaking the strained silence. "Although I've no idea what— that is, perhaps you'd rather not farm . . . I mean . . ." She stopped in frustration. Every topic from what crops they might plant to what animals might occupy the barn seemed intensely personal, and she knew it was because she was planning a future with a man she barely knew.

As if reading her thoughts, Matt said, "It's very hard, isn't it?"

"Yes, it is," Mary answered with relief and no pretense at not understanding what he was talking about. "Are you sure you want to do this?" She shaded her eyes with one hand as she gazed up at him.

Before answering, he studied her for a long moment, his

eyes probing hers. "Yes, Mary Taylor, I'm very sure." His tone left not the slightest room for doubt.

Mary swallowed hard, broke the eye contact, and took up walking again, studying the ground as she went. "Of course. You have no choice," she began.

He stopped her with one hand on her elbow, turning her so that once again they were facing each other. "I have choices," he said softly. "I want to marry you."

Mary was aware of the unseasonably warm Kansas wind whipping at her skirts, tugging at her bonnet and the tendrils of hair that framed her face. His eyes burned into hers, and she knew instinctively that she would remember this moment for the rest of her life.

"I just meant in order for you to—"

"I know what you meant, Mary. Perhaps the real question is, do you want to marry me?"

She opened her mouth to answer, but he silenced her with one finger on her lips.

"And if you do want to marry me," he continued, "the question is why?"

Once again, Mary turned deliberately away to break the contact, to lessen the power he seemed to hold over her just by looking down at her with those penetrating blue eyes of his. "I told you why," she answered defensively. She pretended to scan the horizon. "I can't see Harry."

"Harry will be back shortly. Why me, Mary? There must be a dozen young men in these parts who've courted you . . . or wanted to."

"I told you—I've had beaus," Mary said huffily. "I'm not desperate, if that's what you're implying."

Matt laughed out loud. "Lady, you are about the least desperate female I ever met. If ever there was a woman who knew what she wanted and went after it, it's you. I'm not asking why you want to get married—I'm asking why you're ready to accept me."

Because you have eyes the color of a Kansas sky on a June morning, and when you look at me, I see myself in them and I feel beautiful. And because your hair is like the soft needles of the tamarack tree, and when my fingers touch it, they don't want to let go. And because when you kiss me, my insides feel like a summer storm has taken hold of me. And the only possible shelter is there in your arms. And because when you talk to me in that soft drawl, it makes me want to spend a lifetime listening to your stories, sharing your dreams, building a life with you.

"You need me," she answered with a shrug.

"And what do you need?"

"I don't really need anything. I would like to marry and have a family and travel . . . all the things I spoke of in my advertisement." Mary was becoming increasingly uncomfortable with the intensity of his questioning. Matt was the first man who had ever shown the slightest interest in what her thoughts and needs might be. "I wonder what's keeping Harry," she said.

"Did you have other answers to your advertisement?" Matt asked. He was leaning against a tree watching Mary scan the prairie for a sign of her brother.

"Yes." Mary knew she sounded defensive.

"So, why me?" he pressed.

It was clear that Matthew had no intention of dropping the subject. Mary searched her mind for an answer that would satisfy him. The truth was that in spite of being physically attracted to him, she didn't have a clue as to why on earth she would agree to marry him in less than two weeks' time. "You promised to take me to Memphis," she said.

When he didn't respond, she turned to look at him. He was studying her once again, but this time a slight frown creased his forehead. "And that we will do, Mary. We will go to Memphis as soon as we are married."

She was oddly disappointed . . . in what, she didn't know. Was it the tone of his voice? The lack of enthusiasm? What on earth had she expected? Theirs was an arranged marriage in every sense of the word. The only difference was that she had done the arranging instead of going through a marriage broker as her ancestors might have done in Europe.

"Yes, as soon as we are married, we will go to Memphis to claim your inheritance." Might as well state the terms of the agreement out loud before her fantasies could convince her there was anything more to it than that.

Matt's frown deepened. He pushed himself away from the tree and began pacing the land. "Ah, yes, the inheritance. Well, perhaps we ought to plan this house, Mary. How large shall it be?"

He was striding over the land as if marking off sections of it for rooms, but at the same time everything about his movements suggested barely repressed anger. Mary was as confused as ever.

"Oh, I hadn't thought of size. Something small, I should think . . . at least in the beginning."

"But there's the inheritance," he called as he marked the land several feet from her with a rock and began pacing off another section. "We can afford a showplace."

"I don't want a showplace," Mary said quietly, almost timidly, still unsure of his mood.

He paused in his measurements and glanced back at her.

"I just want a normal life," she added.

Matt abandoned all pretense of surveying and gave her his full attention. "I thought you wanted to travel."

"I do, but . . ." This was quite possibly the most frustrating conversation she had ever had. "Oh, honestly, Matthew Hubbard, I have no idea what we are arguing about. We have agreed to marry. Wouldn't it be best to stop all this nonsense and talk about the important things?"

A hint of a smile tugged at the corners of his mouth, and he visibly relaxed. "Such as?"

"Such as what we're going to raise on this place . . . or whether or not you'll like my cooking . . . or . . . oh, I don't know."

"I like your cooking, judging by the sample I got last night," he said as he walked back to where she stood.

"My mother did that," Mary said, not daring to look at him, thrilled to have him no longer angry at her, but still confused by the effect his smile and proximity always had on her.

Again he laughed.

Lord, if she lived with this man for the next fifty years she would never tire of the sound of his laughter.

"Perhaps the question I should be concerned with is, can you cook?"

"You won't starve," Mary shot back and walked toward the place where Harry was bringing Traveler to a halt. "I thought you'd headed for Colorado," she said petulantly to her brother.

But Harry's high spirits were not to be daunted. He grinned and shrugged. "I figured I'd give the two of you time to get all your kissing done," he answered sassily as he slid from the horse's back.

Matt snapped his fingers as if just remembering something important. "I knew there was something I'd planned on doing while you were gone, Harry." He pulled Mary into his arms and kissed her before she had a chance to protest.

Harry watched them for several long seconds, then cleared his throat loudly. "Maybe I'll just take ol' Traveler for one more ride," he announced.

As her brother's voice finally penetrated the fog of desire that seemed to engulf her whenever Matt kissed her, she pushed firmly away. "Oh, no, you don't," she said. "We're going home . . . now." She turned on her heel and marched resolutely back to where they had left the buggy.

Matt winked at Harry, and Harry just grinned as the two men followed her.

CHAPTER
8

When Mary came back to the store after riding out to the mill to see her father late the next afternoon, she found a meeting in progress. Frederick Winchester was holding forth to Lillie, Maisie, and Minnie. Mary assumed the topic was the Harvest Festival until she heard Minnie say, "Are you quite sure that's proper, Lillie? I mean, it's never been done at any wedding I've attended."

Before Lillie could respond, Maisie interrupted. "Well, of course, it hasn't been done, Sister dear. Nothing about this entire . . . betrothal is what you'd call traditional."

Mary cleared her throat loudly.

"Well, here's the bride-to-be now," Frederick gushed as he moved forward and took both Mary's hands in his. "And where might the bridegroom be?" He peered over Mary's shoulder toward the door as if Matthew might be lurking about outside.

"I assume that Matthew is at the hotel. He said something about going to see my father at the mill this morning. Why?"

"No reason. We were just planning the ceremony, weren't

we, ladies?" He pulled Mary farther into the room and toward the gathering at the counter. "Now then, where were we?"

"You were rambling on about calla lilies," Minnie reminded him.

"Ah, yes, it was the wedding of Lady Eleanor Sutton to Lord Helmsley. Lady Eleanor carried the most spectacular bouquet of calla lilies. It was quite the talk of the event." His eyes practically misted over at the memory.

"Freddie," Maisie shouted as if speaking to a dull student, "this is Kansas. It is October. And we do not have calla lilies."

"I still think some nice Queen Anne's lace would serve the purpose," Lillie suggested, still caught up in the romantic notion that Fred had actually spoken of Mary's wedding in practically the same breath as that of Lady Eleanor's . . . whoever she was.

"I thought perhaps roses," Mary began.

"Well, the Queen Anne's lace might suffice," Fred mused. "Of course, the flowers are a matter of concern, but clearly, ladies, they are not our primary concern at the moment."

"Yes, what on earth will she wear?" Minnie said miserably, as if she were announcing a tragedy. "I mean, there simply isn't time for Jane to stitch up a proper wedding gown even if you had the appropriate fabric in stock, which you clearly don't, Lillie dear."

"Sister, I wonder why it is that every time you're around Freddie here you start talking like you have marbles in your mouth," Maisie said, then added more concisely, "You are babbling, Minnie, about something that is none of your beeswax. Mary will decide what to wear."

"Thank you, Miz Hastings." Finally someone considered Mary as a legitimately important participant in this conversation. "I—"

"I'm not finished, Mary," Maisie announced with a stern frown. "Now, Lillie, if you insist on combining this wedding with a town event, which I do *not* think is at all proper, I must—"

GETTING HITCHED

"May I ask one question?" Mary shouted.

All eyes turned to her.

"Who is getting married here?"

"Well, you are, my dear," Fred said as he solicitously patted Mary's arm and looked nervously at the other three women.

"She knows that, Freddie," Maisie explained impatiently, then turned to Mary. "Though this is probably your mother's duty, may I remind you, young lady, that there is such a thing as respect for your elders?"

"I mean no disrespect, ma'am, but it is my wedding, and Matthew and I have some ideas of our own of what we might like."

Lillie's interest was piqued. "Such as?"

"Well, we had planned to discuss it in more detail tonight at the hotel," Mary replied.

"You will *not* spend one moment in that man's hotel room, young lady. Do I make myself clear?" Lillie announced loudly.

"Mother, we are having supper together in the restaurant."

"Oh. Well, that's another matter. So, what are your ideas?"

Everyone looked at Mary expectantly. "We thought we might like something smaller . . . more . . . less . . . That is . . ."

"Spit it out, Mary," Maisie prodded. "Either you have ideas or you don't, and if you don't, what the devil have the two of you been talking about these past couple of days? After all, you've spent quite a bit of time together—something, I might add, about which the entire town is buzzing." She shot Lillie a look.

"I . . . that is . . ." Mary searched for words as images of the time spent with Matt filled her mind. They had talked. Of course they had talked. All she could think to say was that when he kissed her there was no need for conversation. And how come that particular thought always brought a blush to her pale cheeks?

"I thought as much," Maisie said triumphantly as she leaned close to peer at Mary's flushed face. "Lillie, if you want my advice, you'll move things along with this wedding."

"It's taking place a week from Friday as scheduled," Lillie said through pursed lips, "and how dare you imply—"

"Please, ladies," Fred said.

And then they were all speaking at once . . . except for Mary, who threw up her hands in exasperation and headed for the door.

"Mary Taylor, we are not finished," her mother called above the fracas that surrounded her. "Where do you think you're going?"

"To meet Matthew for supper," Mary replied without a backward glance.

Matthew stood at the window of his hotel room. In his immediate view were the train station and the tracks that had brought him to Harmony . . . and could just as easily take him away. Beyond that in the distance were the outbuildings of the Englishman's farm and a couple of other spreads. Beyond that was the land where he and Mary would spend their lives . . . if he married her.

The land was in one way a symbol of the mystery of Mary Taylor. She had a good life . . . loving family, good friends, nice peaceful town, even plenty of money and her own land. So, why had she mentioned the inheritance yesterday? Why had she actually made a point of it, as if it weren't the obvious reason for going to Memphis?

It should have been enough to make Matt march straight to the train station and buy a ticket out of here. That would certainly please her brother Joseph. But if all Mary really cared about was the inheritance, was she any different from Louisa?

He knew she was. To think of Mary in the same moment as Louisa was to do Mary an injustice. She was forthright in all the dealings she had with people. He'd seen evidence of that more than once in the brief time he'd known her. He'd even felt a bit of her prickliness himself.

But it still didn't add up. Mary already had everything available to her to make the kind of life she claimed to want. Surely there was an adventurous young man out there on that prairie who'd be only too happy to indulge her desire for adventure. Yet she had chosen Matthew. Why?

"Are you gettin' married next week like everybody says?"

Little Amanda Hutton observed him from her position just inside the open door to his room. He'd seen the child around the hotel, watching him from behind her mother's skirts and from behind half-open doors.

"Is that what everybody says?" he asked, bending down so that he was more at eye level with the small dark-eyed beauty.

Amanda nodded. "Who you gonna marry?"

"Who do folks say I'm marrying?"

"Mary."

"Marry Mary?" Matt asked and wiggled his eyebrows until the little girl covered a giggle with one small hand.

"That's what Boom and me heard."

"Who's Boom?"

"He's my dog," she announced importantly and stepped outside into the hall long enough to drag a small wriggling puppy into the room with her.

"He's a fine dog," Matt said.

"You can hold him," Amanda said and pushed the pup into Matt's arms before he could refuse.

"Thanks," Matt shifted Boom until he could hold him with one hand and pet him with the other.

"Do you have a dog?" Amanda asked.

Memories of the pup his father had given him when he was only a little older than Amanda washed over him. He hadn't thought of that dog in years. They'd always had dogs around the farm, of course, but they'd been sporting dogs and were cared for by the servants.

"Mister?" Amanda prodded.

Matt realized he'd allowed his memories to distract him. "Yeah, I had a dog," Matt said aloud and thought, *My father picked him out just for me.*

"Amanda?" Faith Hutton's voice preceded her up the stairway.

"I'm back here talking," Amanda called back. "Me and Boom."

"Boom and I," Faith corrected as she reached the landing and headed down the hall. "I apologize, Mr. Hubbard. Amanda doesn't mean to intrude."

"No intrusion at all, Mrs. Hutton. Amanda was just introducing me to Boom."

"He's gonna marry Mary," Amanda announced and then burst into giggles as she remembered the way the nice stranger had teased her.

"I know he is, dear. Run along now, and let Mr. Hubbard have a moment's peace."

"See ya," Amanda called as she raced down the hall. "Come on, Boom!" she yelled from halfway down the stairs, and the puppy that had had some reservations about tackling the steep stairway plunged down the steps after her.

"I hope she wasn't a nuisance. She's very curious about people," Faith said.

"She's a pleasure," Matt assured her. "You and your husband are obviously good parents."

Faith blushed slightly and smiled. "Thank you." She turned to go, then slapped her forehead with the palm of her hand. "I almost forgot . . . I swear sometimes I have so many things on my mind that I . . . well, never mind. I came up here to let you know Mary is waiting for you downstairs."

"Now?" Matt was surprised. They had agreed to have supper in the hotel dining room, but he'd assumed Mary would expect to be called for and escorted. He knew Lillie Taylor would expect that. Besides, she was nearly an hour early.

"She came in several minutes ago and seemed quite put out about something. When I asked if I could help, she said she was waiting for you."

"I see," Matt said, which was a complete lie since he didn't understand at all. "Perhaps you'd be good enough to give Miss Taylor a cup of tea while I finish getting ready?"

"Certainly. By the way, congratulations, Mr. Hubbard. Mary

is a lovely young woman, and she'll make a good wife." Faith Hutton smiled as she pulled the door closed behind her.

Wife. The word seemed to hang in the air. Mary Taylor, a woman he barely knew, was about to become his wife. He knew the idea should have appalled him, but in truth it made him smile. Though he had his doubts about Mary's motives in this whole venture, his own motives were becoming increasingly clear. Oh, yes, he'd come here to follow the rules set down by his father's will, but that was only a part of it.

At thirty-two he was more than ready for a place of his own, a family of his own. And why not a life with Mary Taylor? She clearly came from a good family. Her background boded well for her to manage a stable home of her own. She also had a sensible head on her shoulders. He wasn't likely to have to coddle her, and common sense would be a good thing for their children to learn from their mother.

On top of all that, she was very pleasant to look at . . . and hold . . . and kiss . . . and . . . What would it be like to make love to her? Matt wondered. If her kisses were any indication, she promised to be a very able partner. And there was the fact of her running that ad, knowing full well that such an action would cause tongues to wag in Harmony for years to come. That alone told him of the woman's spirit. She wasn't likely to get all skittish and prim in the marriage bed.

Matt grinned as he gave his boots a final buffing. Of course, there was also the fact that when he was near her, his own heart hammered in double cadence, and every time he'd kissed her he'd been hard put to remember that though their betrothal might be moving along at a gallop, they were not wed yet. In fact, just last night he'd lain awake for hours, recounting each of their kisses in graphic detail and allowing himself the painful pleasure of playing out what might follow those kisses once they were married. At times like that their wedding day seemed much too far in the future.

Matt checked his appearance in the small mirror on the dresser and then went to have dinner with his intended.

* * *

The hotel dining room was unusually busy for a weekday that evening, and people continued to come in as Matt and Mary sat eating their supper. Faith had seated the couple at a table right in the center of the dining room, though when they'd first sat down there hadn't been another soul in the place.

"It's our best table," Faith had assured them. "The chairs are by far the most comfortable."

"Sold," Matt had said with a broad grin as he pulled out one of the chairs for Mary.

"I feel as if I'm on display," Mary whispered as soon as Faith had moved away.

"She's gone to some trouble, though," Matt said, nodding toward the fresh flowers that adorned the table and fingering the lace cloth. "Let's just make her happy."

"You're right, of course," Mary said, but could not stifle a weary sigh.

"What is it?"

"It's this whole wedding. I know everyone is excited and wants to be nice, but honestly, Matthew, I—"

"Why, Mary Taylor, how nice to see you. And this must be your young man." Bea Arnold gushed as she approached and focused her whole attention on Matt.

Matt shot to his feet and smiled down at the plump gray-haired matron. "Matthew Hubbard, ma'am."

Bea introduced herself and her husband Daniel, who stood uncomfortably in the background. "We don't usually dine out, Mr. Hubbard," Bea said, "but tonight on a whim we decided to come here. You know Faith is famous for her meat loaf, and how fortunate to find you and Mary here. I'm sorry I didn't have the chance to meet you at church Sunday. We've heard so much about you—"

"Bea Arnold, what on earth are you and Daniel doing in town on a Monday?" Minnie Hastings's voice boomed from the entrance to the dining room.

"I might ask you the same thing," Bea huffed as Minnie and

Maisie wove their way through the tables to Mary and Matt's table.

"Sister and I eat here every Monday night—just ask Faith. It gives us a night away from our own cooking, and besides, we occasionally get some business from people staying in the hotel who might be looking for something a bit more homelike." This last was directed at Matthew, who remained standing and smiled at the sisters.

Mary sank lower in her chair. She felt surrounded, ambushed. Matt didn't seem to mind one bit, but the whole business was becoming impossible. She should never have—

"Well, this is quite a gathering." Samantha Spencer entered the room and made straight for Mary's table. "You two have certainly been the talk of the town, and now you are quite literally the center of attention." Her eyes twinkled, and Mary was surprised to hear Matt chuckle as if this were all something quite normal.

Samantha proceeded to introduce Matt to Cord, and the two men were chatting like old friends when Zan and Edward Winchester entered the restaurant. Was the entire town going to show up here for supper? Mary wondered.

"Well, why don't we all move to our tables and let these two lovebirds have a chance to eat their meal," Cord said. "Matthew, nice meeting you. I'm looking forward to getting to know you."

So am I, if the good people of Harmony would give us a moment's peace, Mary thought miserably.

Finally they all settled at their tables, and Matt had resumed his place and began eating as if what had just transpired was nothing at all out of the ordinary. But Mary saw right away that in addition to those townspeople who had made their presence known, there were half a dozen others who had come in, ordered, and were now eyeing Matt and Mary between bites and hushed whispers.

"You're picking at your food, Mary. Aren't you feeling well?"

"I'm sorry, Matt," Mary blurted. "They mean well and they

are all wonderful people, but all this . . . you and I . . . that is, the way we met and how you came to be here, well, it's all very exciting to them. They have little enough drama in their lives so that when something slightly unusual happens they just cannot contain their . . . interest."

Matt was smiling. "Mary, these folks have been quite welcoming to me, and they are clearly happy for you. I find that touching and certainly nothing you need to feel you have to apologize for."

"But surely you understand that most of them are here tonight to watch us?"

"I know that," Matt answered. Then he winked. "And I say we give them exactly what they came for." He gave her a soulful look and covered her hand with his. "Now smile at me as if you and I are the only two people in this room."

Automatically Mary smiled while her thoughts raced with the impact of the feelings the simple touch of his hand on hers aroused.

"By the time we leave, let's give them no reason to doubt that what they have seen is true love that has every chance of working. For that is most definitely what they want to be convinced of. The sooner they believe that all is well for their little Mary Taylor, the sooner they will lose interest in us and find some other project to occupy them."

He delivered all this with a long soulful look at her, in a low murmuring voice as he stroked her palm with his thumb. Only Mary saw his conspiratorial wink.

He was right, of course, and Mary could not help but be impressed with his astuteness in judging the motives of others. She relaxed a bit as she considered what he was proposing. It might be exactly the right thing to do. It might even be fun. She fluttered her eyelashes at him and smiled. Every eye in the dining room swiveled to Mary, and a low hum of gossip spread through the room.

Matt grinned back at her, squeezed her hand and released it, and resumed eating. "You know, given what your sister Sissy told me about your cooking today, we may be dining here often."

"That would be acceptable, Mr. Hubbard," Mary answered with a shy duck of her head that caused tongues to wag once more.

Matt gave her a look of pure longing. "Are you any better at housekeeping and child-rearing?"

Mary could not stifle a giggle at the incongruity of their longing looks and their mundane topic of conversation. "I would say that I should do quite well in the child-rearing department. I do have several younger siblings, you know."

"And the housekeeping?" Once again Matt smiled at her and touched her hand.

"That may take a bit more practice. Perhaps the house should be a small one after all, so there won't be so much for me to manage."

"Then where will we put all the children?" He leaned forward, his expression intense, his posture one of entreaty.

Mary gave him a startled glance, not because of his posture, but because of his question. "How many children were you planning?"

"Oh, I'd like a large family. Having lost my own siblings, and all."

"Three? Four?" Mary began guessing, and with each guess the color in her cheeks heightened. "Six?"

"That would be a good start," Matt said and stroked her cheek with his thumb before leaning back and taking another bite of his meat loaf.

"I see." Mary let out a breath and lifted her glass with a shaky hand.

"Of course, when we travel and seek all that adventure you want, we'll have to figure out a way to bring the children along. But that's all right. I think it's important for children to have a broad education."

Well, at least they were in agreement on that point. Mary relaxed slightly and picked at her food. "I've always wondered what my life might have been like if I'd been born somewhere else."

"I'm not sure where you're born is as important as the people who raise you," Matt said.

"What were your parents like, Matt?"

"My mother was courageous and beautiful and funny, and she taught me so much. My father was away a lot when I was young . . . through no fault of his own. Still, it fell to my mother to see to my education and upbringing."

"But you and your father were close?"

Matt nodded. "We were until—"

"I know—Louisa—but before that. What was he like?"

"Shortly after I left to fight in the war, my mother died. I had never felt more alone or lonely in my life. But my father wrote to me every single day . . . he didn't miss one. Pages and pages about the farm and the neighbors and the family business in Memphis. Sometimes those letters wouldn't come for weeks at a time because I was moving around so much. But then I'd get somewhere, and there would be a whole pack of them waiting for me . . . and I always knew they were out there somewhere. Those letters saved my life because they kept me in touch with the future."

"Our life here must seem a little drab to you after all your adventures. Sometimes I feel as if I haven't done anything at all in my life, and you've experienced so much."

"You ran an ad for a husband," Matt reminded her with a grin.

Mary smiled back at him. "I did, didn't I?"

"And look what happened from that," they said almost in unison and then burst out laughing, which set off a fresh buzz of speculation throughout the dining room.

After that Mary and Matt relaxed and became co-conspirators, seeing how much they could tease the townspeople. They toasted each other with soulful looks behind which both could hardly contain their giggles. Matt reached across the small table and touched Mary's cheek. She fed him a piece of corn bread. Their conversation appeared to be serious and probing, when in fact they were plotting their next move.

"Let your napkin drop to the floor," Matt advised, his expression one of soulful longing.

Mary lowered her lashes, touched the napkin to the corner of her mouth, and replaced it on her lap in such a way that it fluttered to the floor. "Okay," Matt whispered as he focused on the fallen napkin and Mary followed his gaze, "all together now, go for it."

Each of them leaned toward the floor from their chairs. "Stop giggling," Matt whispered.

"I can't help it," Mary replied, and their fingers met. Matt entwined his with hers, then gave her a look that was positively loaded with desire. So much so that there was an audible and communal sigh throughout the restaurant.

Matt gave Mary a quick wink which sent her into a fresh fit of giggles. She kept her head bent to disguise the laughter and hoped the others would think it was a posture of shyness. When they sat up once again, Matt reached across the table and gently replaced a single tendril of hair that clung to her cheek. Then he allowed the backs of his fingers to trail down her cheek before withdrawing his hand.

"Oh my," came Bea Arnold's strangled voice. And indeed, every female eye in the place was focused on her and Matt. The men might be interested in their meals, but food was the last thing on the minds of the women in the room.

"Would you two like dessert?" Faith Hutton asked as she started to clear away their plates. "Why, Mary, you hardly ate a thing," she said.

"Really?" Mary replied, her gaze fastened on Matt. "I guess I'm not all that hungry."

Matt returned her gaze. Faith Hutton might as well have been in another town as far as the two of them were concerned. "Would you care to take a walk, Mary?" Matt asked softly.

Again Mary lowered her lashes. "That would be lovely," she replied in a hushed voice.

Faith raised her own eyebrows to the ceiling and grinned.

"Well, you lovebirds go ahead, then. I'll just put this on your tab, Matthew."

"Thank you." Matt got up and went to pull out Mary's chair for her. "The meal was very good," he added almost as an afterthought.

"Uh-huh," Faith replied with a wry glance at their almost untouched plates.

On their way through the restaurant, Matt tucked Mary's hand into the crook of his elbow. He handled her as if she were precious crystal. For her part she gazed adoringly up at him and seemed completely unaware that anyone else was even present in the room.

Just before they reached the door, Matt leaned toward her and whispered something that made Mary blush and giggle.

CHAPTER
9

~❦~

Outside on the street Mary's giggles turned to muffled belly laughs. Hand in hand, she and Matt practically ran the short distance to the end of the building and around the corner, where they collapsed against the side of the large pink hotel and laughed until tears ran down their cheeks.

"Oh, Matthew, I can't remember when I've had so much fun," Mary said finally, gasping for air. "Did you see the way Bea was looking at us?"

Matt nodded, trying to contain a fresh onslaught of laughter. "I thought she was actually going to swoon when we went for the napkin."

"No, when you touched my cheek," Mary said, and they both burst out laughing again.

"Then there were Maisie and Minnie," Matt began.

Mary couldn't even respond to that. The image they shared of the twins watching their every move did not need words. Mary held her sides and gasped for breath. "Stop," she protested through her laughter.

"All I can say is that after tonight I'd better get you down that aisle quick or the ladies of the town will have my head." He reached for Mary's hand and started walking toward the outskirts of the town where the river ran.

For the first time since Matt had arrived in town, Mary didn't panic at the mention of their impending wedding. In fact, tonight the idea that she would spend the rest of her days with this man seemed an attractive one indeed.

"When I was young," Matt said as he helped her across the railroad tracks and continued their stroll to the banks of the river, "my father and I would often go fishing together in a river near our farm."

"Papa taught all of us to fish in this river," Mary said as they paused near a cottonwood tree and listened to the soft rhythm of the current.

"Even the girls?" Matt asked in surprise.

"Well, not Sissy. She hates putting the worm on the hook."

"And you don't?"

Mary smiled. "I'm not all that thrilled with stabbing the poor little thing with the hook, but I don't mind digging them up from the garden or holding them in my hand, if that's what you're asking."

"How's the fishing on the part of the river that runs past our . . . your land?"

"Our land," Mary corrected softly and glanced up at him. "You'll have to ask Harry. He's out there all the time."

Matt smiled. "Would you like to sit out here with me for a while?"

"That would be nice," Mary answered.

Matt removed his jacket and spread it on the ground for her, then sat next to her with his back against the huge tree. "What would you say about me starting to prepare the land for our house tomorrow?"

"I'd say that was probably a good idea," Mary answered. "My folks have some catalogs at the store we can look through. Libby and Travis ordered their house from the catalog."

Matt nodded. "Maybe you'd rather design your own place."

"Would you?"

"It might be fun," he mused. "Besides, it seems to me you might have some fairly definite ideas about what you want."

"Well," Mary replied and shifted uncomfortably. Did he think she was some sort of demanding harridan? Did he think she was one of those women who had to have things her own way? She recalled the things he'd told her about Louisa. Did he think she was like that? And yet, she did have ideas about the way she'd like her house to be . . . ideas she'd never really seen expressed in the catalogs.

"I know I have some ideas of what I'd like," he continued.

Mary relaxed slightly. "Such as?"

"Oh, well, it needs a great big wide porch. Houses in the South all have big porches—verandas, they're often called. Sometimes on the part where the sun comes in strongest, we'd put up lattice or shutters."

"It sounds nice," Mary said dreamily as she gazed out over the landscape and imagined the house. "I'd like a nice garden for herbs and vegetables and flowers. Have you seen Abby Lee's roses?"

"I saw a white one the day I met you," Matt said softly.

"I'd like roses."

"Then you'd best check with Abby Lee and see what she recommends for the placement of the rose garden."

Mary grinned. "I'll talk to her tomorrow."

They were quiet for several minutes, each lost in pleasant thoughts of the future, lulled by the sounds of the river and the night.

"This is going to work out, Mary Taylor," Matt said finally.

Mary nodded. "Yeah, I think it is." Then she looked at him and smiled. "As far-fetched as the whole crazy idea seemed, I think it's actually going to work."

They grinned at each other, and it seemed the most natural thing in the world for him to reach for her and pull her into his arms, cradling her against his chest as he tilted her head back to receive his kiss. "I'm very glad you ran that ad, Mary," he whispered just before his mouth covered hers.

And I'm so glad you answered, she thought as she once again reveled in the experience of Matt kissing her.

After a moment it was hard to say who was kissing whom. Their mouths and teeth and tongues collided and probed for long breathless moments, then they would pull slightly apart, gaze at each other through eyes glazed with desire, and then kiss again. Mary grasped his thick hair, urging him to deepen the kiss, and when he did, she slid her hand over his shoulders to the hard plains of his back, feeling the dual pounding of their hearts against each other.

For several moments Matt satisfied himself with kissing her, caressing her cheek and throat, and releasing the pins that held her hair; but then he, too, needed more. His mouth moved over her chin and down to her neck, and his palm cupped her breast. When she made no move to stop him, he began a slow massage of her breast, kneading it and teasing it through the fabric of her cotton dress. He felt it swell to fill his hand and felt an answering swelling in his groin.

Their breaths came in sharp gasps as each tried in vain to deal with the confines of clothing and their own rampant hunger to touch and be touched, to taste, to find succor in each other.

Matt pulled back, knowing the move would gain Mary's attention. He could see her clearly now, their eyes having become accustomed to the night. Her lips were full and sensuous from his kisses, her eyes wide with desire. He reached for the buttons of her dress.

She did not stop him. Lord help her, she couldn't have stopped him if she'd wanted to, and that was the last thing she wanted. She felt the cool night air on her skin as he bared each inch. As he opened the buttons near her breasts, she felt a delicious sense of release as if her dress had suddenly become too small to contain her. She gave a sigh of pleasure at the sensation.

When she made no protest, Matt's attention focused on working the long row of tiny buttons, freeing them one by one. When she whimpered in pleasure, he looked at her. She was biting her lower lip, and her head was thrown back to the night sky. The length of her throat down to her cleavage was exposed, inviting.

With a muffled groan, Matt abandoned the buttons and pushed aside the fabric of the dress to allow himself the pure pleasure of tasting her skin made alabaster by the moonlight. And when her fingers burrowed through his hair and pulled him closer, he accepted the permission she had granted and gave himself up to the pure pleasure of suckling and teasing her hardened nipple into bloom.

Mary felt the fabric of her chemise, soaked now with the sweet moisture of Matt's kisses, clinging to her breast. With his tender ministrations, the throbbing that had threatened to overcome her had eased. But now the torturous pain that only Matthew seemed to ease had moved lower. The heat and need that had only moments before pooled in her hardened nipples now cried out for release from somewhere deep inside her.

Without forsaking her bared skin, Matthew shifted their position so that Mary reclined across his lap, her nearness momentarily soothing his full-to-bursting groin. He tugged at her dress until it fell free of her shoulders. He eased the wide straps of her chemise slowly down her arms until the ribbons that held it closed threatened to break.

Their eyes met. She shrugged her arms free of her dress so that it gathered at her waist, and reached for him. "Matthew," she whispered against his ear, her breath sending shivers of fresh need through him.

He raised his head and reached for the ribbons. "If I told you I loved you now, Mary, you wouldn't believe me," he said as he untied each bow and spread the soft fabric until she was fully exposed. "We will be married a week from Friday. We will live together in a house with a rose garden and a large porch over there by the river. We will have children and we will have adventures. We will grow old together, and when we are done we will have known a love like no other."

She was sitting on the banks of the river she'd known as a child, fully a woman now, exposed both physically and emotionally to this man. The words of the wedding vows suddenly filled her head: ". . . plight thee my troth." That was what she and Matt were doing tonight. This was a commitment . . . a promise given and accepted.

With shaky fingers she opened the buttons on his shirt, pulling it free of his tight trousers until she could push it open to expose his tanned and muscled chest. As she worked, he combed her hair with his fingers and watched her. She pressed her palms against his chest and massaged his nipples with the heels of her hands. He ran his hands along the length of her naked back and around to her bare breasts. When he pulled her against him and their skin touched for the first time, they each gave a shuddering sigh before meeting in another kiss.

This time his tongue filled her mouth and held there before beginning a slow, ever-penetrating stroking, sliding against her lips and teeth and out again just to the tip, then back. Her need to have more of him would not be denied. In frustration she straddled him, her skirts bunching above her knees.

With an actual cry of need, his hands tunneled beneath her skirts and settled on her hips, lifting and positioning her until she straddled his sex. For a moment he felt her tense and he broke the kiss.

They stared at each other, their breath now coming in heaving gasps as if they had been underwater. Suddenly her eyes filled with tears.

"Mary, we can wait," Matt said. "It's all right, darlin'." His touch became more soothing than stimulating.

Mary shook her head in frustration. What must he think of her? Was she any better than Louisa, throwing herself at him like this, wantonly inviting him to take her out here on the riverbank? And yet nothing in her life had ever seemed more right. Being with him, touching him, having him touch her, look at her, make love to her. If he had told her he was leaving tomorrow and would not return, she would not regret this night.

"I don't want you to stop," she whispered, then was overcome by actual sobs. "You must think I'm terrible . . .

but this is all so new and . . . exciting . . . and I . . ." She could not go on.

Matt smiled. "Would you believe me if I told you it's all pretty exciting for me as well?"

"Now you're teasing me," she said with a hiccuping sob. "I'm not a child, Matt. I know what's about to happen here."

"No, you are not a child. You are possibly the most beautiful woman I have ever known. From the moment I saw you standing up to your family and practically the whole town, I knew you were someone special." He felt her relax and allowed her a moment to get hold of her emotions.

She was still straddling him. His hands were still resting on her thighs, and she was enticingly naked from the waist up. "It doesn't have to happen the way you think, love."

Her eyes met his. "It doesn't?" Clearly her imagination was trying to deal with this bit of information.

"There are other ways of . . . gaining satisfaction."

"Will you teach me?" she asked after a long moment, her eyes downcast, her voice shaky.

Matt chuckled and turned her so that she was beside him rather than on him. "Yes, love, I will. But not tonight. Tonight I need to get you home before your mother sends out the sheriff." He lifted her off him and knelt before her as he started to retie the bows of her chemise.

Mary giggled. "The sheriff is my brother-in-law," she reminded him.

"Just because you have friends in high positions, don't brag about it," he teased. He tied the last ribbon and stood up. "Finish dressing and fix your hair. I'll be right back."

He walked away from her until he was hidden in the shadows of a clump of walnut trees. Mary stood up and untwisted her dress until she could find the sleeves and pull it on. When she had finished closing the buttons, she knelt and searched the ground for the hairpins and combs Matt had pulled from her hair. Her search turned up one comb and three pins. They would have to do.

As she pulled her hair high off her neck and twisted it into a practiced chignon, she remembered the sensation of Matt's long fingers combing through it, his eyes searching hers, messages that flashed between them like lightning, speaking of want . . . hunger . . . love. Suddenly she saw them in years to come, living in the house they had built with words tonight, raising their children, sharing a life, and for the first time in all her years Mary Taylor felt like a fully grown woman. She recognized her womanly power, her womanly needs, and she knew that this was a night she would never forget. It was the night she had fallen in love.

"Ready?" He stood behind her and put his arms loosely around her waist, pulling her against him. She nodded but made no move to go.

If she could hang on to this night forever, she would, for surely there would never be one sweeter.

Throughout the next several days Mary walked through each hour oblivious to the existence of anyone but Matt. When she wasn't with him she was thinking about him. She allowed herself the luxury of being in love, certain that because by nature she was a practical woman, she would be able to deal with the reality of their marriage of convenience when the time came. She was realistic enough, after all, to understand that while she may have fallen in love, what Matt felt was probably centered more on his physical needs.

With the help of the entire town, her mother filled Mary's days and evenings with pre-wedding activity. If she wasn't at Jane's having a fitting on her wedding gown, she was at the church listening to Lillie make plans for the ceremony with the Reverend Johnson. In the evenings there were parties and suppers to attend so that everyone could have an opportunity to get acquainted with Matt and extend their good wishes.

Mary's entire family was always included in these events, so there was almost no possibility for Matt and her to steal an hour for themselves, much less find the privacy to pursue what they had started that night by the river. When they did find themselves alone for a few minutes, they took full advantage, falling into each other's arms and kissing each other with a hunger that seemed impossible to satisfy.

Their friends tried to assist them. Matt had been helping Jake Sutherland with some blacksmithing, and Saturday afternoon when Mary stopped by to bring lunch for Matt, Jake made some clumsy excuse about needing to be gone for a couple of hours and winked broadly at Matt.

They pretended Jake's absence had no effect on them for about three minutes, then Matt took a repaired bridle into an empty stall, supposedly to hang it with other harnesses.

"Mary, come here a minute," he called.

When she entered the stall, he pulled her into his arms and kissed her with a fervor that was powerful even for them. In seconds her hands were combing through his thick hair, and he was pressing her against the rough wooden wall of the stall. Their clothing seemed to provide more bondage than comfort, and Mary squirmed in frustration.

"Anybody here?" Fred Winchester strolled into the livery stable and called out.

Matt and Mary froze and waited. Perhaps he would assume no one was present and leave.

"Jake? Matthew?" He was moving toward them, down past the fire and huge bellows. "Hello," he called.

Matt released Mary and motioned for her to stay where she was and stay silent. "Coming," Matt called and picked up a heavy bale of hay to cover his reason for coming from an empty stall. "How are you today, Mr. Winchester?"

The two men chatted for a moment. Fred needed a wagon repaired. Matt promised to come out to the Double B as soon as Jake returned and take a look at it.

"Well, that would be splendid," Mary heard the Englishman say as he headed for the door. "Shall we say two o'clock?"

"Two o'clock is fine," Matt replied.

"Very well. I'll say good-bye, then. You have work to do, I see. Carry on, Matthew, carry on." Soon he was gone.

Matt waved and glanced over his shoulder to be certain Fred

didn't return as he headed back to the stall where he'd left Mary.

When he got there he pulled off the shirt that had been hanging free of his trousers when Mary had arrived. He grinned at her wide-eyed perusal of his sweat-slicked chest. "You heard the man," he said softly as he opened the top buttons of Mary's shirtwaist. "He said we should carry on."

Mary smiled and ran her hands across his shoulders, down his arms, and back again. "I think it's an English expression," she said.

"Maybe. But I think the man knew exactly what he was saying."

Mary's hands stopped, and she stared up at Matt with wide eyes. "You don't think . . . are you saying . . . he *knew*?"

Matt laughed and kissed her forehead. "I'd bet the farm on it, love."

"But," Mary began her protest but was silenced when Matt pushed open her blouse and traced his finger along the crocheted border of her chemise.

"God, you are lovely," he said huskily and bent to kiss her neck.

Any further protest she might have made died with the magic of his lips on her skin. The truth was, she had lain awake nights wanting to feel his touch again, wanting to experience that incredible sensation of fire racing through her limbs and threatening to explode like dynamite, wondering what it would be like if it did.

She balanced her hands against his shoulders as he lifted her, cupping his hands under her buttocks. Now his face was even with her breasts, and he took full advantage of the position, working on first one and then the other with his open mouth, teeth, and tongue until her nipples were swollen and dark against the moist cloth.

"Yoo-hoo! Jake?"

There was only one person that particular voice could belong to . . . "Luscious" Lottie McGee of the First Resort saloon.

"Yoo-hoo . . . yoo-hoo . . . Jake . . . Jake."

That would be her pet parrot.

"Jake?"

Jake had married Lottie's cousin, Abby Lee, so it was hardly unusual that Lottie would stop by.

Matt gave a heavy sigh and allowed Mary to slide back to her feet, steadying her there for a moment. He motioned for her to dress and picked up another bale of hay.

"Jake's not here, ma'am," he called as he emerged from the shadows of the stall, hoisting the bale to his shoulder and hoping it accounted for his breathless state. His aroused state would need no explanation to a woman like Lottie, so he tried to stay in the shadows and keep his back to her.

"Oh, you're the new man in town, aren't you? The mail-order groom, I believe? Well, let Lottie have a look."

Matt lowered the bale so that he held it by both hands directly in front of himself and smiled as the woman approached.

Lottie circled him as she might have inspected a prize stallion, her tongue clucking the entire time. "My, you are quite something," she said in a low husky voice.

Hearing this, Mary flinched. Everybody knew about Lottie and her girls. The word was that they knew how to make men cry out with pleasure. Any time a man in town wasn't satisfied with the way courting a respectable girl was going, he threatened to go down to Lottie's where the women knew how to satisfy a man.

Mary peeked around the corner of the stall. Lottie was running her fingers lightly over Matt's bare shoulders.

"Hard as a rock," she said in a voice that might have been taking inventory at the mercantile.

"Hard . . . hard . . . harder . . . faster," the parrot cawed.

Then Mary saw Lottie looking at the way Matt's jeans jigged his narrow hips. "You must have driven those frontier girls wild with that tight ass of yours, darlin'," she said.

"I had no complaints," Matt said with a soft chuckle.

"Put that bale of hay down, darlin', and let me see the whole package."

Mary watched wide-eyed, as with a studied slowness and a lazy grin Matt set the hay inside the nearest stall and turned toward Lottie. When she saw the bulge that pressed against his buttoned fly, Mary gave an audible gasp which was covered only by Lottie's own involuntary exclamation. "Holy shit, darlin', did I do that?"

"Holy shit," cackled the parrot. "Harder . . . baby . . . harder."

Both Lottie and Matt burst out laughing at the parrot's raucous cries.

"Good to meet you, Matthew Hubbard. I'm Lottie McGee, and if you ever have a need for a little tea and sympathy—or something a bit stronger—come see me." The madam extended her hand, but her eyes fastened suggestively on Matt's jeans.

Matt accepted the woman's handshake. "I'll keep that in mind, ma'am," he said with a grin.

Mary practically drew blood biting her lip to keep from speaking out. *He'd keep that in mind?* Over her dead body. If she ever caught him anywhere near . . .

"Well, now, you tell Jake I was here, darlin', and don't be a stranger," Lottie called as she headed out of the stable.

"Come to Lottie . . . come to Mama," the parrot cried as two townswomen made a wide berth around Lottie when she met them crossing the street.

"You can come out now," Matt called as he watched Lottie stroll down the other side of the street. He gave one last chuckle and turned toward Mary.

"I have to go," she said primly as she gathered the basket she had carried his lunch in and fussed with the arrangement of the cloth liner she had used.

"Okay." Matt sounded disappointed and slightly confused. "I'll see you for supper."

"All right," Mary replied through tight lips.

"Is something wrong?" Matt moved closer, blocking her exit.

Mary refused to look at him. "No," she lied.

"You weren't . . . you didn't think . . . ?" He glanced from Mary to the door and back again. Then he burst out laughing. He stood there, all six foot–plus of him, naked to the waist, hair all tousled where her fingers had roamed it, gorgeous and laughing his fool head off at her.

"You certainly seemed to be enjoying yourself," she burst out, "standing there like some prize bull at auction for stud service." Then she sucked in her breath, shocked at her own words.

Matt grinned and reached for her. "Darlin', I—"

"Don't you call me darlin'. That's Lottie's word, and I won't have you using it with me. You save that for one of Lottie's girls on that night when you need tea and sympathy." She grabbed her basket and stepped around him.

But he was too fast for her. Taking her by her shoulders, he hauled her against his bare chest. "I have everything I want in a woman right here, right now. I've no reason to go looking elsewhere, Mary Taylor." Then he kissed her, working at her mouth until she opened to him and then plundering it with his tongue until she felt her knees buckle. "Remember that," he murmured huskily when he pulled away but did not release his hold on her.

"And you remember this, Matthew Hubbard. I will not have people talking about me as if I were some common saloon girl. There will be no repeat of this afternoon's . . . activities. We will wait until our wedding night as a proper and respectable couple should."

To her complete and utter frustration, he did not answer, only lowered his head and kissed her more tenderly and thoroughly. Kissed her until she clung to him. Kissed her until her own mouth moved over his, her tongue danced with his, her hands memorized the muscles of his back all the way from his broad shoulders to the waist of his tight jeans and back again.

"Whatever you say, Mary," he said softly as he broke the kiss and released her.

CHAPTER
10

On Sunday afternoon Mary went to call on Abby Sutherland. Matt was helping Mary's father at the gristmill along with several of the other men in town. This was the busy milling season, and every hour counted.

Ordinarily Mary would have enjoyed a visit with Abby, but the argument she and Matt had had in the livery the previous afternoon remained unresolved. Mary didn't know Abby well, but she did like Jake, and Abby seemed such a quiet and gentle soul . . . not in the least like her cousin Lottie.

Her mission was to arrange for Abby to provide flowers from her garden for her bouquet and the church altar.

"I'm afraid the choice will be small," Abby said apologetically. "It's late in the season even for what is here. We've had such an unusually warm and prolonged autumn . . . it's almost as if God planned it so that there would be something in bloom for your wedding, however meager the selection."

They were walking through Abby's garden, a beautiful

palette of autumn golds and purples and silver grays. "I don't need a large bouquet," Mary said.

Abby stopped and studied Mary for a moment. "No, you are so petite that something smaller would be better." This observation seemed to brighten her spirits considerably. "Well, perhaps we'll have some choices to make after all."

They studied each rosebush for signs of promising buds that might blossom at exactly the right time. "I love them all," Mary sighed.

"Well, I might suggest that there is one last white over there. It may not open in time, mind you, but I seem to recall a white rose played an important part in this whole romance." Her eyes twinkled merrily.

Mary blushed and smiled. "I'm sorry about that—trying to sneak a rose over the fence that way. It was shameless of me."

"Nonsense. It was such fun observing the entire process, especially once Matthew Hubbard stepped off that train. I don't mind telling you he took a little of my breath away. Of course, don't you dare tell Jake I said that, but your young man is awfully good looking."

"I hadn't really noticed," Mary replied primly, and then both women broke into peals of girlish laughter.

"Come over here to the shed, and let's see if any of the dried stuff might work as a filler."

Inside the small shed were bundles of lavender and yarrow, as well as assorted herbs. The two women spent nearly an hour considering the various combinations.

"Well, at least we know even if a frost comes tonight, the bride will have her bouquet," Abby announced. "Each night from now till the wedding or the frost—whichever comes first—I'll bring in whatever buds and promising blossoms there are, and when Friday gets here, we'll see what we've got."

"Thank you, Abby. I can't tell you how much this means to me."

"Nonsense. It's a pure pleasure to be able to do something . . . to take part. Why don't you come inside with me? Dinah hasn't been feeling too good today, so I've let her lay about in our bed. We spoil her shamelessly, especially Jake. Lord, the sun rises and sets on that little girl as far as he's concerned."

Mary followed Abby back to the house. "From what I've seen of the two of them over at the livery, the feeling is mutual."

Abby's smile was radiant. "Yes, it's all worked out so wonderfully. We have been so blessed." She indicated a chair at the small kitchen table and hurried through the small house to check on the child she had been pregnant with the night Jake had first found her on the steps of Lottie's saloon . . . the child he'd helped deliver and then adopted.

Mary glanced around the kitchen, taking in all the small details that spoke of a house filled with love and caring. It was all so foreign to her. She'd spent so much of her time in the store that her domestic skills had been neglected. She wondered how Abby managed to get her pots so clean. She examined the glass chimney on the lamp and could not find so much as a smudge. She sighed and wondered how on earth she was going to learn everything she needed to know in the next few days.

"Well, she's sound asleep. No fever, though, so I'll just let her rest. I caught her eating a handful of dirt. Kids. You try to tell 'em, but sometimes they just have to learn the hard way." Abby stirred the fire in the cookstove and slid a coffeepot into place. "It's leftover coffee, but I've got plenty of milk if it's too strong. Will you have a cup with me, Mary?"

"I'd like that." Mary relaxed and visited with Abby while the coffee heated and Abby cut them each a slice of bread, then offered Mary butter and jam.

"So," she said as she sat across from Mary, blowing on her coffee, letting the steam warm her face, "has it all seemed as much of a whirlwind as it's been for the rest of us?"

Mary laughed. "It's been pretty unbelievable," she admitted.

Abby smiled. "What on earth ever gave you the nerve to run that ad?"

"I've asked myself that a thousand times. What if I hadn't? On the other hand, what have I gotten myself into here?" Mary was smiling, but she did not miss the small frown that crossed Abby's face. "What? Tell me, Abby. What are you thinking?"

"It's nothing." Abby smiled and dismissed Mary's concern with a wave of her hand and an offer of a second piece of bread with jam.

Mary laughed. "I won't fit into my wedding gown if you keep feeding me," she protested.

They sat in comfortable silence for a few minutes, drinking their coffee.

"You know, I was a mail-order bride . . . the first time," Abby said softly.

She was looking out the window, but her gaze seemed to focus on something far away.

"I had heard that," Mary said. "What was it like?"

"It . . . it was all right at first. We had written and we seemed to have a lot in common . . . share the same dreams . . . or at least that's what I thought."

"What happened?"

Abby focused her attention back on Mary. "Well, will you listen to me rambling on like some old woman? I'm sorry, Mary. I just got off track there for a while."

"Your first marriage didn't . . . that is . . ."

"Now, don't you start worrying about ancient history here. My first marriage was a mistake. I was young and foolish. I thought I knew what I was getting into, but really I went into it as blind as a bat. And look how it all turned out . . . I've got Dinah and I've got Jake and I've got this one on the way." She patted her rounded belly and smiled. "So, the way I see it, sometimes the Lord truly does work in mysterious ways. His wonders to perform."

She got up and cleared the table, and Mary helped her. They talked for a while longer about the wedding and the flowers, and then Abby walked Mary out to her wagon.

"Mary, Matthew is nothing at all like my first husband was. He's a good, decent man, and I know you all are gonna be happy as two peas in a pod." She hugged Mary. "May you be as happy as I am," she said softly just before she let Mary go.

"Thank you," Mary said. "For everything."

"Come by any time and bring that handsome groom with you next time. I may be pregnant, but I'm not dead. I still appreciate a good-looking man." She laughed and waved as Mary drove away.

The Sutherland farm was just past her own land. Abby Lee had a garden in town next to the livery, but her garden here at the farm was the one that was remarkable. As Mary rode past the land she would share with Matt, she could see the framework of the house that Matt and some of the men in town had begun putting up. Matt had driven Mary out here to watch the framework as it rose. Mary could hardly believe the changes that were taking place in her life. In a few weeks she and Matt would return from Memphis and set up housekeeping here.

She pulled the wagon over and walked up the slope to the shell of the house—her house—where her children would be born and her days would be filled with all the gladness and sadness that was life. She walked around, trying to imagine how it would all look. Here was Matt's "veranda." Above it on the second floor was their bedroom, and off that the nursery and other bedrooms for when the children were older.

Downstairs Matt had wanted a large dining room where the whole family could gather for holidays and birthdays and other times of celebration. She recalled how he had stood right here, ticking off on his fingers the number of chairs they would need around the table to include her parents and brothers and sisters and their families. She had protested that he was being far too extravagant, but he had reminded her of his inheritance and kept on counting chairs.

As she walked around the outside of the house, Mary could not shake a feeling of uneasiness. Clearly Abby's experience as a mail-order bride had been unpleasant, even disastrous. Rumor had it that her first husband had beaten her, even when she was pregnant, and that he had turned into a drunk and a gambler.

Abby had indicated that in the beginning she had thought they shared the same goals and dreams. They had talked about the future just as she and Matt had. But Abby had also indicated that her dreams had disappeared . . . at least in that marriage. Did Mary really know Matt any better than Abby Lee had known her first husband?

"Well, nothing bad is going to happen to me," Mary said aloud, talking to the horse as she climbed back into the buggy. "This is an arrangement Matthew and I are entering into . . . we both know and appreciate that. Neither of us is expecting true love. It is a practical decision we have made, and thankfully we seem well suited to each other. In time we will probably be the best of friends, even if it is a loveless marriage," she mumbled to herself as she drove back toward town.

She had no doubt that in the beginning they would share a grand passion, for she was new to the act of making love, and Matt seemed to enjoy that. But once that had passed, she would not kid herself now or in the future. The likelihood was that he would seek other releases for his obviously lusty nature. Although seeing someone like Lottie McGee touch his bare skin had been enough to set her teeth on edge, Mary knew that she would just have to find a way to adjust.

"But in the meantime, there are certain agreements that we have made and which we both should be held accountable for," she lectured the horse as the rainbow-colored buildings of Harmony came into view.

"Mary, the preacher's waiting for you. Where have you been?" Sissy stood at the back door to the store, her small hands firmly planted on each hip.

"I was at Abby's picking out flowers. What are you talking about?"

"The Reverend Johnson is upstairs in the parlor right now, and Matthew's there with him. Did you forget he wanted to meet with the two of you so he could give you some idea of what you're getting into?"

Mary swallowed nervously and smoothed her skirt. She hadn't seen Matthew since the episode in the livery stable. When he'd come for supper the night before as if nothing had happened, she'd pretended a headache and stayed in her room, trying hard not to eavesdrop when she heard his wonderful laughter echoing down the hall from the dining room. He had not attended church this morning.

"How do I look?" she asked Sissy as she snapped the reins around a hitching post and hurried toward the back stairs.

"Like warmed-over potato soup," Sissy observed. "Bite your lips and pinch your cheeks. You're as white as a sheet."

As Mary hurried up the stairs, she followed her younger sister's advice. Why on earth had she stopped at the house? How could she have forgotten this appointment with the reverend?

She rushed down the hall and into the parlor. "Reverend Johnson, I'm so sorry. I—"

Both the Reverend Johnson and Matthew stood the moment she entered the room, but Matthew held her gaze. Was she destined to have her breath stolen away every time she didn't see him for twelve hours?

As usual his presence filled the room . . . more so because he came immediately to her side and took both her hands in his. "How are you feeling today, my dear?" he asked as he led her to a chair as if any moment she might collapse in a heap on the braided rug. "Mary wasn't well last night," he said to the preacher.

The Reverend Johnson made appropriate conciliatory sounds and waited for Matthew to retake his seat, which he did right next to Mary, holding her hand as if any moment he might be called upon to spring to her assistance. But Mary understood that this was his way of letting her know that he knew she had faked illness to avoid him. His grip on her hand told her that he would not allow her to elude him any longer.

The preacher cleared his throat and bowed his head. "Let us

begin with a word of prayer," he said, and launched into a monologue to God that included blessings for the bridal couple, their families, their future, the weather, the crops, the need of the church for a new minister, the need of the church for a new steeple, and a plea for lost souls who might live in or near the town of Harmony to find their way to Jesus and to church.

Through it all Mary kept her eyes on her lap, but she was keenly aware that Matt's eyes, while lowered, were focused on her.

"Amen," the minister finally said, and Mary and Matt added their own amens.

"Now then," the Reverend Johnson said, "it is my duty as well as my pleasure to spend the next hour or so with you to help you examine this contract of holy matrimony you are about to join in."

After the single word *contract*, Mary heard little else. Of course, that was the perfect answer. They would draw up a contract, her expectations and his, stated simply and plainly on a sheet of paper they both would sign. It was exactly what was called for in these unusual circumstances, and Mary considered it a sign from heaven that the idea had hit her in the presence of the Reverend Johnson, which to her was tantamount to the presence of God's own messenger.

She glanced at Matt and saw that he was listening intently to what the preacher was saying. Discussions like this were important to Matthew. He liked to have details spelled out, he had told her once. He had admired the way she had been so practical in running the ad and then standing up to her family in the face of actually achieving her goal. She could hardly wait to present him with the contract. How clever he would think she was! How he would admire her ingenuity! She smiled and tried to focus on what the Reverend Johnson was saying.

On Monday morning Matt hurried to get back to work on the house he was building for himself and Mary. Their meeting with the minister had seemed a turning point in their relationship. Soon

140

after the Reverend Johnson had begun talking to them about marriage and the commitment it implied, Matt had felt the change in Mary. It was as if everything had suddenly fallen into place for her. She had relaxed and listened attentively to the preacher, a contented smile lighting her beautiful face.

Their spat over that foolishness with Lottie McGee seemed to disappear, and by the time the minister stood up to leave, Mary was holding on to Matt's arm as if being at his side were the most normal thing in the world. That night at supper with her family and later at the evening church services, she had been talkative and gay, willingly enduring the teasing of her friends and family about the impending wedding.

And she had never been more desirable. Her sparkle and wit made her even more beautiful in his eyes. Although he would have preferred to have her all to himself so that he could kiss her and touch her and make love to her, he was content to enjoy the moment, knowing that in a few short days they would begin a lifetime together and could be alone whenever they chose, at least until the babies started to come.

Matt climbed the ladder to the place where their bedroom would be, above the large porch. It seemed impossible that in less than two weeks his entire life had changed. He had found a place where he could feel at home, people he could see forming lifelong friendships with, opportunities to make a home, build a business, be part of a community. Most of all, he had found a woman to share his life with, to make it all have meaning.

Mary. The mere thought of her brought with it such a sense of satisfaction, a sense of fulfillment. He had no trouble at all seeing the future . . . their future. Every time he came out here to their land and the house, he saw images of their life together everywhere. Here was where she would birth their children. Here was where they would share joy and endure sadness. Here was where they would live out their lives . . . and their love.

For Matt had no doubt that he was indeed in love with Mary. Though some might say two weeks was a whirlwind courtship, he knew that what he and Mary had now had grown steadily over the days of that time. How they had begun and where they were now were not the same. They had begun as partners in an unlikely business arrangement. By the time they met in front of the altar of the Harmony Methodist Church, they would be partners for life. The vows they would repeat would not be a formality. They would hold meaning and promise and be backed up with love.

"Need some help?"

Matt looked down to see Joseph Taylor looking up at him. Mary's brother Joe had maintained his reserve with Matt, but Matt had silently claimed a minor victory when the man had stopped challenging his motives at every turn.

"Always glad to have help," he called back.

Joe nodded and moved a second ladder into place a few feet away from where Matt was working. When he had climbed the ladder and pulled a hammer from his belt, he started nailing the boards to the supports.

"I appreciate this," Matt said as the two worked in tandem.

"Not much going on at the station," Joe said around a mouthful of nails.

"Must get kind of boring with just the one train coming and going in each direction each week," Matt noted.

"Yep."

They didn't say anything for several minutes. Then they worked together to reposition the ladders and start on another section of the house.

"Are you feeling any better about me marrying your sister?" Matt asked.

Joe shrugged and pounded in another nail. "She seems happy. You seem a decent sort."

Matt smiled. "Thanks for the vote of confidence."

Joe almost smiled, but then he leveled his hammer at another nail and focused all his concentration on that. "I reckon you know what you're getting into . . . marrying Mary."

"Well, I think I do . . . but if there's something I should know . . ."

This time Joe did smile. "She's got a temper."

Matt grinned. "Yeah, I found that out the other day."

"And she's a dreamer."

"Funny, she says the same thing about you."

Joe shot Matt a look and resumed his work. "She also talks too much," he muttered.

"Well, she'll be glad to know we've got your blessing. It means a lot to her what you think."

Joe's eyes lit with surprise and pleasure.

Later, when the two men stopped to eat the lunch Faith Hutton had packed for Matt that morning, they talked easily of farming and life on the prairie as opposed to life out on the range. Joe shared his dream of heading west and his idea of starting an import business in San Francisco, mostly to give himself the opportunity of seeing the world.

"Speaking of seeing the world," Matt said, "I need to make some reservations for Mary and me to get to Memphis."

"What'd you have in mind?" Joe asked, and took another dipper of water from the pail to wash down the cold meat sandwich.

Matt grinned. "What I had in mind was asking you to make the best reservations you could for us. But I guess between building the house and meeting the preacher and all, I clean forgot."

"I'll take care of it," Joe said. "'Course, you understand it won't be nothing fancy till you reach at least Topeka."

"That's okay."

"And it could get expensive." Joe looked out toward the horizon when he said this, but Matt knew that he was once again being tested.

"I can afford it," he said quietly.

Joe nodded and took another bite of his sandwich.

"You know, it'd be nice to have somebody at the wedding to stand up with me," Matt mused after a while when they had resumed their work. "I've got no family of my own, but on his wedding day a guy can use some . . . support."

Joe grinned. "Are you asking me?"

"Are you accepting?"

"Yeah. I figure you'll need somebody to hang on to the ring till you need it."

Matt's eyes went wide with shock. "The ring. Damnation! I never even thought about it. Where the hell am I gonna find a wedding ring around here?"

"Well, knowing Ma, she probably has a stock of 'em at the store," Joe said.

"Uh, no offense, but I don't want Mary's ring to be something she's already handled a dozen times showing it to some other customer. It should be special."

Joe nodded, and the two men sat perched on their ladders trying to figure out where Matt might get a ring by Friday.

"I suppose I could ride over to Salina," Matt said without much enthusiasm.

"Or you could talk to Jake."

"Jake?"

"Well, yeah. He works with metal all the time. Maybe he could make something that would do until you got to Memphis, and you could buy Mary a proper ring there." Joe seemed quite taken with his plan.

Matt grinned and hurried down the ladder and over to where he'd left his saddle so Traveler could graze without the weight of it while Matt worked.

Joe watched from his vantage point on the ladder as Matt rummaged through the pockets of his saddlebags until he pulled out a bandanna and carefully began unfolding it.

"Do you think he can work with silver?" Matt called as he held up a nugget the size of a small rock.

"Lordamighty, Matt, where'd you get that?" Joe almost fell getting down the ladder to have a closer look.

"A guy I did some scouting for out in Colorado paid me with it. I've always carried it for luck." Matt grinned as Joe hefted the weight of the piece and gave a low whistle.

"Let's go talk to Jake right now," Joe suggested. Clearly he was almost as excited about the project as Matt was.

GETTING HITCHED

*   *   *

"A wedding ring for Mary?" Jake scratched his whiskers and looked skeptically at the nugget Matt held out to him. "I don't know. Mary's awfully particular."

"But will you try?" Matt asked.

"What if I ruin it? Or worse, what if I do something to the silver that takes away the value? Then you not only don't have a ring, you ain't got the silver, either."

"Damnation, Jake," Joe blurted, "the man's rich. He's heading for Memphis to claim an inheritance . . . going first class, too. Do you think he needs a little piece of silver like this?"

Matt smothered a smile and stared pleadingly at Jake. "Just give it a try, Jake."

Jake took the rock, turning it over, polishing the jagged edges with his huge thumb. "How do I know what size?"

Matt and Joe looked at each other dumbfounded. Then Joe snapped his fingers. "You could get her to try on rings at the store, like you were gonna buy her one of them, then bring the one that fits here to Jake."

"When will you need it?" Matt asked Jake.

"The sooner the better," Jake said. "I need to see what I'm working with."

"I'll go now," Matt answered and headed for the mercantile.

"I'll come with you," Joe called, slapping his hat on his head and hurrying after Matt.

"Will there be anything else, Miz Parker?" Mary asked politely as she tied up in brown paper and string the ribbons and findings Minnie had selected.

"I reckon not. But don't you tell Maisie I was in here. She has a perfectly good hat for the wedding, but if she knows I'm fixing to freshen a bonnet of mine—which I have had since the year one, I might add—nothing will do but that she'll have to have something new as well . . . and she doesn't need it."

"Yes, ma'am," Mary said absently. Her mind was still at her writing desk upstairs. She had started working on the contract last night, and the task had been far more complicated than she had imagined.

"Oh, your head is in the clouds, Mary Taylor. Just look at the mess you've made of that string. I'll need Zeke's barber scissors to cut through those tangles." Minnie snatched the package and turned to go. "Ah, Matthew . . . and Joseph," she said with delight as the two men raced into the store as if the sheriff himself were after them.

"Ma'am." Matt whipped off his hat and nodded to Minnie Parker, but his eyes were on Mary. "Mary, I came to buy you a wedding ring," he announced.

"Oh, how romantic," Minnie tittered and rushed out of the store in search of someone she could share the news with.

"Show him the selection, Mary," Joseph urged as he crowded up to the counter behind Matt.

"Well, there isn't much, but—"

"How about that one?" Joe said, leaning over Matt's shoulder and pointing to a simple band as Mary pulled the small box of rings out from behind the glass door where her mother kept the best laces and fancy handkerchiefs.

Matt looked skeptical. "I don't know. Maybe this one?" He held the ring up and showed it to Joe.

Mary cleared her throat to remind them she was there and waited.

"Here, try this one on, Mare," Joe urged as he shoved the ring in the general direction of her ring finger.

"It's a little large," she said wryly as the ring slid easily off her finger the minute she dropped her hand.

Joe and Matt glanced at each other dejectedly. "How 'bout this one?" Joe asked, grabbing another ring from the small selection.

"May I ask just one question here? Well, actually, two questions." Mary smiled sweetly at her brother and her fiancé.

They nodded in unison and waited impatiently.

"Why are we in such a rush? And," she said as she turned her full attention to her brother, "why do you care at all?"

"Joe here has agreed to stand up with me at the wedding," Matt explained with a triumphant smile.

His announcement had the predicted effect. Suddenly Mary was beaming. "Really?" she squealed and came around the counter to hug her brother. "Oh, Joey, thank you. You've made me so happy."

Joe grinned and winked at Matt over Mary's shoulder.

"So, we need to decide on your ring so Joe here can hang on to it for me until the big day," Matt continued.

Their panic-stricken rush to shove rings on her finger forgotten, Mary became a willing participant in the process. She tried on every ring until they found the one that seemed to come closest to fitting. Of course, every one of them was too large, but there was one that she could have on her finger without it falling off every time she moved her hand.

"That's it!" Joe cried triumphantly and jerked it off Mary's finger. "Come on, Matt," he called as he headed for the door.

Mary looked confused. There was, after all, the matter of his paying for the ring, and on top of that, this whole business had been about the least romantic undertaking she'd ever participated in.

"Let your mother know which one we picked, Mary, and I'll settle the bill with her," Matt called as he raced out after Joe.

"Nice doing business with you," Mary muttered to herself as she reshelved the remaining rings.

Down the street Joe and Matt were already handing the ring over to Jake. "This one . . . only smaller," Joe ordered.

"And prettier," Matt added. "Like Mary."

CHAPTER
11

❧

On Tuesday night the whole town was invited to come help with the decorations for the Harvest Festival and to stay for refreshments provided by Lillian and James Taylor in honor of their daughter's wedding. Everyone was in high spirits as they decked Main Street with pumpkins, gourds, corn shocks, and garlands of herbs and flowers. The men lugged bales of hay onto the boardwalk so folks would have a place to sit when they were tired of dancing.

Matt helped Jake, Joe, and Travis build a platform where Zeke could stand to call the steps for the square-dancing. Faith and Kincaid pulled tables out to the boardwalk from the hotel dining room in preparation for the food that would be offered the following day. Even Cord Spencer and Lottie McGee got into the act, trimming the fronts of their respective saloons with bunting and lining up rows of chairs for their customers to sit in while they viewed the festivities.

Mary was busy at the church. Abby Lee had arrived with baskets of dried flowers just after supper, and Mary, her sister

Libby, and Abby Lee were hard at work transforming the plain church sanctuary into an autumn garden, mixing Abby's flowers with evergreens and ribbons and candles. Mary could not have been more excited . . . or more in love.

She found herself constantly dreaming of Matt. They had managed to steal a few minutes to be together last night, and the moment they were alone they fell into each other's arms, devouring each other with kisses accompanied by hands moving over body parts that were frustratingly armored by clothing. Mary was spending a great deal of time imagining what it would be like Friday night after they were married, when they could touch each other any way they liked, whenever they liked.

The thought of Matt's hands on her bare skin, of his mouth kissing her all over, the way he now trailed kisses down the length of her throat, of him pressing himself to her, his need for her blatant and thrilling . . .

"Mary, I said what do you think?" Libby demanded as she shook her younger sister by the shoulder. "Is there enough greenery on the windowsills?"

Mary felt her cheeks redden as if Libby could know what she was thinking. "I think it's lovely," she enthused.

Libby rolled her eyes and winked at Abby Lee. "Oh, you're thinking of something lovely, all right, my sweet little sister, but my guess is that it's Matt Hubbard stark naked."

Abby Lee and Libby started to laugh, and after a weak protest at her sister's shocking talk, so did Mary.

"Seems to me that gettin' hitched agrees with your Mary," Maisie commented as she and Lillie Taylor stood at the back of the church and watched the younger women trim the altar.

"She is happy, more so than I've ever seen her, especially these past few days. Why, I don't think that girl's feet have touched solid ground once in the past week." Lillie puffed out her ample chest in pride as if she were personally responsible for the success of the match.

Minnie frowned and rushed forward toward the altar just as

Abby Lee placed several long stems of dried yarrow in the main bouquet. "Oh, Abby Lee, I do hate to interrupt, but—"

"Then don't interrupt if it bothers you so, Sister." Maisie hurried along right behind her sister. "The girls are doing a fine job."

"Oh, yes, they are, but—"

"Just go on with what you were doing, girls. Sister, I need to talk to you now." Maisie took Minnie firmly by the arm and turned her toward the exit.

"But . . ." Minnie protested.

"It's Mary's wedding," Maisie hissed. "If she wants dead flowers on the altar, it's her business."

Abby quirked a doubtful eyebrow at Mary, who took the remaining stems of dried flowers and tucked them firmly into the arrangement. "There," she said as she took a step back to survey her handiwork. "I think that's splendid."

Abby flushed with pleasure. "Now then, I've been saving this till last," she said shyly as she uncovered the one remaining basket to reveal its contents. "And if you'd rather not carry it, I'll understand."

Mary watched as Abby lifted a small nosegay of dried lavender, silver artemis, and dried purple rosebuds from the basket. The bouquet was trimmed with lace Abby had stiffened with a flour starch and cascades of ribbons in shades of lavender, blue, and orchid. "Jane gave me the ribbons," she said as she handed Mary the nosegay, then turned back to the basket for one more item.

"It's beautiful," Mary said softly and showed it to Libby, who nodded her enthusiastic agreement.

"I thought we could add this on Friday just before the service," Abby said and showed them a small vase that held a white rose that was just beginning to spread its petals. "If this one opens too much, there's one more in my garden that just might make it till Friday."

"Oh, Abby, it's perfect. Thank you." Mary hugged her new friend. When they pulled apart, both women had tears in their eyes. "We're going to be the best of neighbors," Mary added with a huge grin.

Then they were laughing, and Mary was rushing up the aisle to show the nosegay to her mother, Maisie, and Minnie. Abby followed, carrying the basket she had used to bring the bouquet with her. "You can keep it in this until Friday," she offered.

Lillie took the basket and carefully removed the bouquet from Mary's hand. "Thank you, Abby Lee. It is quite lovely." She carefully placed the bouquet and the vase in the basket and covered them. "Now then, young lady," she said, turning her full attention on her daughter, "I would suggest that you say your good nights to that young man of yours."

"But, Mama—" Mary protested.

"Your mother is right," Minnie agreed. "You wouldn't want to have dark circles marring that pretty complexion of yours come Friday. I do believe a good night's sleep is just what is called for."

"Honestly," Maisie huffed. "It's hardly likely the girl will have a good night's sleep for the next two weeks. She's all keyed up about getting married, and from what I've seen of Mr. Matthew Hubbard, I doubt very seriously he intends to leave her alone once they're legally hitched."

"Maisie!" Minnie and Lillie chorused.

"Well, don't act so all-fired shocked. Surely both of you remember those first nights following the wedding. If you weren't kept awake by—"

"Maisie, that's quite enough," Lillie ordered, noticing how Mary was far too interested for her own good in what Maisie was about to reveal.

"Really, Sister, sometimes you can be so uncouth," Minnie reprimanded.

Maisie clamped her lips shut.

Libby laughed out loud and took hold of Mary's arm. "Come on, sis. Abby and I can tell you anything you want to know."

"Libby, you just mind your own business," Lillie warned.

"I think I'll go find Matthew," Mary said shyly, her face flaming from all the innuendo that surrounded her.

"Well, there goes any chance at a good night's sleep," Libby said with a laugh. "You'll be lucky if you see either one of them again before the ceremony on Friday, Ma."

"Oh, but surely you can't mean . . . that is, it's bad luck for the bride and groom to see each other on the wedding day until the ceremony," Minnie fussed.

"Thank you for telling us all something we already knew," Maisie said dryly.

Mary's eyes widened as the full impact of the event began to penetrate. "It's really going to happen," she whispered and looked around the church as if she were seeing it for the first time.

"So go find Matthew," Libby urged, giving her sister a gentle push toward the door, "before he has a chance to get cold feet."

Accompanied by the music of Libby's teasing laughter, Mary practically ran from the church and hurried up the main street in search of Matt. Along the way she was stopped several times by well-wishers and those who needed to tease her just one more time about the way she'd chosen to get herself a husband.

Then she looked up, and he was standing there watching her . . . waiting for her. On Friday he would stand at the altar just like this, waiting for her to come to him; and when they left the church they would be man and wife. She slowed her step and moved toward him, barely hearing the comments of those she passed now. She saw only Matt.

"Can we take a walk?" he asked when she was within a few feet of him. "I feel as if we've never had a moment alone since this week began. And if I don't kiss you in the next ten minutes, I may die."

"I know," Mary agreed and then blushed when Matt laughed softly. "That is, I'd like to have a moment to give you something."

His eyes widened in surprise and pleasure. "A wedding gift?" he asked.

Mary laughed. "Well, in a way . . . yes."

Matt offered her his arm, and they walked off toward the river together, oblivious to the townspeople's tittering and buzz of speculation that followed them down the street.

When they reached the large cottonwood they had come to think of as their own special place, Matt pulled Mary into the shadows of its branches and kissed her. And when at last they paused to catch their breath, he smiled and then kissed her again. After several moments of kissing as if they would never have their fill of one another, they pulled a little apart. Then Matt hugged her hard and lifted her so that he could swing her around in an impromptu dance.

"Oh, Mary, it'll be here before we know it. Our day. By this time Friday we will be on the train and on our way."

"To Memphis."

"Not only to Memphis—that is just the beginning of our journey. We will be on our way to a new life . . . both of us. Are you ready for that, Mary?"

She laughed and held on as he swung her around and around. *It's going to work,* she thought happily.

"Look out there," he whispered when he had stopped swinging her around and stood holding her. "Our house is out there waiting for us, for the children we'll bring up there, for the days and nights and years we'll share there."

Mary's eyes brimmed with tears. How on earth had she been so fortunate as to find this wonderful, decent man? She was so in love with him that she felt if she didn't say so, she would burst. But she forced herself to remain silent. A declaration of love at this point might ruin everything. There was time enough someday to tell him how she had felt on this night.

"Now, what is this gift you have?" Matt asked.

His face was very near, and in the bright harvest moonlight she could see that he looked expectant.

She pulled two sheets of paper from her reticule and presented them to him. "Here," she said as he accepted the papers. "This is my gift to you, Matthew Hubbard."

Matt unrolled the papers she had tied with a velvet ribbon and moved into the moonlight to try to read them. He was smiling. "What is it? A poem? Did you write me a wedding poem, Mary?" he asked with a delighted chuckle as he held the first page up and tried to read it.

"It's better," Mary said. "It's a contract. It assures you that I accept that ours is an arrangement with certain understandings and expectations. See?" She took the pages from him and held up the first one. "Here I've listed my expectations of you once we are married. They are pretty much the same as those I originally outlined in the ad. And here . . ." She fumbled excitedly to switch to the second page. "Here is your list for me . . . or at least what I thought you expected of me. You're free to add things before we sign them."

"Thank you," Matthew said quietly and took the first page once again from her fingers.

So excited was Mary that she had actually thought to do this, she completely missed the change in Matthew's demeanor.

"Perhaps you might remind me just what's on your list here," he said. "The light is so poor."

Mary did not need the light. She had spent so many hours working on the list that she had committed it to memory. "It says that you will father our children and help me to raise them, that you will provide for the children and myself either through your inheritance or honest labor of your choosing here in Harmony, that you agree to live here in Harmony, that you will not drink or smoke excessively, and that should you find the need to . . . to seek . . . pleasure somewhere other than our bedroom, you will be discreet about it and not bring shame to me or the children. It says that you will never strike me or the children and that, as time and money allow, you will make possible travel to places of interest to me and the children."

She whirled around and grinned up at him.

Now his face was in shadow, and he stood very tall. Mary assumed he was surprised.

"And in return?" he asked.

"In return I agree to accompany you to Memphis and stay there as long as it takes to sort out the business of your inheritance and dispose of your father's estate. I agree to make a home for you and our children, to cook and clean and manage that household, to provide for the proper upbringing of the children, and to care for you and the children whenever you are sick. It says that I will also contribute to the financial support of our household by giving you the land my father has given me, our house, and all property that may come to me as the result of my parents' gifts or as a part of their inheritance once they die." She paused for breath. "Of course, there's space here for you to add any items I may have overlooked."

Matthew took the papers from her hand. "I can think of only one thing you've missed," he said quietly.

Mary frowned, suddenly aware of his shift in mood. He was definitely upset. What could she have forgotten? She had thought of nothing else but this contract for days. She was certain she had not missed a thing. "What?" she asked anxiously.

"This sounds like a bill of lading you might get at the mercantile or a contract your father might draw up with neighboring farmers," Matthew said as he crumpled the papers in one fist and allowed them to drop to the ground.

"It is a contract." Mary was dumbfounded. That was the whole point. She was giving him proof that she did not expect love . . . that she did not delude herself . . . that he needn't worry. "I wanted to assure you that I wouldn't expect things to . . . that is, that we . . . what I mean is I wanted to assure you that I didn't expect . . . you know . . . love," she stammered.

"Oh, really?" His voice shook. "Well, let me give you a piece of information, Mary Taylor." He took her by the shoulders and pulled her close. "I'll admit our courtship has been unusual, but the first time I kissed you, the first time I touched you, the first time we both went up in flames with need and desire, I was pretty damned sure that this was more than a simple business arrangement. We are talking about the rest of our lives here, woman." He released her as suddenly as he had grabbed her, leaving her rocking uncertainly on her heels as he stalked away.

"Matthew, wait!" she cried as she ran after him.

He whirled around and shook one finger at her as he continued to walk backwards. "Get something straight, Mary. I know what I expect from this little *arrangement* of ours, and I damned sure don't need you to spell it out for me. So stay away from me. I need some time here, and I won't be responsible for what I do or say if you don't leave me alone."

Everyone had gathered outside the mercantile to partake of the cider and apple cake Lillie had prepared for the evening's refreshments. There was a lot of laughter and chatter, but it all came to a halt when the crowd saw Matt Hubbard stalk back into the light of the street, give a fierce and yet bewildered look around, and then head back around the mercantile to the hotel. Ten seconds later they heard the unmistakable sound of a door slamming.

Ten seconds after that they saw Mary standing forlornly at the end of the street looking toward the hotel. Then she glanced at the crowd, straightened her shoulders, and walked determinedly toward the hotel entrance.

"Matthew Hubbard, you open this door," she called after repeated knocking had brought no response.

"Go away," came the muffled reply.

"I am not leaving," Mary warned as she rattled the doorknob and found it unlocked.

The door swung in, carrying her with it.

Matt was lying on his bed, his booted feet propped on the footboard, his hat low over his forehead and eyes.

"You owe me an explanation," Mary began primly.

"Ha!" It was a single explosive expletive.

"Then you owe me the courtesy of allowing me to explain—" she began, but stopped as he swung both feet to the floor, stood, and tipped his hat back so she could see his blazing eyes glaring at her.

"I don't owe you a damned thing, Miss Taylor. I am *not* for hire . . . as your husband or anything else."

Mary bristled and stood her ground. "I never thought you

were for hire. I thought we had an understanding—a mutual agreement that would serve us both nicely."

"Well, you were wrong!" he roared. "Clearly we are not in agreement on anything, and even if we were, what gives you the right to lay down the rules? If this *agreement* is so all-fired mutual, where do you get off—"

"I told you that you could add anything you wanted!" Mary yelled back, placing her fists firmly on her hips as she glared right back at him. "I worked for hours . . . days . . . on that paper you so callously wadded up and threw away back there."

"Oh, yeah, well, I could have saved you some trouble," he bellowed.

"I thought you would be pleased to see that I wasn't going to expect . . . more than you might be able to give," she argued.

"I'll decide what I can give!" he yelled. "And until then I think we should postpone any talk of getting married."

"Fine!" she shouted and turned on her heel. "When you've figured it out, please let me know in writing so there can be no further misunderstandings." She exited the room, slamming the door behind her.

The conversation in the street had resumed at a much more subdued level once Mary headed for the hotel. Everyone kept one eye and one ear on the lighted second-floor window as they pretended to enjoy the refreshments and camaraderie. Lillie clung worriedly to James Taylor's sleeve. Maisie and Minnie and Bea Arnold stood off in a little group clucking their tongues and shaking their heads as they strained to catch each new outburst. Frederick Winchester moved from one knot of people to the next, muttering, "Oh, dear. Oh, dear."

When Mary reappeared on the street, the crowd made no pretense of not seeing her. They all waited, holding their communal breaths to see what she would do next. They didn't have to wait long.

With a purposeful stride that practically dared anyone to try to stop her, Mary marched past them. When her mother made a movement to intercept her, she did not miss a step.

"The wedding is off," she said through gritted teeth as she entered the store and stomped up the wooden stairs to her room.

"Oh dear," Fred moaned.

Mary refused all attempts by her family to discuss her announcement that the wedding would not take place. Until well after midnight a steady stream of relatives and friends took their turn standing outside her door and pleading with her to let them in.

Finally—blessedly—she heard the calm voice of her father. "Let's just let the girl sleep on it. Clearly what we have here is a case of prenuptial nerves. It's understandable, especially in this case. Now, everyone, just go home, and we'll see what happens in the morning."

Mary heard a fading sputter of protests from her mother and Libby as her father herded them back down the hall and away from her door. At least there was quiet and she could think.

She tried to interpret what Matt had been yelling at her. What had he said exactly? More to the point, what did it mean? She couldn't for the life of her understand what possibly could have set him off. If he had had other ideas, didn't it make sense that he would have let her know what they were by now? Honestly, sometimes men did not appear to use the good sense they were born with.

Mary went to the window and leaned out until she could just see the corner where Matt's room was located. Dark as a tomb. Damn the man. How could he sleep after what had just happened? How dare he calmly turn out his light and go to bed as if this were just some ordinary night?

She uttered a low growl and plopped down at her dresser. In the mirror she could see the dress Jane Evans had created for her wedding hanging on the door of her chifforobe. It was a work of art, and in it Mary felt and looked like a fairy princess.

On her bed was the basket that held the bouquet Abby Lee had created for her.

She felt huge hot tears plop onto the backs of her clenched fists. Oh, why did this have to happen tonight of all nights? Why couldn't she just go back to an hour ago when everything had been perfect? Why was she sitting here, on what should be one of the most wonderful nights of her life, crying? What on earth was she going to do about it?

"Think," she muttered aloud as she swiped at the tears with the back of her hand. She got up and began pacing, her hands clenched behind her back as she stalked around the small room.

"Okay," she told herself, "perhaps all is not lost. You love him. If only he loved you as well, there would be no problem."

But clearly there was a problem. She and Matt were furious with each other . . . not speaking and most definitely not getting married.

"Okay," she began again. "He still needs a wife in order to claim the inheritance, and time is running out. Even if he doesn't love me right at this moment, he did say love might develop, which is, of course, what I thought, too, until the first time he kissed me and touched me and . . . well . . . no time necessary . . . I was in love."

So, that was a given. She was hopelessly in love with Matthew Hubbard, and no matter how angry she was with him at the moment, the truth was if he walked out of her life tomorrow, she would simply not wish to exist.

Mary gave a long sigh and gazed out the window. Her eyes scanned the view and settled on the train station. Good Lord, what if he left on the train as planned . . . but without her? Worse yet, what if he just got up tomorrow and saddled Traveler and rode out of town? How on earth was she going to convince him to stay long enough for her to persuade him that this whole night had been a misunderstanding and they should go ahead and be married as planned?

Mary paced, racking her brain for an idea. She considered kidnapping him. Or telling Papa she was pregnant, in which case Papa would make him marry her. But then in a few months everyone, including Matt and Papa, would know she had lied. Was she that desperate to keep him?

Yes.

"Think," she commanded to herself.

She could court him. Not exactly the way things were traditionally done, but then neither was ordering a husband through the mail. Why not? Perhaps they had rushed into this too hastily. Why not carry this to the next logical step and court the man? It was the perfect plan . . . or would be if she had a little time . . . and if she knew anything at all about how to woo a man.

"Oh, sweet heavenly stars," she moaned and collapsed on her bed.

Lillie Taylor tiptoed down the hall and put an ear to her daughter's door. Mary was still pacing. It was well after midnight, and the girl was still walking the floor. What on earth had happened tonight? Lillie wrung her hands to keep from being tempted to knock once more on Mary's door.

She had asked Travis to check on Matt, but he had reported that Matt had refused to discuss the matter and had said, "Mary is in charge here as she has been from the beginning. After all, she's the one who placed an order for a husband. I just answered the damned ad."

Travis had apologized for repeating the profanity.

"Yes, yes," Lillie had replied, brushing away the swear word—which normally would have sent her into a swoon—as if it were nothing. "But did he say what happened? I mean one minute they were both floating on air and the next they are calling off the wedding. Something must have happened when they went for that walk." Then she had given a strangled cry. "Oh my heavens, he attacked her."

"Mother, he did not attack her," Libby had insisted. "Rumor has it that while they may not have . . . consummated the marriage . . . they have certainly explored the possibilities."

Swearing was one thing. The idea that another of her daughters might actually have made love without benefit of matrimony was quite something else. James had caught his wife in mid-swoon and led her to the nearest chair. It was shortly after that that he had prevailed on everyone to get some rest and take a fresh look at the situation in the bold light of day.

"Mama?"

Harry stood at the end of the hall rubbing sleep from his eyes.

"Go back to bed, Harry dear," Lillie whispered.

"Is Mary all right?"

"Yes, dear, she's fine."

"Is she gonna marry Matt?" Harry came to Mary's door and whispered his questions to his mother.

"I'm sure it will all work out. Now, go back to bed."

"I'm just gonna sit out here in case Mary needs me," he said, and slid down the wall to sit on the floor.

Lillie considered this. There had always been a special bond between Mary and Harry. Oh, they fought like barnyard cats most of the time, but let one of them be in any pain or trouble, and the other was always right there. "All right. If she needs me, come and call me."

Harry nodded sleepily and curled up on the scatter rug next to Mary's closed door.

Just before dawn Mary eased open the door to her room. She had been dressed for hours and waited for the first streaks of light to appear in the East. She'd been over her plan a dozen times, looking for any flaws. She would have to act quickly if she hoped to prevent Matt from leaving today.

She tiptoed into the hall and turned to pull the door closed behind her. It was best if everyone thought she was still in there.

"Mare?"

Mary gave a startled gasp and looked down to see Harry leaning against the wall at her feet.

"Where ya goin'?"

"Shhh." Mary knelt next to her brother. "I have to do

something. Just keep quiet, and I'll see that you get to ride Traveler whenever you want after Matt and I are married."

Harry grinned. "So, the wedding's gonna happen."

"Shhh!" Mary placed her hand over her brother's mouth as his whisper became a croak of sound. "Of course. I just need a little time. It may not happen this week but it will happen."

Harry struggled to his feet. "I want to help," he whispered loudly.

"Then stay here and cover for me. Don't let anyone in my room. Say that I'm sleeping . . . that you saw me and I was sleeping. Don't let anybody in."

Harry nodded. "You wanna use my secret way so nobody sees you?"

Mary blinked. Of course. Her little brother's exploits were practically legend in the household, and he never got caught. Would she like to know how he did it? Positively. "Show me."

Feeling quite important, Harry led the way down the stairs to the store. Though it was pitch-black, both Taylor children knew the store as well as they knew their own rooms, so they had no trouble maneuvering through the barrels and shelves and narrow aisles.

At the back of the storeroom Harry pushed aside a supply of feed and flour sacks and pointed to a hole in the wall. "Can you get through that?"

"Where does it come out?"

"Outside under the stairs, next to the rain barrel. When you're ready to come back in, take off the three boards with the red paint marks on them and slide through. Then just pick up a pile of stuff and stroll on into the store like you was back here counting sacks or something."

Mary grinned and ruffled her brother's red hair. "What about the boards?"

"Soon as I see you're back, I'll replace them."

Coming back unobserved was the one part of her plan Mary had not been able to work out, and now Harry had saved the day. "Thank you, Harry," she said, and bent to give him a quick kiss.

"Ah, quit it," he muttered and wiped away the kiss with one hand. "What time will you be back?"

"As soon as I can," Mary answered as she headed for the door.

"You can't go out that way," Harry said in a panicked voice as she reached for the knob.

"Shhh," she demanded.

Harry pointed to the bell above the door that let them know whenever a customer entered or left. Mary let go of the doorknob as if it suddenly had become a hot poker. Harry rolled his eyes at her stupidity and led the way back to the storeroom.

"You better leave that skirt here and put these on," he said, handing her a pair of jeans.

They were three sizes too big, so Harry hunted up a piece of twine to tie them on with.

"Okay," Mary said more to herself than to him. She rolled her skirt and hid it behind the feed sacks, then shimmied through the hole, pushing the loose boards out with her hands and barely keeping them from crashing down against the rain barrel.

"Shhh," she heard Harry whisper right behind her. "Get going," he ordered, "I'll take care of the boards."

Lillie Taylor rang up another sale and bid good-bye to her customer with an absentminded wave of her hand. She glanced up at the ceiling to about the location of Mary's room, her ears tuned for any sound of movement.

"Are you sure she was sleeping that soundly?" she asked Harry, who had been hanging around the store most of the morning.

"Yes, ma'am. She was plumb tuckered out."

Fred Winchester burst into the store. "Lillian, I'm afraid we have another catastrophe that needs our immediate attention," he announced from the doorway, then turned on his heel and hurried up the street in the general direction of the church.

Lillie looked from the door where Fred had been, to Harry

and back again. "Can you manage for a few minutes, Harry?"

"Yes, ma'am."

As soon as Lillie left the store, Harry hurried into the storeroom. Where was Mary? She'd said she would be back before anyone knew she was gone. It was already getting to be midmorning. Town was busy. Somebody was gonna see her if she tried to come back now, and how would they explain her being in the storeroom when he'd been telling everybody she was sleeping? "Sisters," he muttered aloud.

"Harry?" The muffled whisper came from behind the feed sacks.

"Where've you been?" Harry fussed as he shoved the stack of sacks aside and bent down to the hole.

"For the last hour I've been stuck," Mary said with a sardonic smile.

Harry gave a closer look. She was wedged all right. He considered the options. If he tried to get her to back out, no telling who might happen to wander by and see her . . . not to mention that it would expose his secret entrance to the whole town.

He sat down on the floor and braced his feet against the wall to either side of the opening. "Give me your hands," he ordered.

Mary looked doubtful.

"Right now. Mama will be back any minute."

She wriggled her hands free and took hold of his.

"Now kinda roll to your side."

She did as she was told.

"Okay, you push off with your feet, and I'll pull . . . on the count of three. Ready?"

"Ready."

"Suck in real skinny and one . . . two . . . threeee."

"Ow!" Mary yelled as she came flying into his lap.

Harry pushed her away as if she might be contaminated. "Geez, you're a mess," he said as he stood up and brushed off the seat of his pants.

"Thanks," Mary replied as she hurried to pull her skirt on over the jeans. "Go fix those boards before somebody sees."

Harry nodded and hurried out of the stockroom.

Mary had just managed to refasten her skirt and adjust her blouse when she heard her mother return to the store . . . with Matthew.

CHAPTER

12

"I'm sure you're wrong, Matthew. Mary has been in her room all morning," Lillie reported as she followed the young man into the store.

Matt strode up and down the aisles of the store and even glanced inside the storeroom. Mary ducked behind a barrel just in the knick of time.

"She took Traveler," Matt announced, "and I intend to find out where she's taken him."

"Now, Matthew," Lillie began, but that was as far as she got.

"The woman took my horse, Miz Taylor. She knows I won't leave town without him." Matt shouted this last in the general direction of the ceiling where he thought Mary's room might be. "I don't know what kind of game she's playing with me now, but I've just about reached my limit!" he shouted.

Lillie's spirits brightened considerably. Perhaps all was not lost after all. "Oh, that is a shame—about your horse, I mean. But I'm quite certain that Mary would never dare to—"

"She ran an advertisement for a husband," Matt roared.

"There's not a whole lot that woman won't dare when it comes to having her own willful way."

"Now, Matthew, if you would just calm down and stop shouting at the ceiling, I'm sure we could—"

"*Mary!* Get down here!" Matt shouted as he stormed halfway up the stairs.

"If you yell any louder, the whole town will be here," Mary said as she emerged from the storeroom carrying a stack of feed sacks. She walked right past him and began placing the sacks on the shelf behind the counter. "What is it that you want?"

"I want my damn horse!" Matt roared as he followed her down the aisle to the sales counter.

Lillie gave a little gasp.

"Please don't faint, Mother," Mary said calmly. "I really have enough to deal with here without having to revive you."

Lillie frowned but regained her composure.

"Well?" Matt leaned both palms on the counter and swayed toward her.

"Traveler?" Mary gave him a wide-eyed look of innocence from her kneeling position behind the counter. "I thought he was at Jake's livery."

"No, he's not at Jake's livery." Matt mimicked her guileless tone.

Mary stood and looked at him with genuine concern. "You're serious, aren't you? Traveler is missing?"

Her concern momentarily took Matt aback. He nodded and eyed her suspiciously.

"That's terrible," Mary said almost in a whisper.

"Maybe he ran off," Harry mused from his position near the back door of the store.

Matt whirled toward the red-haired kid. Could he have taken the horse? "Traveler wouldn't do that," Matt said. "You haven't seen him by any chance, have you, Harry? Because I'd be a bit upset, but I wouldn't be exactly mad if you were to tell me that you just thought you'd take him out for a little—"

"Just stop that," Mary demanded as she came from in back

of the counter and pulled Harry protectively against her side. Her eyes flashed as she looked defiantly up at Matt. "How dare you accuse my brother? Honestly, Matthew Hubbard, sometimes I don't think I know you at all." She nudged Harry toward the door, and the boy did not have to be asked twice to get out of there.

"Have you spoken to Travis about this?" Lillie asked.

Matt nodded. He was still watching Mary, who was going about her business as if this were just another day in the store instead of the day after they'd called off their wedding.

"Well, I'm sure Travis will get to the bottom of this," Lillie assured Matt. "He's very good at being a sheriff."

Matt nodded absently and wondered what to do next. He watched Mary. Lord, she looked wonderful this morning. There was that smudge of dirt that streaked her cheek. Probably from the storeroom. And her hair was haphazardly piled on top of her small head. He relaxed slightly and took inventory of her face, which looked tired. Perhaps she had slept no better than he had. Her clothes were rumpled as if she'd taken little notice of what she had put on. Even her shoes . . .

He stared at her shoes. They were caked with mud, as if she'd been walking through fields or crossing streams.

"How did you get your shoes so dirty?" he asked quietly.

Mary froze in the act of replacing bolts of calico on the shelves and glanced at her shoes. "I . . . uh . . ."

"Really, Mary, you might have cleaned them off before coming to work this morning. I suppose that's what comes of allowing you to go walking with young men by the river at night." Lillie gave Matt a glance that was unmistakably a reprimand as she brushed past him on her way to the counter. "Now we'll have to sweep, as if I didn't have enough to do." Lillie headed for the broom, but Mary was ahead of her.

"I'll do it, Mother. Why don't you go see what's needed for the festival?"

Lillie began to protest but then glanced from Matthew to Mary and smiled. "Yes, well, Fred Winchester may need some help at that. You two will be all right here?" she asked as she untied her apron and hung it on the peg behind the counter.

"We'll be fine," Mary said. "I'll finish up here, and then I'll come and help you."

"Change your clothes first, dear," Lillie whispered. "You're looking quite rumpled."

Mary nodded. As soon as her mother was gone, she began sweeping the floor.

"Where's Traveler, Mary?"

"I haven't any idea," she said and didn't even cross her fingers, for it was the truth. The minute she had handed the horse over to Abby Lee, she had hurried back to town and she had no idea where Abby had taken the animal.

"I need to get to Memphis," Matt continued.

"We'll find Traveler," Mary assured him, "and besides, you have at least a week before you have to be in Memphis. I'm sure your horse will turn up by then."

Her concern seemed so genuine, and yet all the evidence pointed to her involvement—the shoes, not to mention her adamant defense of Harry. The two were in cahoots on this one. Matt would have bet his lucky silver piece on it if he hadn't already given the charm to Jake to fashion a wedding ring for Mary.

"But if you don't find him, what will you do?" Mary asked softly as she continued to sweep the same square yard of floor over and over.

"I'll find Traveler and then be gone—either by train or on horseback." He watched her face for any sign of panic or regret, but she kept her head down, concentrating on her sweeping.

"Yes, but what if you don't find Traveler in time?"

"I have to go, Mary."

His voice was soft and even a little sad. Was that because he was thinking of his father and the task ahead? Or because he regretted leaving Harmony? Mary risked a glance.

"My offer stands," she said.

They stood there looking at each other for a long moment,

and then he slowly pulled the wrinkled remains of her contract out of his pocket. "This offer?"

Mary nodded, surprised to see that he had evidently retrieved the pages from where he had discarded them by the river last night.

Matt looked at her and then at the papers in his hand. "It might have been all right at first, Mary," he said sadly as he laid the papers on the counter. "If you had drawn this up before we . . . On the other hand, it probably wouldn't have worked out after all."

He turned and walked out of the store past James Taylor, who had stood there unnoticed during this last exchange.

"Everything all right, Mary?" James asked as soon as Matt had left.

Mary nodded and threw her whole being into sweeping the floor. She hoped her father would not notice the tears that blinded her as she swung the broom, that he would not notice the white-knuckled grip she had on the handle, and that most of all he wouldn't try to pursue the conversation.

"Well, then, I'm headed for the mill. If you need something, or if your mother's looking for me, I'll be there."

Mary nodded and bent to sweep the dust onto a folded paper. She heard her father moving toward her on his way to the rear entrance of the store. As he passed her he placed one hand on top of her head, pausing for just a moment. "It'll all work out, Mary," he said softly, then kept on walking.

Mary held a sob until she was certain she was alone and then let it out. Now the tears came in a flood. She had ruined everything. How could she have been so stupid? She would have done better to have admitted the truth of her love to Matt and suffered those consequences. He might still have left, but at least he wouldn't hate her.

There just had to be a way to win him back. If she had more time she could show him that a marriage with her was still worth his consideration. After all, he had talked about the importance of settling down and having a family of his own. Did he really want to go looking for another wife? Could he do any better than the life that waited for him right here in Harmony?

"Mary?" Jake Sutherland stood just inside the rear door of the mercantile. "You okay?"

Mary wiped her face with the back of one hand and stood up. "Just feeling a little stupid and sorry for myself," she admitted with a smile.

"So, is the gossip true? Is the wedding off?"

Mary shrugged. "I suppose it is."

Jake frowned. "It's not like you to give up so easily, Mary Taylor. Why, from everything I've seen about you, it seems to me that when you set your mind to something, everybody else just might as well stand back and give you some room."

Mary gave him a skeptical glance and leaned on her broom.

"I mean it. I can't imagine the gumption it took working up the nerve to run that advertisement in the newspaper," Jake insisted.

"Maybe I'm getting soft," Mary answered, pouring herself a cup of the strong coffee brewing on the potbellied stove and then offering one to Jake.

"Thanks." He blew on the steaming coffee, then took a long swallow. "So, is Matt leaving town?"

"As soon as he finds Traveler."

Jake frowned again. "I just don't understand it. I thought I knew everybody in these parts, and I never reckoned there was a horse thief in the bunch. I guess I'll have to hire somebody to sleep in the livery overnight. Bet when Travis catches this varmint, he'll lock him up for good."

Talk of stealing and jail made Mary a little apprehensive. After all, she had only borrowed Traveler for a while, just long enough to convince Matt that marrying her wasn't the biggest mistake of his life. "Is Travis looking for anyone in particular?" she asked nervously.

"There's talk of forming a posse to ride out and around the countryside. A horse as grand as that one would be real easy to spot."

"I imagine he would be," Mary said. Her mind raced. She

and Abby had agreed that only they could know Mary had borrowed the horse. But what must Mary have been thinking? How in the world was Abby going to hide any horse, much less one the size of Traveler?

"Well, it's a slow day. Thought I'd go home and surprise Abby for lunch," Jake said.

"No!" Mary shouted. When she saw the startled expression on Jake's face, she added, "Abby and I are having lunch so we can finish planning the flowers for the wedding."

"I thought the wedding was off," Jake said with a puzzled frown.

Mary's face flamed red. She had never been a good liar. "Well, it may be, but you said yourself, Jake, that it was unlike me to give up so easily."

Jake smiled. "Thatta girl. How can I help?"

"As a matter of fact, you could help. That is, well, I need to . . ."

"Spit it out, Mary. If it's mine to give, it's yours."

"What do you know about courting a man?" Mary blurted.

Jake looked confused, and then he started to laugh.

"I'm serious," Mary protested. "If I'm going to win Matt back, it's going to be through some good old-fashioned courting. Trouble is, I don't have the foggiest idea what men like."

Given a choice, Mary would rather have sought advice from someone like Travis or Cord. After all, Jake Sutherland was hardly an expert on courting. He'd been so tongue-tied when he was mooning around over Abby Lee that it was a pure miracle the two of them had ever gotten together at all.

Jake continued to laugh and shake his head.

"Are you going to help me or not, Jake Sutherland? I haven't got a whole lot of time here." That was the brunt of it. Jake was here, not Travis or Cord, and she needed help right now. Surely marriage to Abby had taught the man something. If she could just get him to stop laughing for two seconds, maybe she'd get some helpful information.

"What's so funny?" Joe asked as he entered the store.

"Mary here want to go courting," Jake said through barely controlled guffaws.

Joe frowned and turned to his sister.

"Now, Joseph Taylor, just don't start up with me," Mary fussed. "I am about to see the best thing that ever walked into my life walk right back out again, and I aim to do something about it."

"I'll have no sister of mine——" Joe began.

Mary gave a heavy sigh. "Are you ever going to make it into the nineteenth century, Joe? This is a new world. Women do stuff with or without a man's permission. I'm going after Matt. If you want to help, then fine. If not, get out." She wheeled around to face Jake. "That goes for you as well."

The two men eyeballed each other over the top of Mary's head. Then Joe grinned and said, "Why don't you send him some flowers?"

"Or some perfume?" Jake added with a chuckle.

"Or write him a mushy poem," Joe choked out between giggles.

"Enough!" Mary shouted, then swung the broom at each of them. "Out! Both of you! Out!"

"Ah, Mare," Joe placated.

"Yeah, Mare, we were just having some fun with you," Jake added.

Both men had backed away from her and her weapon.

"I don't have time for fun," Mary moaned. "Oh, what's the use? Just leave me alone."

"Now, Mare, we want to help," Joe said as he eased back toward her.

"Yeah. We'll be serious," Jake added.

Mary cast a suspicious eye at them as she leaned the broom against the wall, then pulled a pad of paper and pencil across the counter to where she could make a list. "So, what do you think? How can I court Matt?"

Joe and Jake thought about it for a long moment.

"Why don't you make him a special supper?" Jake asked.

Joe made a face. "Have you tried Mary's cooking?"

The two men resumed their pacing. Mary made an entry on her list. *Special supper.*

"How would I get him there? To supper, I mean?"

"Mary, forget supper," Joe warned. "You're trying to win the man back, not scare him off for good. There'll be plenty of time for him to find out how bad your cooking is once you're married."

"Maybe Abby could give you a hand," Jake mused. "You could maybe do a picnic. Abby sure knows how to make a picnic special," he added, more to himself than to anyone in the room.

"It's October, Jake," Joe reminded him.

"Yeah, but—"

"I could do it up at the new house," Mary said, and started making notes. "And I will get Abby's help. Thanks, Jake."

Jake beamed with pleasure.

"What else?" Mary demanded.

The two men who had assumed they were off the hook just stared at her. "What else?" Joe asked.

"Yeah. What next? A special supper and then what?"

"Well, uh . . ." Jake stammered and glanced helplessly at Joe.

"Why don't you kiss him about a thousand times?" Harry asked, coming out of the storeroom.

"Harry Taylor, how long have you been back there eavesdropping?" Mary demanded.

Harry shrugged. "So, you could kiss him, right?"

"Maybe," Mary said.

"'Cause if there's one thing he seems to like, it's kissing you. Sure as the devil, he's gonna like that a sight better than eating whatever you feed him. Maybe you oughta kiss him first," Harry decided.

"I don't think—" Joe began, but stopped the minute Mary turned on him.

"Supper and kissing," Mary repeated as if reading from her list. "What else?"

"Jeez, Mary, you've only got a couple of days," Harry protested. "How much do you need?"

"I need whatever it takes," Mary answered.

"Well, I've got an idea that might work," Jake said. "It's not courting exactly, but I know one thing that's always impressed me about you, Mary. You're a real hard worker. I mean, if you were to go up there and start working on that house and Matt was to hear about that . . ."

Mary started to smile, and then she started to laugh. "I see what you're saying. It might work. It might just work. Oh, thank you, Jake," she gushed as she gave him an impetuous kiss on the cheek. "You are positively the brightest man."

"Hey, I came up with the kissing idea," Harry protested. "Give a guy a little credit here. After all, if it hadn't been for me, Jake and Abby would probably still be moping around all moon-eyed over each other instead of married. Not to mention that without me, Mary Taylor, you never woulda been able to take Trav—" Harry clamped his mouth shut immediately.

"You took Traveler?" Jake asked.

"I only borrowed him for a bit. I was desperate for a way to keep Matt from leaving town. I was afraid he wouldn't wait for the train but would ride east to one of the bigger towns and take the train from there. Don't you see?"

Jake frowned. "I do see, but Mary, stealing a man's horse . . . Where'd you hide him?"

Mary's blush deepened. "He's just hidden, okay?"

"Mary," Joe said, "Matt's bound to find the horse, and when he does . . . well, he's going to be pretty upset with you."

"I know," Mary said miserably. "But I don't know what else to do. If I tell him where Traveler is, he'll leave. If I don't and he finds out later that I tricked him, he'll leave."

"You really love him?" Joe asked.

Mary nodded.

"Then we'll tell him I took Traveler."

Everyone looked at Joe in surprise.

"I'll tell him that as his best man, I felt it was my duty to give the two of you a chance to work out your differences."

"You'd do that for me?" Mary asked, her eyes brimming with tears.

"Don't go making a big case out of this. I'm just trying to get you settled so you'll stop scandalizing the family name with stunts like ordering a husband through the newspapers. Now, you'd best get yourself up to that new house of yours and get to work. Jake and I'll send Matt along directly."

Mary stood on tiptoe to kiss her brother. "Thank you, Joey," she whispered.

"I'm leaving," Harry announced. "I don't want Mary kissing on my face."

"You are in no danger," Mary sassed back as she brushed past the youngster on her way out of the store. "Stay here and take care of things till Ma gets back," she ordered.

Mary was astonished to see how much work had been done on their house in just two short weeks. The outside was practically done and just needed painting. Inside she found the whitewash and brushes stacked next to the fireplace in what would be their parlor.

Outside she looked out toward town for any sign of Matt's approach and then started to paint. She kept herself amused by planning out the color schemes and furniture arrangement for each room in the house. Of course, there wasn't much furniture yet. Perhaps that would bother Matt. After all, he might have lived for several years on the prairie, but that didn't mean he couldn't recall what must have been the luxurious surroundings he'd grown up in.

When Mary had asked him to talk about his family, Matt usually ended up talking about the land or the house. He was reluctant to talk about either parent, especially his father. The wounds were still too fresh, Mary surmised. But because she felt it helped him to remember the wonderful times he had known, she encouraged him to talk about the house and the land, quizzing him about the particulars of his surroundings.

She heard the approach of a horse and rider. Nervously she doubled her strokes, splattering paint across her arm and nose as she worked. What if this was Matt? She hadn't figured out what to do once he actually came. What was she going to say? She risked a glance over her shoulder. It was him.

"What are you doing?" he asked as he reined in the horse a few yards from where she stood painting the side of the house.

"I'm painting a house," she replied evenly and kept working.

"I can see that. Why?"

"Because it needs to be done. There's a lot of work yet to be done, and winter is coming on fast."

She heard him dismount and hobble the horse, then nothing.

"Did you find Traveler?" she asked, not daring to look at him.

"No."

"I'm sorry."

Neither of them said anything for several minutes. Mary kept painting. The birds chirped. The wind rustled through the dry tall grasses.

"Can I show you an easier way?" Matt asked.

Mary nodded and shielded her eyes with one hand against the midday sun as she held out the brush to him.

"If you use a stroke like this, you'll get more paint on the board and a little less on yourself," he said.

Mary glanced at her arm where a large drop of paint had plopped. She smiled and took back the brush to resume painting. "Thank you."

Matt continued to stand next to her, watching her paint. "Are you going to live here, then?"

"Yes." *With you,* she thought.

Matt nodded. "Could get lonely."

"It could," she agreed.

"I guess I could give you a hand—that is, until I find Traveler."

"That would be nice," Mary said.

Matt walked inside the house and returned with another bucket of whitewash and a brush. "I'll start down at this end," he called, and moved to the far end of the wall.

"Fine. We can meet in the middle," Mary said, and hoped he caught the double meaning of her words.

They worked until the sun was low in the sky. They didn't say much, but the tension between them eased somewhat as the afternoon moved along.

Around four Jake galloped up with a basket. "Mary, Abby thought you'd like some supper," he called. "Oh, hello, Matt. I didn't know you were here," he said.

"Tell Abby thanks," Mary said as she took the basket. "Would you like something?" she asked Jake politely.

"No. I guess I'd best get on home. Matt, nice seeing you." He extended his hand to Matt and then tipped his hat at Mary and winked as he rode off.

"Oh, this looks really wonderful!" Mary exclaimed as she uncovered the contents of the basket. "I hadn't realized it was so late or that I was so hungry."

"I'll put the paint away," Matt said and began gathering their supplies.

"Would you like to share some of my supper, Matt?" Mary asked shyly a few minutes later when she had followed Matt into the house where he was storing the paint. "There's so much food here and—"

"That would be nice," Matt answered.

"Maybe we could build a fire," Mary suggested, shivering a little against the evening chill.

"I'll do that," Matt said and hurried from the room.

Tarnation! Matt thought. If he lived to be as old as Moses, he would never understand this woman. She was acting so strange. Not mad at all or hurt or anything. As if he were some stranger she was being kind to. As if he'd never held her or kissed her or touched her or wanted her in all the ways a man wants a woman. As if in his arms with his lips on hers she had never melted and responded and practically begged him to keep making love to her. As if all afternoon he hadn't been thinking about them together in that bedroom above the spot they were painting . . . making love, making babies, making a life.

Now he was supposed to sit down in front of a fire with her and try to eat? If he had a lick of sense he'd mount up and head right back to town. But that would be as good as admitting he couldn't take it . . . couldn't stand the idea of leaving her.

"I've got the wood," he announced brusquely as he reentered the parlor.

He busied himself with building the fire, working at keeping his attention on his work and off the way she looked sitting there on the floor, her skirts spread out around her, her hair black as night against the pale skin . . . the skin he itched to touch and stroke and uncover.

"Ow!" Matt dropped a log and sucked the spot on the back of his hand where the spark had landed.

"Let me see that," Mary demanded, immediately kneeling next to him, her face level with his, her eyes riveted on his hand.

"It's okay," he protested, incapable of managing the desire that sprang to life the minute her fingers touched his hand.

She ignored his protest and examined the burn. "Yes, I think it is all right," she said and kissed the spot lightly. Then she smiled. "My mother used to say that was the best medicine," she said amicably and returned to putting out the food.

If he had had any ideas before, that for Mary as for him their arranged marriage had grown into something more, they disappeared in that moment. How could she so blithely touch and kiss his hand? How could she so nonchalantly return to laying out the food? No, he was clearly the fool here—the one who had lost perspective and made the mistake of falling in love. For Mary, their relationship was what it had always been: an arrangement . . . a contract and nothing more. He couldn't take that, and he couldn't be responsible for his almost desperate need to try to convince her otherwise by kissing her senseless and making love to her right on the floor of the house they were meant to share.

"Aren't you going to eat?" Mary bit into a piece of cheese and studied him.

"I . . . uh . . . that is, I need to get back to town."

"But you have to eat," Mary protested.

"No, I'm not that hungry. I'll stop by tomorrow and work on the house some more if you don't mind."

"That would be all right," Mary answered, her eyes on the fire.

"You'll be all right here?"

"I guess I'd better get used to it if I'm going to live here alone," she said with a wry laugh.

"Than I'll head on back."

"Good night, Matthew."

"Good night."

For the second time that day Mary held at bay the sobs that threatened to engulf her until she heard Matt ride off. Then she sat in front of the fire he'd built, rocking her body back and forth as the tears came and the flames leaped.

I should have never kissed him, even on the hand, she chastised herself. *He probably thought I was throwing myself at him . . . like Louisa.*

After she had cried herself out, she carefully put out the fire, packed up the basket, and drove the buggy back to town.

At home she climbed the outside stairs to the family living quarters and let herself in. Her mother and father were sitting in the kitchen going over the ledgers. They looked up worriedly as she came in.

"Mary? Are you all right?" Lillie asked, half rising from her place at the table as she studied her daughter.

"I'm going to bed," Mary said softly. "I need some rest."

From her room she heard her mother talking to her father. Lillie's voice dominated the conversation. The only thing Mary heard clearly was, "You have to do something, James. Our Mary is miserable."

Our Mary was miserable all right. In fact, her heart was breaking.

CHAPTER
13

The following morning Matt decided that until he could locate Traveler, he might as well stay busy. The best escape from the questioning looks and whispered comments of the good citizens of Harmony was to go out to the house he'd been building for himself and Mary. He was just leaving the hotel on his way to work on the house when he heard the commotion down near Cord's saloon. He walked the length of Main Street to where the small crowd had gathered.

"Here he is now," one man said as Matt approached the group. "You gonna have her arrested, mister?"

The group parted, opening a path for Matt. The curious onlookers buzzed among themselves as he walked through their midst. He heard one woman say that a thief was a thief no matter whose daughter she might be.

Then he was in the clear and saw Mary holding Traveler's reins.

"Here's your horse, Matthew," she said as she handed the reins to him. "I'm sorry I took him. I just thought . . ."

Her eyes were not large enough to contain the tears pooled there. She ducked her head and walked away in the direction of her parents' store, head high, back straight.

"Did you want to press charges, Matt?" Travis asked.

Matt hadn't even noticed the sheriff's presence.

The crowd waited, eager for the possibility of a little scandal.

"Nope. It was just a little misunderstanding," Matt said, loud enough for everyone to hear. "No harm done."

The people were clearly disappointed, grumbling among themselves.

"That's it, folks," Travis announced. "Move on about your business now. Go on."

Matt looked back across the street, but Mary was nowhere to be seen. He tied Traveler to the railing outside Cord's saloon and headed for the mercantile.

"Where is she?" he asked as soon as he'd cleared the door.

Lillie was standing in the center of a chattering bunch of women near the stairway. She glanced up toward the living quarters and then back at Matt. "I don't think Mary wishes to have your company just now, Mr. Hubbard."

"I'm not real interested in what Mary wishes right now, ma'am. I want to know what she thought she was going to accomplish by stealing my horse."

He took the stairs two at a time, and the tin pots and pans hanging from the rafters of the store vibrated as he strode down the narrow hall, pounding on every closed door as he went. Lillie and her friends climbed the first several steps to the landing and waited.

"Mary? We need to talk!" Matt bellowed. "Right now!"

The door to Mary's room slowly opened. "You don't have to shout," she said softly. "The whole town can already hear you."

He made a move to enter the room, but Mary blocked his way. "Whatever you have to say can be said from there," she ordered with a little more conviction.

"All right. Why did you take Traveler?"

"Because I had this crazy idea that if you didn't know where he was, you wouldn't leave."

"So, you wanted me to stay?"

"I did," Mary admitted. "But . . ."

"But what?"

"But now . . . that is, I recognize that you were right. It was a stupid idea from the outset. I'm sorry for everything, Matthew. Not only for taking Traveler . . . which is the least of my errors in all of this. But for running the ad in the first place. I can't marry you." *Because I love you, and it would break my heart to spend the years with you knowing you didn't love me.*

"Can't or won't?" He hadn't moved from his position outside her door, yet there was a tension between them that connected them as surely as if they had been in each other's arms.

"What does it matter? I was a fool to think I could actually make a marriage that wasn't based on love."

Her words came like a slap in the face. She didn't love him—she was as much as saying so. He'd been the fool, it seemed.

"Very well," he said softly. "I'll go, then."

Mary nodded and studied the toes of her high-topped shoes.

There was a long moment when neither of them moved, and then he started to walk away. He paused just at the top of the stairs and looked back. "I hope you find happiness, Mary," he said softly.

James Taylor had joined the group of ladies listening at the foot of the stairs. Matt tipped his hat to the man who would have made a good father-in-law and kept walking.

"Matthew." James Taylor followed Matt as he crossed the street and headed for Traveler. "I think we'd best talk, son."

Matt started to protest politely that there was nothing to talk about, but Taylor took a firm grip on his arm and detoured him through the swinging double doors of Cord Spencer's Last Resort.

"Cord, two whiskeys," Taylor ordered as soon as they were

in the saloon. Still holding Matt's arm, he led the younger man to a table in the corner of the deserted saloon. Cord Spencer glanced up from the ledger he was working on at a table near the bar, pushed back his chair, and got the whiskeys.

"Anything else?" he said as he delivered them to the table and placed one in front of each man.

"Some privacy," James replied, not taking his eyes off Matthew.

Cord returned to his ledger, seating himself so that his back was to James and Matthew.

James tossed back his drink and then ran one finger around the rim of the shot glass.

Matt followed suit, feeling the fire of the liquor warming his insides as it slid down his throat.

"You and me had a bargain, son," James began quietly.

"Sir?" Matt was not at all sure where this was going.

"We had us a bargain that you wouldn't hurt my girl."

Matt said nothing. He thought about ordering a second round of drinks but decided that would not be the wisest move. James Taylor was running this show.

"Mary's hurting. I don't know what happened with the two of you the other night or last night or why, but I do know that my daughter was happier than I've ever seen her just two days ago, and today she looks like she hasn't a friend in the world."

Matt opened his mouth to offer a defense, but Taylor just kept talking.

"Now, I like you, son. I like the way you've come in here and tried to just kind of fit in. Another man might have tried to take over, but you didn't, and I respected you for it. Truth is, the more I saw of you, the more I knew you were exactly right for our Mary."

Once again Matt opened his mouth. Once again he closed it as Taylor continued stroking the rim of the glass, focusing on the scarred wooden table and talking in that low, calm way of his.

"A man like me marks the value of walking around on this earth pretty much by what he's gonna leave behind . . . by his children and how they turn out. 'Cause if they turn out spoiled or rotten in some way, it's gonna reflect back on that man. The other measure is whether or not he can see them all settled and satisfied before he leaves this world."

He glanced up at Matt, but this time Matt just met his gaze and remained silent.

"Son, Mary has fallen in love with you. I'm pretty sure she's tried to convince herself otherwise, but the fact is, she's gone completely 'round the bend for you. Hell, half the women in town are mooning over you. But I don't care about other women . . . I care about Mary. We had a deal, son, that you wouldn't hurt her. Well, she's hurting. What are you gonna do about it?"

Taylor released the empty glass, leaned back in his chair, and folded his hands over his stomach. It was clear that he'd said his piece, and now it was Matt's turn.

"What do you want me to do?" Matt asked, intuitively understanding that this was not the time to suggest that perhaps Mary might have had a hand in spoiling their relationship.

"I want you to go before the Reverend Johnson tomorrow afternoon just like you planned."

Matt's eyes widened. "I'm not sure Mary would agree with that," he protested.

Taylor waved his hand impatiently as if shooing a pesky mosquito. "Mary's upset and doesn't know what she wants. You're a good bit older, son, and I hope a little wiser. I think you understand that what's going on between you and Mary has not one danged thing to do with how she really feels about you and how you feel about her."

"How do you know how I feel about her?" Matt asked. "She thinks all I want is to use her to get my inheritance."

"Well, of course you do. That's a piece of it . . . not the whole pie."

Neither man said a word for several minutes. Cord's hand had stopped moving across the ledger sheet, although he remained hunched over the thick book.

"What if she won't agree to the wedding?" Matt asked.

"She'll agree," Taylor said firmly. "Does that mean you'll go through with it?" He leaned forward, his hand and forearms on the table, his eyes piercing as they bored into Matt's eyes.

"Why are you doing this?" Matt asked.

"Because life is hard and sometimes lonely out here in spite of how good the folks of Harmony are. Mary's not likely to find anybody else who'll give her the kind of life she thinks she wants. If you get on that train tomorrow and ride out of her life, she'll always wonder. I don't want her to do that."

"What if it doesn't work out?" Matt asked. "Mary and I are coming at this from two very different directions, sir."

For the first time since the conversation had started, James Taylor smiled. Actually he grinned and then slapped his thigh as he gave out a hoot of laughter. "Hell, son, how do you think any two people end up sharing a lifetime together? They each start out thinking they know where they're goin', and then one day they look around and see to their surprise that they're both heading exactly in the same direction, and they don't have one notion in hell how they got there." He stood up and pulled on his hat. "Isn't that right, Cord?" he called across the saloon.

Cord stood as well and turned to the two men with a big grin. "That's pretty much the way of it, I reckon," he said.

"Well, I better go tell Lillie there'll be a wedding. She'll be put out with me if I don't give her enough time to fret and worry over this thing. See you at the church, son," he called as he ambled out the door, tipping his fingers to his hat as he passed Cord.

"Papa did *what?*" Mary could not believe what she had just heard out of Samantha Spencer's mouth.

"He told Matt to marry you . . . tomorrow . . . just as planned," Samantha said. "Go ask Cord. He was there the whole time."

"I don't believe this." Mary felt as if she had not yet awakened from a bad dream. First the fiasco with trying to court Matt last night and now this? Was there no limit to the ways in which she would be humiliated before this business was over? "I just wish people would mind their own business," she muttered half to herself.

"But isn't it the most romantic thing?" Samantha babbled.

"Romantic? It's . . . it's . . . barbaric!" Mary shouted. "And I'll have no part of it."

"But you told Libby that you thought given time you could get Matt to come around," Samantha argued. "And you asked both Jake and Joe what would please them if a woman wanted to . . . court them."

Damn small-town gossip, Mary thought as she clenched and unclenched her fists and tried to think where she could best hide to avoid the mortification of this entire affair.

"Well, we can't do it tomorrow, James," Lillie argued as she entered the store with her husband behind her.

"Why not?"

"Because Fred and I have already made alternate plans for the festival."

James laughed. "Is that your best argument? Because I gotta tell you, Lil, it's pretty weak."

"It's just not right after all that's gone on," Lillie replied with a determined thrust of her jaw.

"Well, the thing that's not gonna be right is if that boy gets on that train tomorrow afternoon and we have to live with Mary's long face for the next several years. And you know how stubborn she can be. If Matt goes, she won't marry anybody or else she'll run off with the first no-good who rides through town, just to spite Matthew."

Lillie could not argue with that.

But Mary could. As she stood on the stairway and listened to her parents debate her future, she exclaimed, "I am not about to throw my life away on—"

"Now, you listen to me, young lady. You started this. I had my reservations, as did everybody else, but Matthew is a good man, and you could do a lot worse."

"But he doesn't love me!" Mary yelled.

Her father threw up his hands in frustration. "So what? Most of the marriages in this town started out without love. Love came . . . it grew. I don't think you love him or he loves you at this point. The two of you are pups when it comes to knowing the slightest thing about love. You think it's all giggling in the shadows and kissing under the cottonwood, but that ain't love, Mary."

Mary's face flamed red when her father mentioned the cottonwood. Good Lord, did the whole town know that Matt and she had practically . . . ?

"I think—" Lillie began, but at that very moment Maisie, Minnie, and Bea collided at the door, each trying to enter the store at the same instant.

"We heard," Minnie said breathlessly as she pushed past the others and rushed to Lillie's side. "What can I do?"

"You can show up for the wedding like everybody else," Maisie declared as she righted her bonnet which had been knocked askew.

"Lillie," James said in a voice that held more authority than he usually used with his wife, "go on over to the church and tell the Reverend Johnson there's going to be a wedding after all."

"But, James—" Lillie protested.

"Go on now," James urged. "I'll take care of things here." He looked directly at Mary.

With a worried glance at Mary, Lillie hurried out of the store.

"Now, Papa," Mary began, "I cannot agree to—"

James took a step toward her and said in a quiet but firm voice, "Make up your mind to this, young lady, there is going to be a wedding with or without your agreement."

"Well, I certainly cannot condone this," Bea huffed.

"Oh, quiet, Bea. Would you rather the man left town and Mary's belly started to swell up?" Maisie whispered in a rasp that everyone heard.

All eyes swiveled to Mary.

"We have not . . . I am not . . . Of all the . . ." Mary found she was so mad she could not finish a single thought. Instead she flounced upstairs and slammed the door.

"Well, thank heavens she's not—you know . . ." Bea whispered.

"Pregnant, Bea. The word is *pregnant*," Maisie hissed.

"Oh, dear heavens," Fred Winchester murmured in disbelief and shock as he entered the store and joined the ladies. "Oh, this is quite unsettling. Our little Mary . . . that is to say . . ." Unable to utter the word, Fred patted his own rounded belly.

"No!" Minnie, Maisie, and Bea shouted in unison.

"Excuse me, folks," James Taylor said as he moved past them and mounted the stairs to the living quarters. "Mary, this is your father, and we are going to talk," he announced in a voice that left no room for argument.

Everyone in the store moved a little closer to the foot of the stairs.

The door to Mary's room opened and closed.

Fifteen minutes later James emerged and walked back down the steps. "You might want to see if she needs any help packing for the train trip," he said as he passed by Lillie, who had just returned to the store, a gasping Reverend Johnson in tow. "Fred, let's go see if we can round up the groom."

That evening James insisted the family go about its business as planned. This included the scheduled pre-wedding supper at the hotel restaurant. Determinedly he gathered his flock at the appointed hour and marched with them down Main Street to the hotel.

"Faith, please let Mr. Hubbard know that we are here," James requested as Faith and Kincaid greeted the family and showed them to the large round table reserved for them in one corner of the restaurant.

"I'll go," Amanda announced and raced toward the stairway with her dog Boom nipping at her heels before anyone could stop her.

"Matt!" she could be heard shouting as she raced down the hallway and up the stairs. "Mary's here."

Mary's cheeks flamed red, and she looked at both of her parents with barely concealed fury.

"You look lovely, daughter," James said with a smile and squeezed her hand.

"Papa, please stop pretending this is all going according to plan," she whispered.

"Why, Mary? I believe it *is* all going according to plan." He glanced up and spotted Matt coming through the door. "Yes, absolutely according to plan."

As usual Matt looked wonderful and took her breath away. Why couldn't he be one of those men who are good looking in the beginning but the more you know about them or the more time you spend with them, they turn out to be slightly sleazy? Mary wondered.

Matt risked a glance at Mary and immediately focused his attention on her father. In ordinary everyday clothes the woman made him breathless. Here she sat all done up in her Sunday best and looking thoroughly miserable, and she was absolutely the most beautiful, most desirable woman he'd ever laid eyes on.

"So," James boomed, "here we all are. Faith, some wine, please," he called.

When the wine had been delivered and served, James insisted on making a toast. "To Mary and Matthew," he said. "May they find as much happiness together as Lillie and I have had."

"Here, here," Travis and Libby echoed and sipped from their glasses.

Joe lifted his glass in Mary's general direction and then drank. Harry and Billy mimicked the actions of their elders with glasses of fruit punch. Sissy, thrilled to be included among the grown-ups, raised her own glass, which contained just the barest sip of the wine.

Mary risked a glance across the table at Matthew. He was holding his glass aloft and watching her. When their eyes met, he lifted the glass a fraction higher and then drank. Mary took a sip of her own wine and promptly choked.

GETTING HITCHED

In seconds she was surrounded by family members and other people dining in the hotel's restaurant, pounding her on the back, offering advice and solace.

"I can't do this," Mary gasped when she had finally regained her breath. She looked at Matt and then her father. "I just can't do this," she said, and fled from the restaurant.

Everyone at the table sat motionless. Matt half rose to go after her, but Lillie stayed him with a hand on his. "Let me talk to her, Matthew," she said, excusing herself to follow Mary from the hotel.

Mary was sitting on the bottom step of the outside stairway to their living quarters when Lillie found her. She was crying so hard that she didn't even hear her mother's approach.

"This used to be your special hiding place when you were little," Lillie said softly as she squeezed herself onto the step beside Mary and offered her a handkerchief. "I used to worry so much about you. Libby would argue things out, but you always seemed to need to go off by yourself and puzzle your problems out on your own."

"Oh, Mother, it's such a farce," Mary said, weeping.

"Perhaps it is, dear. But you must look inside your heart and tell me one thing. Do you love Matthew?"

Mary broke into fresh sobs and nodded.

"Then I believe it will all work out. He needs you, Mary dear. With you at his side, he can reclaim his family's name and reputation. Clearly this is most important to him. And if it's that important, he's not going to treat it lightly."

"But . . . he doesn't . . ." Tears prevented Mary from finishing the statement.

"Love you?" Lillie chuckled. "Don't tell your father I said this, but I expect he's right about love and the two of you. You've known each other such a short time—how can either of you possibly have the slightest idea what love is all about? Give it time, Mary."

"Did you love Papa when you married him?"

"Absolutely. But if you ask me if I thought he loved me back? Heavens, no. The man was so handsome and popular,

193

and who was I? Some little farm girl from over at Salina. I didn't have any idea why he chose me."

Mary's sobs had quieted as she listened to her mother's story. "But he always said you were the most beautiful girl in the whole territory," she reminded her mother.

Lillie smiled. "He still thinks that," she said softly.

They sat in comfortable silence for several minutes. Lillie's arm was around Mary's shoulders, and she rocked her daughter gently back and forth as they looked up at the star-filled sky.

"I do love him, Mama," Mary said after a while, her voice heavy with the emotional exhaustion of the last several days.

"I know, honey, and love can work miracles. You'll see. Now, let's go on upstairs, and you get ready for bed while I make you a hot cup of tea."

Mary nodded and allowed her mother to lead the way to the only home Mary had ever known. She hoped Mama was right because with all that lay in store for her tomorrow and the days after that, there were going to have to be more than a few miracles.

Matt had excused himself from the fiasco of a pre-wedding supper soon after Lillie had gone after Mary. He heard James insist that the rest of the family stay put and eat their meals. The last thing Matt wanted was food. What he needed was some air.

He'd walked outside and started down the street. As he neared the mercantile from the opposite side of the street, he'd spotted Mary and Lillie sitting on the step. He could hear Mary crying all the way across the street, and the sound of it tore at his heart. Mary hadn't seen him, but Lillie had, and the older woman had waved him impatiently on.

Not knowing what he could possibly say to make Mary feel better, he had kept walking. The truth was he wanted to marry her under whatever circumstances might be available. The fact that it was her father insisting and not him should count for something, he figured. Once they were on the train and away from Harmony and all its busybodies, maybe he and Mary might actually come to some understanding that would carry them through at least these hard first days of a life together.

Matt was determined that later Mary would come to love him, and barring that, he was determined that he would give her everything she could possibly want to make her happy. He'd buy her presents and take her on trips and do whatever she wanted. And maybe in time . . .

Mary's wedding day dawned with a sky leaden with storm clouds and a cold wind whipping around the building. She shivered and burrowed back under her covers. There was something both ominous and appropriate about the weather.

She could hear the rest of the family moving around the house, having breakfast, getting ready for work and the festival as if this were any other day. Her mother was fretting over the weather and its effect on the festival plans.

"What about Mary's wedding?" Sissy lamented.

"Mary's wedding will be inside the church, stupid," Billy replied. "What about the horse race?"

One of the alternate plans Fred and Lillie had come up with when it appeared the wedding would not be the highlight of the festivities as planned was a horse race open to all young men over the age of sixteen. Harry had begged his mother to lower the limit to fourteen so that he could enter, but to no avail.

"You know, you could be a little more concerned about Mary," Sissy retorted, "and don't call me *stupid*."

This last was delivered as Sissy flounced down the hall toward her room and past Mary's door. Mary sighed and got up from the safe warm haven of her bed. She might as well face the day.

The morning was a rush of activity. Samantha and Libby came to do her hair in an elaborate arrangement that Samantha assured her was all the fashion out East. Jane came by for one final fitting on her wedding gown and chastised Mary for not eating and losing weight so that she had to take the gown in in three new places. Abby Lee stopped by to bring Mary the last of the roses, among which was one perfect white blossom to match the one in the vase on Mary's dresser. Abby placed both in the bouquet.

Even through her closed window, Mary could hear the excited chatter of everyone who had come to town for the festival as well as the wedding. The street was full of carriages and wagons and people. Some firecrackers exploded . . . Harry and his friends, no doubt. If it hadn't been for her wedding, she might have been out there enjoying herself as well.

By noon the clouds had blown over without leaving a single drop of rain, and the wind had abated. The sun shone on what was left of the last of the fall colors, and the sky was a blinding clear blue.

When Mary ventured downstairs just after noon, thinking that a walk might do her some good and steady her nerves a bit, she was instantly shooed back upstairs by Maisie and Minnie.

"Heavens, child, have you no sense of tradition?" Maisie chastised her as she physically escorted Mary back to the stairway.

"My stars, Mary, what if Matthew had seen you?" Minnie protested.

"What if he had?" Mary replied with a shrug.

"It would be bad luck," Maisie and Minnie announced together.

Mary resisted the urge to laugh at the irony of that superstition. After all, how much worse could her luck get? Her father was forcing a man who didn't love her to marry her, all because of her own stupid idea to order a husband through the mail. So much for tradition.

"Now, get back upstairs," Maisie prodded.

"Yes, dear, why don't you lie down for a bit? You're looking quite peaked," Minnie added.

Mary saw that she had little choice but to follow their orders. She went back upstairs and restlessly paced the small confines of the family's living quarters. Once she stepped out onto the outside landing, thinking she could sneak down the outside stairway to take her walk, but the minute she emerged, Bea

Arnold shooed her back inside. Apparently Lillie had sentries posted everywhere.

Mary sighed and went to the kitchen. Suddenly she was ravenous. She stuffed herself on leftover gingerbread and milk and then searched the pantry for something more. When she came across the canister of brown sugar her mother used for baking, she used a spoon to shovel the sweet lumps straight into her mouth.

"Mary, what on earth?" Libby started laughing as soon as she saw her sister hasten to hide the evidence of her sugar binge. "I was the same way," Libby said through her giggles. "So nervous that I was absolutely starved . . . couldn't get enough, except instead of sugar, for me it was potatoes!"

Mary managed a smile. Then she started to cry. "Oh, Libby, what am I doing? We're not like you and Travis. Matt doesn't love me."

"But you love him," Libby said firmly, "and that can be enough at least at the beginning. Now, come along and let me help you dress."

An hour later Mary walked down the stairs as if she were approaching the gallows. Libby and Abby Lee had assisted her with the final arranging of her hair and putting on the beautiful gown . . . the gown she had lovingly watched being created stitch by stitch as she imagined how enormously happy she was going to be the day she finally put it on.

"You look just beautiful, honey," her father said quietly as he offered her his arm and led her out to where the whole town—and Matthew—waited.

Outside the church Abby Lee fussed over the arrangement of Mary's skirt one last time and handed her the bouquet. The white roses rested right in the center of the silver and lavender dried flowers and gave off a sweet perfume. The ribbons tickled the backs of her hands as she grasped the nosegay as if it alone would get her through this.

Abby gave Mary a tentative smile and then a light kiss on the cheek. "It'll all work out," she whispered, and faded into the crowd.

Mary saw little except the narrow planks of the church floor and the feet of the guests lining the route as her father led her down the aisle. There was music . . . Zeke on his violin. She was aware that the perfume of the dried herbs had permeated the church and given the air a sweetness she would have savored under other circumstances.

Her father stopped, so she did as well. Then he lifted her fingers from the crook of his arm and placed her hand in Matt's. The minister started the words . . . familiar, precious . . . the vows she had waited all her life to take. She was aware of Matt's strong fingers grasping hers, of his height next to her, and yet she could not bring herself to look at him.

If he had hated her for suggesting the contract and kidnapping Traveler, what must he be feeling now? How had her father persuaded him to go through with this sham of a marriage? Of course, there was the inheritance. Time was running out, and what choice did he really have? She understood that it wasn't so much the money as his family's honor. Well, she would make sure that she supported him every step of the way, and perhaps in time he would forgive her and even come to accept the marriage.

The preacher called for the ring. Mary waited for the plain band Joe and Matt had made her choose in a rush that day in the store. That should have told her something right there. The way it hadn't seemed to matter what the ring looked like, just that it would do for the occasion. She'd been too wrapped up in her happiness that Matt and Joe had become friends to notice how unimportant the ring seemed to be to Matt.

She glanced down as Matt slid a beautiful silver ring onto her finger. It fit perfectly and it was perfectly lovely . . . delicate, with a design of entwined vines running the circle of it.

Surprised, she glanced at Matt. He was watching her intently, but she could not read his expression.

The Reverend Johnson asked if she took him and he took her, and they both mumbled agreement, without once breaking eye contact and without even so much as a hint of a smile.

Zeke played something festive, and the reverend beamed. The crowd tittered, and Joe and Libby nudged the newlyweds into the ceremonial kiss.

Matt's face came slowly down to meet her upturned lips. Mary closed her eyes to hold back the tears that threatened. His kiss was sweet and gentle, not at all the way he had kissed her before. But one thing would never change — she would always wish the kiss could never end. When he pulled away, she wondered if for the rest of their lives he would always kiss her in this polite, distant way.

Then the congregation was cheering and Zeke was playing and they were being herded along back up the aisle and out into the sunshine of the autumn day.

At Lillie's urging, a reception line was formed, and Mary and Matt stood side by side without speaking to each other for nearly an hour. One by one each citizen of Harmony filed past to offer their good wishes and to try to decide for themselves whether or not this match had a snowball's chance in hell of working out. When the last guest had passed by and everyone had turned their attention to eating and minding the kids who had been cooped up in their Sunday best for too long and admiring the displays of the festival, Matt and Mary found themselves alone for the first time.

"Well, Mrs. Hubbard, shall we lead this dance?" Matt said somberly as he held out his hand to her and Zeke struck up a waltz.

So this was the way it would be — politeness, not passion; reality, not romance. She placed her hand in his and allowed him to lead her to the center of the street. When he placed his large hand across the span of her slim waist and spun her into the dance, a cheer went up from the crowd. Then they were surrounded by other couples . . . happy couples. Libby and Travis. Abby Lee and Jake. Faith and Kincaid.

"Thank you for the ring," she said softly.

Was it her imagination or did his eyes soften just a bit? Did his hand on her back tighten just a fraction?

"You're welcome," he answered, his eyes intent on her face

as they spun around the street. "So tell me again why you took my horse."

There was no use denying it. "I told you. I thought perhaps if you didn't leave right away, there would still be time enough to work this out between us. Instead . . ."

"Instead the whole town got involved, and here we are," Matt finished for her, but his tone held no rancor.

"Mary," her mother called, "you have to change. Oh, James, there was supposed to be more time," she moaned as she rushed Mary past her father and into the store.

Jane Evans had made Mary a traveling suit of pale blue wool with a hat to match. Lillie handed her a pair of leather gloves, a blue velvet reticule, and a small, ribbon-tied package. "Open it," she said.

Inside were a pair of the most beautiful silver earrings Mary had ever seen.

"They were your grandmother's," Lillie said. "I wanted each of you girls to have one nice piece of jewelry on your wedding day as a symbol of the love and happiness this family has always known."

"They're beautiful," Mary said softly as she put the earrings on, bending her knees to see herself in the small mirror on her dresser. The face staring back at her was different . . . she was a woman now, fully grown, her life decided. There was no turning back. She just had to make this work out with Matthew.

She turned and gave her mother a hug. "I'm ready," she said as she released her mother, and both women understood the multiple meanings in those two words.

CHAPTER
14

Matt finished loading Mary's trunk into the freight car of the snorting, panting train and then moved to the entrance of the passenger car to wait for her. The sun was getting lower in the sky. By the time they returned to Harmony, the days would have shortened considerably, and winter would have set in. He turned and glanced out toward the horizon where the house they had begun stood silhouetted against the pink-streaked sunset of the Kansas sky.

Jake and Joe had assured Matt they would organize work parties to finish the house while he and Mary were gone so that they could be in by the first snowfall. The scene before him was of a shell of a house on a mild autumn day, but in his mind he was seeing the house against a gray winter sky and wondering if it would be as cold and dark as its surroundings, or filled with the warmth of Mary's laughter that he had grown to want and need.

His revelry was interrupted by the excited chatter of the townspeople moving toward the train. He turned and saw Mary coming toward him, surrounded by her family and friends . . . his family and friends too now. She was smiling, but it was a sort of brave little smile that held no confidence at all. He wanted to tell her he knew how she felt.

She looked so fragile that he was tempted to move forward and sweep her up in his arms and carry her the last few steps to the train. But that would not do. They had a lot to work out, which would take some time. He just hoped the days it would take them to get to Memphis would be enough time.

James Taylor had said Mary was in love with him. At the time he hadn't disputed it, but the truth was he didn't think so. If she was in love with him she would have seen that he was in love with her . . . she would have trusted in what they were building together. She wouldn't have felt the need to label it or write up a damned business agreement just in case there was any misunderstanding.

Joe walked importantly along the side of the train shouting, "All 'board!" and urging them to hurry if they expected to make it to Salina by nightfall. Faith Hutton pressed a wicker basket of food into Matt's hands.

"For the long ride," she said.

Matt mumbled his thanks and set the basket on the steps up to the passenger car. When he turned back, Mary was standing next to him. She'd never looked younger . . . or prettier . . . or more terrified. He took her hand and helped her up into the car, then joined her as the train eased slowly away from the station.

"Good-bye," Libby called, and the chorus of farewells swelled throughout the gathering.

Lillie Taylor was crying on her husband's shoulder. James was looking straight at Matthew. Maisie and Minnie were arguing about something and gesturing toward the train. Abby Lee and Jake stood to one side, waving and calling out something that was lost in the rumble and screech of metal wheels on metal tracks. And standing by himself, near the corner of the stationhouse was Harry, watching the train go, his hands thrust into his pockets, his shoulders slumped in a sadness Matt doubted the boy even understood.

"We'll be back," he called to the youngster as the train picked up speed. "Take care of Traveler for me."

Harry's spirits lifted noticeably, and he flung one last wave in the general direction of the train, then ran off toward the livery stable.

Matt stacked their luggage in the aisle and under the seat to allow people to pass and to give him and Mary the maximum amount of room when they sat down. There were not many other travelers, so they had space to spread out over the two facing seats. He held up the basket of food Faith had prepared for them.

"I'll put this here in case you get hungry," he said as he placed the basket on the seat opposite Mary and sat down next to her. His demeanor was one of polite civility.

Mary scooted a fraction of an inch closer to the window to make more room for him, but saw by his expression that he thought she was trying to keep herself as far away as possible from him.

"I can sit opposite you, if that will make you happier, Mary," he said, and this time his voice sounded sad and weary.

"No, I . . . that is, I only thought I would make a little more room. The seat is narrow, and your legs are so long." She blushed. His legs were not just long. They were encased in pants that seemed to accent every muscle, and in so doing reminded Mary of how powerful those legs were when pressed against her own smaller body. The fantasies she'd been having that night as she and Libby and Abby Lee decorated the church had not been the slightest bit dampened by the fact that she and Matt had fought.

Matt sat down and shifted his long, lanky frame until he was comfortable. "We'll have a berth from Salina to Topeka and then a hotel car from there to Memphis."

"That's nice," Mary replied politely. Under other circumstances she would have plied him with questions. She had ridden this train before, but she had only heard stories of berths and hotel cars from Joe and the drummers who came to town to sell their wares. It had all seemed so exciting a few days ago when the most important thing on her mind had been how she was supposed to behave and dress and act on this trip. Now, of course, the transportation seemed decidedly unimportant in the face of spending the next few weeks in close confines with a man who had been forced to marry her.

The train bumped and swayed, and Matt and Mary both pretended to watch the passing scenery. "There aren't many travelers today," she commented after a while.

Matt glanced around, noticing the two rough-looking men at the back of the car, the family two rows in front of them, and the elderly couple at the very front of the car. "We'll probably pick up more passengers as we go," he replied.

Both of them sighed.

Mary glanced around again. Even if they'd wanted to talk things out, they could hardly do it under such surroundings. They seemed doomed to travel in silence or make attempts at polite meaningless conversation, at least until they got to Topeka. What a way to start a marriage.

Matt put his feet on the facing seat and slouched down a little so that his shoulders rested against the low back of the seat. He was very aware of Mary next to him. She was so petite and she looked so pretty in her new blue traveling suit. There seemed to be no color that didn't make her look wonderful, but he thought the blue was exceptionally becoming. He wished he knew what to say to her.

"You look very nice," he said.

"Thank you," she responded as she brushed a bit of soot from the skirt of her suit. "So do you."

Mary turned away from him on the pretense of looking out the window, but actually she did not want him to see the tears of sadness and exhaustion that welled in her eyes. How had they come to this? The days leading up to their wedding had been filled with discovery and excitement and happiness. Now, on what should have been the happiest of all those days, she was sitting next to this virtual stranger and feeling as if she had just made the biggest mistake of her life.

"I think I'll just close my eyes for a bit," Matt said as he pulled his hat low over his eyes and folded his arms across his chest.

Mary continued to stare out the window, seeing nothing in the gathering darkness. The train was hot and dirty. The upholstery on the narrow hard seat was frayed and scratchy to the touch, and the springs were so weak that every movement of the train seemed accented. There was an odor of muskiness and stale air in the close car, and one of the men in the back was smoking a huge smelly cigar. When it was nearly dark outside, the conductor lit a single kerosene lamp at either end of the car.

In the semidarkness, the swaying and jostling of the car seemed even more pronounced, and Mary was more keenly aware than ever of the lack of air in the car. She began to feel nauseated and longed to go and splash a little cool water on her face. But that would involve waking Matt or climbing over him, which would be most unladylike. Besides, he was sleeping soundly, and why shouldn't one of them have a little peace after what they'd just been through? Instead she took off her hat and shrugged out of her suit jacket. She fanned herself with her hat and closed her eyes.

But the rising bile would not be stanched. She rummaged through her reticule for her handkerchief. Clutching it to her mouth, she tapped Matt's shoulder.

"Matthew?"

Instantly he was awake. He swung his feet to the floor and sat up straight. "What is it?" His eyes focused and widened in alarm the moment he saw how distressed she was.

"I think I'm going to be——" She crammed the handkerchief more forcibly against her mouth and stood up. As she lurched down the aisle toward the toilet, Matt hurried to catch up to her.

The elderly couple glanced up with concern as Mary stumbled against their seat. Matt caught her elbow and righted her and then half carried her the last few steps to the toilet, where he shoved her inside the tiny space, propped her against the tin basin, and grabbed for the slop bucket in one swift motion.

Mary had thought there could not possibly be another moment of humiliation contained in this day. Yet here she was. Matt was holding her, steadying her as she heaved and gasped for air, then heaved again. She was vaguely aware of not only the strength of his arm steadying her as she retched, but of his calm, soothing voice.

"It's okay, Mary. You'll be all right. Just a little too much excitement. Take it easy, darlin'."

At last a shudder ran the length of her body, and the bout was over. She felt weak and disheveled, but she was no longer nauseated.

"Better?" he asked as he sat the bucket on the floor and wet his bandanna in the clean water provided for washing. He gently wiped her face with the cool cloth, brushing her hair back from where the fever of her sickness had plastered it to her cheeks.

She took the cloth from him to wipe her lips and mouth and try to rid herself of some of the foul taste. Matt offered her a dipper of water.

"Here, take a mouthful and swish it around and spit." He held up the slop bucket for her to spit in. "Better?"

She nodded and looked directly at him as he raised the dipper to her mouth again.

"Now, this time take a little drink, but not too much at first." He was frowning as he levered the dipper to her lips, but it was a frown of concern rather than irritation.

She took a sip of the water. A little ran down her chin, and Matt wiped it away with his finger. "In sickness and in health," he said softly and smiled.

This time there was no holding the tears back. Mary started to sob, and all the pent-up emotion of the last two days spilled out in those sobs.

"Hey, hey, hey," Matt crooned as he pulled her against his chest and held her, his body blocking the doorway from the curious looks of the other passengers. "It's all right. Shhh. It's all right."

Mary could not have said anything if she had wanted to. Her nerves were as frayed as the upholstery on the railroad car seat they'd sat on, and her mind was a jumble of conflicting thoughts. She hiccuped and sniffled as she fought to stop crying.

"Why don't we go outside on the platform? Some fresh air might be just what you need."

Mary nodded and wiped at her tear-streaked face with the back of her hand.

Matt dipped the bandanna once again into the clean water and wrung it out with one hand. The other hand he kept securely wrapped around Mary's waist, steadying her as the train chugged through the night.

"Here," he said, and gave her the cool cloth.

Once again she wiped her face, and it did help. She gave him a wan smile.

"Lean on me now," he said as he led her out. He ignored the sign on the exit door that said PASSENGERS NOT PERMITTED TO STAND ON PLATFORM, and opened the door. The minute they stepped onto the small narrow platform that connected the passenger car to the freight car, they were greeted with a rush of cool air. "That's better, isn't it?" Matt asked as he closed the door behind them.

Mary nodded and turned her face up to the wind. She gulped in the air, and immediately the dregs of her nausea disappeared. "Much better," she said in a voice left raspy by the vomiting and the crying.

Matt stood behind her, his hands resting loosely around her waist, steadying her against him as he swayed with the train to hold their balance. "It's going to be all right, Mary," he said softly, his mouth next to her ear.

Mary felt her heart swell. Perhaps they could find a way after all.

Matt added, "Lots of folks have started out with less feeling for each other than we've got and made it work. At least we like each other. Friendship is as good a basis as any to build on."

Mary's heart plummeted. She didn't want him to just like her; she wanted his love. She didn't want just his friendship; she wanted his passion.

"So could we call a truce?" he asked, turning her so that they faced each other.

"Truce," she agreed with a bright smile.

He studied her for a long moment, but in the darkness she could not read his expression.

"Salina," the conductor called as he entered the car from the opposite end. "Salina," he repeated as he neared the door to the platform and rapped on it to get their attention.

Matt nodded and opened the door. The other passengers were beginning to gather their belongings, preparatory to leaving the train. Mary put on her jacket and hat.

Once more the conductor strolled through the car. "Salina. Change for Wichita, Topeka, and St. Louis."

The depot at Salina was only slightly larger than the one Joseph ran in Harmony, but it was far busier. As soon as the train stopped, the other passengers rushed for the exits.

"Why is everyone in such a hurry?" Mary asked as she was bumped by one of the children from the family on their train.

"They want to make sure they have a chance to get something to eat before the next train leaves," Matt explained.

Mary recalled Joe's stories of Eastern trains with elegant dining cars where passengers were served wonderful food right on board as the train raced through the countryside. But the smaller trains and those that ran west of the Mississippi River rarely had such luxuries.

Mary and Matt entered a waiting room crammed with other travelers.

"Wait here while I see about our connecting train," Matt said.

Mary glanced around the room. Several of the people looked as if they had been there for some time. Children were crying or complaining to their mothers. Several men were asleep on the floor, using their luggage for pillows or backrests. A trio of young ruffians eyed her from their position near the door, and no one looked as friendly as the people she knew in Harmony. She wished Matt would hurry.

"Well, we may have a little wait here," Matt said when he returned from speaking to the stationmaster. "It seems the eastbound train that was supposed to come through here this morning broke down and never made it. Now those folks plus the ones who were scheduled to be on the train tonight will all have to share one train."

"But we have reservations," Mary protested.

"So do they," Matt pointed out as he pocketed the tickets. "Anyway, it'll be an hour or so before the train gets here. Why don't we take a walk and stretch our legs?"

"What about our things?" Mary asked, glancing once again at the three young men by the door.

"I'll ask the stationmaster if he can keep them behind the ticket window there."

Matt carried his saddlebags and her carpetbag over to the ticket window. Mary had checked a small trunk, which Matt had assured her would be transferred by the train crew from one train to another. She looked down and saw the wicker basket.

"Matt," she called as she picked up the basket and hurried across the room.

"Let's keep that with us," Matt said. He gave the stationmaster some money and tipped his hat to the man.

"Okay, let's take that walk," he said, relieving Mary of the basket and taking her elbow as they walked toward the door.

"Evening, ma'am," one of the young men said as she and Matt passed by.

She nodded but did not look at him.

"Nice shade of blue, ma'am," said another.

She felt Matt's grip on her elbow tighten.

"Looks especially good on you," the third called as they turned and walked down the platform.

Mary felt Matt falter. "Come on," she urged. "They're just trying to get you angry."

"Well, they're succeeding," Matt said through gritted teeth.

Mary looked up at him in surprise. Could he possibly be jealous? The idea gave her a great deal of pleasure, and suddenly she felt much better. "Why don't we sit over there on that bench and eat what Faith prepared for us?" she said. "Suddenly I'm famished."

Matt's grip relaxed slightly. "Good idea," he agreed. "Remind me to thank her when we get home. The last thing you need tonight is the food they serve in these railroad diners."

He had called Harmony *home*. It had rolled off his tongue without the slightest hesitation. Mary savored this revelation.

The bench was around the corner from the entrance to the station and out of sight of the other travelers. For the first time since early this afternoon, Mary and Matt were alone.

Mary covered her nervousness at the realization by fussing over the spread of food. "As usual Faith thought of everything," she said as she set each item between them on the seat of the bench.

There was a hunk of cheese, fresh bread, apples, and gingerbread cookies. They were both hungrier than they had realized, and they ate the food with gusto and without conversation. It occurred to Mary that this was their first meal together as a married couple. Would he remember this meal years from now? She would.

"You must be feeling better," he said as they reached for the last cookie at the same time. "Your appetite seems to have returned."

She handed him the cookie. "You take it. I've had plenty."

He broke the cookie in half. "We'll share," he said softly and offered her a bite of one half of the cookie.

"Thank you," she murmured. His feeding her felt far too intimate for their situation, so she took the rest of her piece from him to eat herself. She knew he was trying to be kind, to relieve some of the tension between them. But it was dangerous to allow such intimacies, she decided. They only led to false hope.

"Let's take that walk." He stood up and stretched.

Quickly she stuffed the leavings of their meal back into the basket and looped it over her arm. "Where should we walk?" she asked, looking around. The town was to their left, and they could hear the sounds of business in the saloons.

"This way," Matt said and headed off in the other direction.

As the shadows and the silence of the countryside enfolded them, Mary began to visualize the months and years ahead. Would they settle into some accepted pattern of behavior that was based on this same sort of polite small talk and long silences? In the days before their argument, she had always thought about their future in terms of spring or summer settings. It seemed that in the last two days whenever she thought of their married life, the setting was always a bleak winter day or a raw, gray November one.

"Are you cold?" Matt asked.

She had shivered, but not from the night air. "I'm fine."

"We'd better go back. I'm not sure you should be out in this night air after being so sick on the train." He turned and headed back toward the station.

"I'm not that fragile," Mary protested.

"Nevertheless, we have a long trip ahead of us, and it won't do for you to be sick."

So it was just a long trip, not their wedding trip. And his concern was probably that she not slow him down once they arrived in Memphis so he could give his full attention to the business of regaining his inheritance. Oh, why did she delude herself? Matt was basically a decent man, so of course he would try to make the best of a bad situation, but anything beyond that was purely a figment of her own fantasies.

Mary gathered her skirts and marched back to the station. Matt rubbed his chin in frustration. *Now what?* he thought as she walked ahead of him, chin high, shoulders rigid. He seemed doomed to say the wrong thing. What had happened to them? Two days ago he could have teased her or sweet-talked her into anything. Now he had to watch every word that came out of his mouth.

"Maybe that's our train," Matt said when they reached the platform. "I'll get our luggage and be back in a minute."

It seemed everyone rushed out of the station at once. Everyone was talking and pushing and yelling, and by the time Matt found her, Mary was looking more than a little terrified. "I'm here," he told her. "Just hang on to my arm."

He plowed his way through the masses of people and pulled her onto the train. "Okay?" he shouted above the fray that surrounded them.

Mary nodded and followed him through one car after another until he had located a place for them.

The train from Salina to Topeka was luxurious compared to the one they had ridden from Harmony. Though the passenger cars were jammed with people on every available seat and in every available sleeping berth, Matt and Mary were once again fortunate. They had been able to claim a folding sofa with an upper berth in the observation room.

The porter showed Mary how to open the folding sofa and helped her make it up for the night. He pulled down the upper berth and made that up as well. Heavy dark green curtains pulled along a metal track enclosed the beds once they were made.

It took nearly an hour of standing in line to get a turn in the toilet. Matt had taken his turn while Mary was making up the beds. Now he stayed with their things while she went. By the time she returned, he had hoisted himself up to the upper berth and given the conductor his boots to store for the night to assure that they would not be stolen while he slept.

Mary got into bed still fully clothed except for her shoes and jacket, which she carefully folded and placed inside her carpetbag. Matt pulled the curtain closed and left them in darkness. It was nearly midnight by the time the train pulled out of the station, and Mary thought she had never lived a longer day in her life.

GETTING HITCHED

"Good night, Mrs. Hubbard," Matt said.

Mary lay on her back and stared up at where her husband lay above her. "Good night, Mr. Hubbard," she replied, and remembered how silly she had thought it was to hear married people call each other by such formal names. Was this the reason? Was the use of courtesy titles indicative of a passionless marriage? A marriage contracted for simply because it answered a need?

Suddenly she thought of a couple who came to the store once a month for supplies. They always came on the first Saturday of the month around nine in the morning. The list was always the same, and there was not one item on it that spoke of anything other than the necessities. They said almost nothing to each other, but when they did, he addressed her as Mrs. Hatfield and she called him Mr. Hatfield.

They never smiled, and there was not even the slightest hint of tenderness between them, although they were unfailingly courteous to each other. They had been coming into the store for as long as Mary could remember, which meant they had been married for a long time. They had children who sometimes accompanied the parents on these monthly shopping sprees. But the children, Mary now recalled, were as dour and lifeless as the parents.

Was this the life she and Matt faced? And what of their children? How could she bring children into such a serious atmosphere? Would they just go through the steps of life, cautiously following the steps of some country dance, always looking at their feet, careful never to make a mistake?

She clenched her fists and bit her lip to swallow a sob. She would not cry one more time today. There had to be some action she could take, some plan she could devise that would save them both from a lifetime of boring civility.

Now think, she ordered herself, and tried not to be distracted by Matt flopping around trying to find a comfortable position above her.

The issue was, to find a way of regaining the rapture they had experienced with those stolen kisses, those fervid moments of touching and exploring their most intimate parts . . . well, not *the* most intimate, but certainly close enough. What had there been about her that had stirred his ardor? Was she simply a challenge for him?

On the other hand, he had expressed admiration for her spunk. He had admired her courage in placing the ad, taking the initiative. Perhaps her original idea of courting him to win him back had been a good one. Perhaps she had given up too soon or been too unconventional in her methods.

She tried to remember what other ideas Jake and Joseph had suggested that might work should a woman decide to court a man. Jake had been reluctant to enter further into the conversation at all, but she and Jake had been friends since they were babies, so she knew exactly how to get the information she needed.

"What do you like that Abby Lee does?" she had asked coyly.

Jake had blushed red to the roots of his whiskers. "Ah, Mare," he'd protested. "That's private stuff."

She had placed both hands on her hips and given an exasperated sigh. "I'm not asking for the intimate details, Jake. There must be something she does that . . . you know . . . leads to that."

Jake had stroked his chin and thought about it for a moment. Then he had grinned and declared, "She makes me feel like she needs me."

She makes me feel like she needs me. Oh, there was a complete recipe for getting a man to love you if ever Mary had heard one. What the devil did that mean? And what if the man had already admired how much you *didn't* seem to need him? How you could take care of yourself?

Well, Jake Sutherland had never been especially good with expressing his thoughts, Mary mused. Now, Joseph was another story. Her big brother had the soul of a poet . . . a dreamer. Why, he'd taken the railroad job for just one reason—it brought him that much closer to living out his dream of traveling to far-off places.

And once he had calmed down and stopped acting completely silly, Joseph had not disappointed her. At one point he had waxed poetic for nearly half an hour on the tributes of the woman of his dreams. How she would be interested in everything he thought about or dreamed about. And how she would know how to listen without always just waiting for her turn to talk. How she would hear what he was saying and help him find the way to make it all happen. How she would surprise him once in a while by turning the tables.

At the time Mary had dismissed his ramblings as unrelated to her own case. But now she tried hard to recall exactly what he had told her. Something about gifts . . . how the man always brought flowers or something. Well, she could hardly present Matt with a bouquet . . . he'd be convinced he'd married a total lunatic if she did that. But perhaps another gift . . . something special just for him. . . .

As the rhythm of the train rocked her in the narrow berth, Mary considered what Jake and Joe had told her. She weighed their advice against what she knew about Matt so far. Perhaps she should take more initiative. After all, Matt had responded to the ad . . . he hadn't been completely scandalized by the idea that a woman would dare such a thing.

By morning they would be in Topeka. The drummers who had come through Harmony selling their wares had told wonderful stories about Topeka, about the sights there and the stores there. Perhaps she should buy Matt a gift in Topeka . . . a wedding gift.

But what? Something personal but not too personal. Something to wear perhaps. But she'd have to guess at sizes, and there would be no time for exchanging something that was wrong.

She sighed. Her eyes had grown accustomed to the dark of the enclosed berth, and there was a little light from the moon. She spotted Matt's hat hanging on a hook next to the window. A new hat? Mary smiled. Perfect . . . not too intimate, yet clearly something just for him.

Papa had given her some money before she left, and then

Mama had stuffed a roll of bills into her reticule just as she was leaving her room for the last time. "In case you need it," she had said when Mary protested.

Mary sat up and immediately cracked her head on the hard bottom of Matt's berth. "Ow," she whispered as she rubbed her head and waited to be sure Matt was still sleeping. When she was certain, she carefully took Matt's hat from the hook and tried it on.

It was loose but not huge on her. Still, trying on a hat for Matt was a guess at best. Mary frowned and wore the hat, trying to memorize the exact feel of its fit on her own head. There was no way she could take the hat with her when she went to buy the new one. Matt would be wearing it.

Then she gave a stifled mutter of triumph as she squirmed to reach her own bonnet, tucked into the small shelf above her head. The bonnet had long grosgrain ribbon streamers she tied in a bow just under her chin when she wore the bonnet. Using one of the ribbons, she carefully measured the inside of Matt's hatband.

To her delight the measurement was exactly the length of the ribbon. She measured again just to make sure, and again it came out to the exact length.

Mary grinned and reshaped the brim and creases of Matt's hat before carefully replacing it on the hook. She would buy him a hat. Men bought women a frilly new bonnet as a token of their affection. Why, that bonnet Samantha had been choosing the other day at the store had been a present from Cord. Mary could still see him standing there, leaning against the store counter as Samantha tried on one style after another. In the end when she'd been unable to choose, he had laughed and bought her three bonnets.

So, she would buy Matthew a hat and surprise him with it once they were on their way to St. Louis. Something dashing and handsome . . . something that would send the clear message to anyone who might oppose him in Memphis that this was a man not to be trifled with.

Mary smiled happily and lay back down in the narrow berth.

Suddenly the rhythm of the train seemed soothing . . . promising. She had begun an adventure, a wonderful adventure, and all things were possible.

Within minutes she was asleep.

What the devil was going on in that beautiful head of hers today? Matt wondered as he sat across from Mary at breakfast.

She had still been sleeping soundly when he returned from taking care of his morning rituals in the communal toilet. He actually had to wake her.

Of course, first he had taken a long moment to luxuriate in the sight of her sleeping. She slept curled on her side, one hand bent to cushion her head. She had removed the pins from her elaborate hairstyle, and the black curls were spread over her shoulders and cheek and the thin blanket the conductor had brought to her last night.

The blanket was drawn up to her chin. Her lips were relaxed and slightly parted, and her lashes were as black and thick as her hair. Her small frame seemed to take no more room in the narrow berth than would that of a child. Matt sat on the edge of the berth and gave in to the urge to stroke his finger lightly across her cheek.

Her skin was so beautiful . . . not weathered and aged like so many young women he had met on the range, not dried and blemished from the overuse of cosmetics like the women who worked the saloons and brothels. Mary's skin was luminous, a perfect background for the perfection of her dark eyes and full lips.

She had stirred, and he had withdrawn his hand and called to her. "Mary? Time to get up."

Her eyes had opened and focused on him, and she had smiled. Lord, how he had wanted to climb into that berth, pull the curtains around them, and spend the morning there in bed with her.

"More jam?" Mary said, jarring him back to the present and the breakfast table between them. The porter had put up the beds and turned their little area back into a sitting area for the day. Then he had delivered them breakfast.

"Thanks," Matt replied and accepted the small pot of strawberry preserves.

"Anyway," Mary said, clearly continuing a conversation he had not heard as he wandered around in his memory of Mary sleeping. "I thought while we were in Topeka, I might like to go shopping. I know how boring it can be for a man like you, so I thought perhaps while you were attending to the travel arrangements and such, I could just . . ."

Matt nodded absently. He was still trying to put his finger on the change in her from yesterday to this morning. It was like being with another person altogether. Yesterday she had been glum and nervous and thoroughly depressed. Today she was more like . . . Mary, his Mary, the woman he'd fallen in love with.

"Then you don't mind?"

"Mind?" he asked absently.

"If I go shopping while we wait for the train to St. Louis," she replied with more than a little exasperation. But then she smiled and reached across the table to knock lightly on his forehead. "Hello? Is anybody home in there?" she teased.

"Sorry," he answered with a sheepish grin. "I guess I was thinking of something else."

Immediately her light mood turned to one of concern. "Of course, how foolish I must seem to you. I am sorry, Matthew. I know you're worried about getting to Memphis and what awaits you there. Please forgive me."

She was dead serious, he realized. Her concern was genuine. Matt tried to deal with the relatively new sensation of having another person actually worry about him. It had been a long time since he'd had anyone he could count on other than himself. "It's okay," he said softly and took another bite of the hard biscuit.

"Not exactly up to the standards of Faith's biscuits, is it?" Mary said wryly as she watched him chew the tough doughy mass.

"Not exactly," he agreed and relaxed. Whatever was going on here was a huge improvement over the tense undertones of the past couple of days. "So, you want to go shopping in Topeka," he said with a teasing smile. "Maybe I'd better go with you."

"No." The idea of his going with her seemed to cause her a moment's panic. "That is," she added more calmly, "there's not a lot of time and . . ."

Matt frowned. "All right. When we get to the station we'll ask the stationmaster if it's safe for you to wander about on your own."

What was she up to?

Once they reached Topeka, they had four hours before their train left. Mary had been a delight to watch as she had discovered the sights and sounds of the city, and Matt had begun to feel a certain pride that he was the one who was providing her with the opportunity.

They had walked along the streets, pausing now and then for Mary to exclaim over something she saw in a store window or whisper excitedly about the fashions worn by the society ladies who passed by in their fine carriages. She had worried over her own simple, unbustled suit and seemed pleased when he told her how he thought it was more becoming than any of the ridiculous swagged and bustled styles they saw. They had their lunch in the small but elegant dining room of a hotel near the train depot.

The more time they spent together, the more easily they talked and laughed and shared their reactions to everything they saw. "It's like a wonderful dream," Mary said with a sigh as she paused on one street corner just to take in everything surrounding her. "I never could have imagined something so wonderful."

Then she hugged Matt. "Thank you," she said, her voice muffled against the fabric of his jacket.

When she released him she smiled, but her smile had been tinged with something less than the pure joy she had exhibited throughout the morning. There had been a certain sad wistfulness in that smile.

Matt recalled every detail as he walked from one end of the station platform to the other, watching for any sign of her. Suddenly the sad melancholy of her smile assumed an import he had failed to give it at the time. Had there been some signal there? Some message of regret at an action not yet taken? Had she decided the marriage could not work after all?

Everything began to come together in a crazy sort of order—her dramatic change of mood this morning, as if during the night she had come to some decision. Not that he hadn't welcomed the change. Yesterday had weighed heavily on both of them, and there had seemed to be nothing he could do to lift her spirits. Indeed, during the night he had lain awake for hours listening to her tossing and turning, at one point so animated in her misery that she had actually cracked her head against the hard underpinnings of his berth.

It had been all he could do to keep himself from going to her at that moment. But he knew that for him, consoling her would lead to touching her, and touching her would inevitably lead to making love to her, and he would not force himself on any woman, much less his wife.

By the time he had finally drifted off into a restless sleep, he had decided that he'd been a fool to agree to being rushed into the marriage. He should have told her father what they needed was time. Time for him to court her properly. Time to show her that what he wanted—needed—in his life was her, the inheritance with all its attached strings be damned.

He had decided to tell her that the following morning, to give her the opportunity to get out of the marriage now before it was too late.

But then she had seemed so happy and talkative, and Matt had assumed that she had come to her own decision to make the best of a bad situation. So, at breakfast his own resolve had changed from letting her back out of the marriage to making her realize that she had made the best possible decision in choosing him.

And at first he had been certain that progress had been made, and even dared to hope that by the time they reached Memphis they might have made at least a start toward building a normal life together.

But now she had disappeared. She had walked away from that corner, gathering her skirts in one hand as she hurried across the street. She had never once looked back.

Matt had been vaguely bothered by that but had put it out of his mind as he walked back to the station to see about the transfer of Mary's trunk from one train to the other and send a telegram to the lawyer in Memphis to tell him of their expected arrival. All the time he had kept one eye out for her return, anxious to hear all that she had seen and experienced, certain that she would keep him entertained for hours with her stories.

But when the train had arrived and the other passengers began to board, and still there was no sign of Mary, Matt began to pace. He began to worry that something had happened to her. She could have been lost or accosted or robbed or . . . Then his fear settled into a dull dread that she had left him.

Again and again he recalled the sight of her rushing away from him, crossing the street without a backward look. The way she had looked up at him with that melancholy smile after hugging him as if she were reluctant to let him go haunted him as he anxiously paced the perimeter of the depot in search of any sign of her return.

CHAPTER
15

Mary had not imagined how much time she would need to find exactly the right hat for Matthew. As she hurried along the street toward the train station, she could hear the engine snorting and sighing impatiently. The late afternoon was growing dark, and she could just make out the familiar form of Matthew as he paced the station platform.

"Boar-r-d," the conductor called.

Mary quickened her step, the hatbox bumping against her side as she ran the last block to reach the station.

The train whistle blasted, and the conductor's call echoed once more. She could see the last of the passengers hurrying aboard, the porters helping them up the metal steps to their car. The train was lavish, its polished varnished sides decorated with hand-painted scrolls and lettering gleaming in the setting sun. Unlike the train they had taken from Harmony or even the one they had been on last night, this one had so many cars that Mary could not count them all.

"Matthew!" Mary shouted, realizing quickly that he'd never hear her above the noise of the train.

To her surprise, he turned immediately and strode across the platform to meet her. When he reached her, he swept her up in his arms and headed straight for the train.

"I thought you'd gotten lost," he said as he tightened his hold on her, settling her firmly against his solid chest, his eyes studying her for signs of misfortune. "I thought you'd changed your mind," he added, once he'd satisfied himself that she was unharmed.

"No," she replied almost in a whisper. *Never,* she thought as he carried her the last few feet and deposited her on the small platform outside one of the passenger cars. Just as the train started forward, he swung himself up behind her.

They stood there crowded onto the platform for a moment, looking at each other as the train started to gather speed.

Being in your arms again was like being back in my fantasy, she thought.

If you had left me, I would not have wanted to go on, he thought.

"I'm going to kiss you, Mary Hubbard."

Mary nodded, her eyes unable to look away from his.

They swayed toward each other, and only a part of the motion had to do with balance and the movement of the train. He cupped her chin with his fingers and lowered his face hesitantly toward hers. She raised onto her toes to meet his kiss.

As their lips met, the train whistle shrilled a long blast, but they heard nothing, were aware of nothing but desire too long suppressed, passion too long denied.

I don't care . . . I don't care . . . I don't care, Mary thought in rhythm with the train's wheels clicking along the tracks as she met Matt's kiss and answered it. *I don't care if he doesn't love me. I love him and for however long he's willing to stay with me I won't waste a moment of it. I won't regret a moment of it.* She buried her fingers in the hair that skimmed the collar of his shirt, nudging aside his hat in her need to hold him more possessively.

Suddenly his hat was flying through the air, spinning along the ground where it landed and got smaller and smaller as the train ran away from it.

Mary gave a cry of alarm and made a move as if to recover it, but Matt pulled her back into his arms. "I can get another hat," he said and then kissed her again . . . sporadic wet kisses along her temple and down to her chin. "Maybe I'll wear your hat," he teased, and held up the hatbox he had taken from her as he'd scooped her up into his arms at the depot.

"Maybe you should," she answered and smiled.

The conductor stepped onto the small platform from the adjoining car and cleared his throat. "Newlyweds, are you?" he asked with a wry smile.

Matt grinned. "Yep."

"Well, I believe you'd be a sight more comfortable inside, folks. Trying to keep your balance out here is pretty dangerous." He opened the door and held it for them.

They entered what Matthew had described as a hotel car. It was similar to the arrangement they had had on the train out of Salina, only more elegant. Here there were plush chairs next to reading tables. The berths were hidden behind beautifully detailed panels that ran the length of the car. There were several other people already occupying the car. Mary noted that all of the men looked successful, and the women were beautifully dressed.

Matt led Mary through the length of the car to the seating they had been assigned. Mary was pleased to see that they had been given an area at the far end of the car, and for the time being no one sat directly across or next to them. She sank into one of the luxurious chairs and sighed. She felt like one of those wealthy Eastern ladies Samantha was always prattling on about.

"Matthew Hubbard?"

Mary glanced up to see a tall, distinguished elderly man in a beautifully tailored suit. Matthew turned and immediately grasped the man in a fierce hug. "Byron!" he cried with obvious delight.

"I thought it was you I saw there at the station, my boy. Please tell me that you are on your way home to claim your rightful inheritance."

Matthew nodded and then hugged the man again. "I can't believe it's you," he said, the words catching in his throat in a way that made Mary want to comfort him.

"And this must be your beautiful wife," the gentleman said, turning his full attention to Mary.

"Mary, this is my father's oldest and dearest friend and business partner, Byron Hill."

"Ah, Mary . . . such a classic name for such a classic beauty. We always knew our Matthew would catch the most beautiful woman in the country. It is an honor to make your acquaintance, my dear." With that the silver-haired gentleman bowed low over Mary's outstretched hand and kissed it gently.

"It's very nice to meet you, Mr. Hill," Mary said shyly.

"Oh, my dear, we mustn't be so formal. Why, we are practically family. Please, I insist you call me Byron, and may I presume to call you by your given name as well?"

"I'd like that," Mary replied.

Throughout this exchange Matt stood beaming down at the two of them. "What are you doing here?" he asked when the introductions and pleasantries had been dispensed and Byron had taken a seat next to Mary.

"A little business . . . a little pleasure. I've been in Kansas City, Topeka, and on the way home will stop in St. Louis. Will you and Mary be staying in Memphis indefinitely?"

"It's hard to say," Matt answered with a slight frown. "It depends on what we find when we get there."

"Ah, yes, well, this is hardly the time to fret about such matters. Tell me, Mary, have you traveled to Memphis before?"

"Oh, heavens, no. This is my first real train trip anywhere other than to Salina, which is just a short distance from Harmony."

"Harmony?" Byron asked with a puzzled frown.

"Kansas," Mary supplied. "I grew up there, and my whole family is there, and after Matt and I get back . . ." Mary faltered, aware that she was prattling on when she really didn't know what Matt's plans were. What if he decided they should stay in Memphis?

"We're building a home there," Matt finished for her. "This is sort of a wedding trip for us aside from the business."

Byron smiled broadly. "Well, why didn't you say so? You must allow me to treat you. I've rented a private car for my travels. At my age it becomes tiresome to always have to make polite conversation with other passengers who may be sharing the car," he explained to Mary. "I hope that doesn't make me sound stuffy or boorish. It's just that sometimes I need to concentrate on my business and get a good night's rest. Besides, I can afford it, thanks to Matt's father and his head for business."

"We'd be delighted to join you for dinner," Mary said, glancing at Matt, who nodded his agreement.

"Oh, my dearest Mary, I wasn't speaking of dinner. You two newlyweds surely have better things to do with your time than spend an evening with an old man like me. No, no, no. I insist we exchange accommodations. I will take your place here, and you will spend the rest of your journey in my private car."

"We couldn't," Mary protested, though she wanted very much to see what a private car looked like. All she knew was what Joe had told her he'd heard about.

"You can and you must or you run the risk of offending me deeply," Byron replied sternly.

"Well, we wouldn't . . . that is . . ." Mary stammered.

Byron laughed. "I'm only teasing you, Mary, but please indulge me. It's been a long time since I played Cupid, and I've missed the fun of it."

"Byron introduced my parents," Matt explained.

"I did more than introduce them. I take full credit for their marriage. The two of them were so stubborn, they might never have gotten together at all had it not been for me."

Mary laughed. "Well, I'll leave it to Matthew," she said.

"Oh, heavens, if you leave it to Matthew, we could be here all day. Matthew inherited both parents' stubborn pride, I'm afraid. No, Mary, I'm quite sure that in this matter you must decide."

"Well, it would be fun to see what—"

"Then it's decided," Byron said triumphantly. He hailed a passing porter and gave the man instructions. "Our friend here will show you to your car, Mr. and Mrs. Hubbard. Enjoy. I will see both of you in Memphis." He leaned down to kiss Mary's cheek, then once again hugged Matthew. "Good to have you back, Matt," he said softly, and Mary noticed the tears that welled in the old man's eyes as he said it.

"Why don't we get together for dinner?" Matt said as he gathered their belongings in preparation for their move.

Byron winked. "My boy, if you'd rather have dinner with an old man than to spend the evening alone with this ravishing creature you've been wise enough to marry, then you are not worthy of her."

Matthew actually blushed. "I just thought we could catch up," he said.

"We will . . . in Memphis. Now, go. The porter has his instructions, and you are keeping him from his duties."

"So nice to meet you," Mary said. "And thank you again." She stood on tiptoe and kissed his cheek.

"Ah, such a lovely creature, Matthew. Now, go, both of you."

The porter led the way to the very rear of the train through two other passenger cars. When he opened the door of Byron's private car, Matt and Mary both stopped dead at the door. Here was a level of opulence and luxury neither of them could have imagined.

While the porter lit lamps and checked to make sure the supply of towels and bed linens was adequate and the wine stock had been replenished, Mary and Matt walked slowly through the car. First there was an elegant parlor, and behind that was a bedroom with a canopied bed, swathed and draped in brocade curtains. Beyond that was a private bathroom, larger than Sissy's bedroom at home. A second porter delivered Mary's trunk to the room, and a third brought a tray of cheeses and fruits and placed it on the sideboard in the parlor. Then all three porters bid them good evening and left.

When Matt returned from following the porters out, he found Mary in the bedroom removing her hat and the jacket of her suit, which she folded with studied care and placed on a side chair. Now that they were alone, the noise of the train was muted, and the room seemed inordinately quiet.

"Mary." Matt came up behind her and took the bonnet from her, tossing it onto the chair with her jacket. Then he began moving the pins and combs that held her hair in the intricate arrangement she had styled that morning.

"Matt, I—" Mary began, but Matt shushed her and continued arranging her hair, lifting it with both hands once all the adornments were removed and letting it slip through his fingers.

"Don't talk," he said softly and bent to kiss the lobe of her ear. "Byron has given us a gift of time and privacy. Let's not just waste it. Back there at the station when I thought you had left me, I—"

Now it was Mary's turn to shush him. "You talk too much," she whispered and kissed his ear. He shuddered and gathered her into his arms, burying his face in the curve of her neck.

Instinctively Mary stretched her neck to give him greater access and felt his mouth open and hot against the high lace collar of her blouse. She clung to him, her fingers digging into the hard muscle of his shoulders and upper arms as he continued kissing her neck.

Matt took a step away and concentrated on opening the row of tiny buttons that held her shirtwaist closed, pulling it free of the tight waistband of her skirt. Without a word he continued undressing her.

She also made no sound, fascinated by the ballet of him undressing her, his large fingers working the delicate closings and fastenings of her garments, his hand steadying her as she stepped out of her skirt and petticoats, his eyes appreciating each new revelation as one by one her garments lay pooled at her feet.

When she was wearing nothing but her chemise and drawers, he turned and pulled down the covers on the bed. Then he lifted her and placed her in the center of it, sealing the action with a kiss that assuaged any doubts she might have.

As she reclined on the bed, he stood next to it, undressing without any hint of shyness, taking his time, watching her reaction. First he shrugged out of his shirt, allowing it to join her clothes on the floor. Then he released the buckle of his belt and pulled the leather strap free of its loops. It dropped with a soft clunk to the floor.

When he sat on the edge of the bed to pull off his boots and socks, the lamplight played over the smooth muscles of his back, and it was all Mary could do not to run her hands over his skin, probing each shadow and highlight. He stood once more and released the first button on the fly of his pants.

Immediately Mary's eyes were riveted on the action. She could see how his manhood had swelled against the bondage of his clothing, and felt an answering tightness in her own body.

"Do you see how I want you, Mary?" he asked in a voice hoarse with need.

She nodded.

"You don't have to do this," he added.

"I'm your wife," she answered and made room for him on the bed.

Matt hesitated. *Oh, Mary, don't come to me out of duty,* he thought. *I love you.*

"It's all right," she said when she saw his hesitation. "I want you to . . ." *make love to me,* she almost said. "I want this too," she managed.

The bed sagged under the weight of him. He lay down and turned toward her, his eyes dark and shadowed. Slowly he loosened the ribbons on her chemise, spreading the garment open until he exposed her breasts. Then he opened the buttons of her drawers and eased his hand between the loose fabric and the smooth skin of her stomach, down between her thighs.

Mary jumped when he touched her there and realized he had found the center of all she had been feeling ever since he had first lifted her into his arms and carried her onto the train.

He knelt next to her and slowly removed her drawers, his fingertips skimming over the skin of her thighs, her calves, her feet. Then he kissed one of her ankles and allowed his mouth to trail up the side of her calf. Mary closed her eyes and willed herself to experience every facet of the multiple sensations that assaulted her senses.

Next she felt the roughness of his tongue on the soft tender skin of her inner thigh. Instinctively she flinched and tried to pull her legs protectively closed, but his hand was there between her thighs, touching that place he had discovered when removing her drawers, stroking her and then suddenly probing her with the length of one finger.

She realized she was wet there, but it was more like a balm than liquid. She opened her eyes and saw Matt kneeling between her spread legs, watching her as his fingers slid in and out of her in a rhythm that soothed and demanded.

Her body answered, arching in protest each time he pulled his hand away, tightening with each new thrust. Just when she thought nothing could give her more pleasure, he found an even more precise center, a point where the instant he touched it, she bucked like a wild mustang.

"No," she whispered, battling her embarrassment at her complete loss of control and her fascination with her feelings.

"Let me show you, Mary," he answered. "It's all right, love. Let it happen. I'm right here."

She had thought she knew the ways of a man and a woman when they made love. But nothing could have prepared her for this. She was coming apart, and yet nothing in her sense of self-preservation would allow her for one moment to relinquish the sensations created by him touching her there. She reached for him, but he pulled back.

She gave a cry of anguish at the loss of his touch there, and her eyes flew open. He was standing next to the bed, stripping off the last of his clothing.

"It will hurt," he said as he covered her body with his own. "But only for a moment, love, I promise."

She grasped at his buttocks, beyond caring whether he ripped her apart as long as he was the one inside her. She felt the probe of his sex and opened to him. He slid partway in and withdrew. She growled and urged him to come back.

He tunneled his hands under her hips and lifted her slightly, then plunged himself into her, feeling the tear as he did so, feeling her sudden surprise and gasp of pain. His instinct was to pull out at once, but she held him there, and he felt her body closing around his, joining his, making them one.

Balancing himself on his arms so he could see her face in the lamplight, he pulled out, then buried himself in her again. This time she arched to receive him. In seconds the pace of their lovemaking created its own rhythm in counterpoint to the movement of the train along the tracks.

With each thrust Matt felt the explosion coming nearer. He heard her breath coming in gasps and whimpers, heard his own voice urging her to stay with him, to hold on. He felt her tighten and saw her reach a pinnacle as she arched one last time and stayed there, clinging to him.

Matt knew the sensation of that instant of complete release, knew the need to make it last, knew the regret of feeling it drain away. Satisfied that he had given her the gratification she hadn't even known she sought, he unloosed his own barely contained climax.

Mary felt him pouring himself into her and experienced a feeling of contentment and rapture such as she had never imagined possible.

Moments later, as she lay cradled against his chest, his heart steadily beating against her ear, she thought once again of their future. Whatever become of them in years to come, she would always have this day. He had been tender and patient with her, for he was a good and decent man. At least in that, her choice had been a wise one. She might never have his love, but she knew that she could count on his loyalty. In marrying her, Matthew had made a commitment that he would honor.

"Are you hungry?" he asked after a while.

"Not especially," she replied, unwilling to allow anything to interrupt whatever might be left of this magic time they had just shared. "Are you?"

He chuckled. "Now, darlin', that's a leading question if ever I heard one."

She smiled and punched playfully at his stomach. "I told you not to call me that . . . to save it for Lottie's girls."

His arm tightened around her, and she felt his kiss on the top of her head. "I don't think I'm going to be having any need to be calling Lottie's girls or anybody else darlin', Mary."

It pleased her to know that she might have performed her part in this mysterious ritual well enough to elicit that kind of compliment from him.

"I have a lot to learn," she answered and knew that she was blatantly fishing for yet more praise.

Again he chuckled. "Remember when we started our lessons?"

She nodded.

"Well, what happened tonight was what I wanted to happen the first time I kissed you," he told her.

"Is that why you stopped the lessons?"

"Yep. I had counted on your not being quite so good a student."

She raised up until she could look at him to see if he was teasing her, but his face was serious. "I . . . uh . . . guess you're a pretty good teacher," she said and ran the flat of her palm across his chest.

This time he released a full-blown laugh and patted her bottom as he levered himself to a sitting position. "Oh no you don't, Mrs. Hubbard. We are going to get something to eat and then we are going to get a decent night of sleep." He reached for his pants and pulled them on, then rummaged around in the pile of clothes for his shirt.

While she was in the toilet washing herself, she could hear

him moving around in the other room. When she emerged, she found him in the parlor, setting up plates and utensils for a meal of the fruit and cheese. She felt some disappointment that he had set up the meal in the parlor.

"You could have stayed in bed," she said shyly. "I would have served you."

"If we had stayed in bed, I don't think I would have had much interest in cheese and fruit. Besides, I don't remember anything in our contract about you serving me," he teased her.

Mary realized the moment of intimacy had passed. They were back to being good friends once more. Oh, why had she spoiled everything with that stupid idea of a contract? He was never going to forget it.

Matt brought them each a glass of beer and was surprised to hear that Mary had never tried the drink even once.

"Not a taste on a special occasion?" he asked.

"No. Mama didn't allow it."

He smiled at her. "What your mama thought never seemed to bother you too much," he reminded her.

"Well, I'm trying it now," she said and took a sip, then instantly made a face.

Matt laughed. "I'll get you something else."

"No, wait. It just takes a little getting used to," she replied and took another sip. "It's fine. In fact, it's really not so terrible."

"Well, don't get to liking it too much," he warned her with a laugh.

As they ate, Matt told Mary all about Byron and his family. The man had been more than a friend of the family. He had been almost a second father to Matt, and Mary saw that her husband loved Byron very much.

"You must be tired, Mary. Why don't you get ready for bed?" Matt said after the conversation had slowed and they had finished the last of the cheese.

Suddenly shy, Mary went into the bathroom to undress and put on her nightgown. When she came out, Matt was still dressed. He watched her steadily from the moment she emerged from the bathroom.

"Aren't you coming to bed?" she asked shyly.

"I think I'll go see if Byron is still awake," he answered. "I won't be long. You go on to sleep."

Mary climbed into the bed, and Matt lowered the lamp. "Good night, Matt," she said.

"Good night, darlin'," he replied and kissed her lightly on the forehead.

Sometime during the night the train stopped in St. Louis. Mary realized Matt had not returned to the private car. He'd been gone for a long time. She looked out the window to see what she could of St. Louis and was surprised at the amount of activity at the station. Several tracks ran alongside each other, and people were working and talking and laughing as if it were the middle of the day instead of the middle of the night.

She spotted Matt standing near a support post talking to Byron. Then Byron gave Matt one final hug and headed toward the station. Matt continued to lean against a pillar, watching the train crews go about their work. Occasionally one of the workers would direct a comment at him, and Matt would smile and make a response. But most of the time he just stood there, his eyes following the action without really seeing it.

When the conductor yelled for boarding, Matt sighed and pushed himself away from the support post and walked slowly back toward the train. Mary wondered if he truly dreaded the trip so much. Or was he thinking of Memphis at all? Perhaps he was thinking of their marriage and wondering just what he had let himself in for.

As the train started to slowly move out of the station, she heard Matt softly open the door to their car. She hastened back to bed, pretending to be asleep.

Matt entered the room, but instead of undressing and getting into bed, he came and sat beside her.

"Mary," he whispered, shaking her gently, "wake up."

She blinked and turned over as if just waking. "What is it?" she asked. "Is something wrong?"

Matt got up and took Mary's wrapper from the wardrobe. "Here, put this on. I want you to see something."

He sounded excited . . . happy. He was smiling at her as he held the robe for her.

She lifted the weight of her hair to free it of the robe and then belted the garment.

Matt was leading the way to the back of the private car. "Come on," he whispered, indicating the outside door.

"I can't go out like this," Mary protested.

"Come on," Matt urged and grabbed her hand, pulling her along.

"I don't have shoes on," she argued. "I—"

Matt stopped and picked her up in his arms, then continued on his mission.

He carried her out onto the large platform at the very back of the train, which was picking up speed. Matt balanced her on a railing and held on to her. "Just look," he whispered.

"What on earth?" Mary asked in an excited whisper.

"Look out there, Mary," he said.

She peered into the darkness. It took a little time for her to realize what she was seeing.

"It's the Mississippi River," Matt said reverently.

"It's so big," Mary whispered back. Indeed it seemed to be as wide as any ocean. She was speechless. It was as if the train were running right on the water itself. The night air was split by a duet of the shrill whistle of the train and the answering call of the steamboats and tugs.

"It's like another world," Mary said in a hushed voice.

"It *is* another world," Matt agreed. "Once you cross the river in either direction you've left something behind and moved on to something else."

"For you this side of the river is home," she said softly.

He wrapped his arms around her and held her against his chest. "It was . . . once," he agreed.

"It's almost as if I can feel the difference. Oh, Matt, thank you for waking me. This is wonderful." She looked up at him, and he smiled.

She reached to kiss him. She had meant to kiss him in gratitude, a quick meeting of the lips to express her delight at this impromptu adventure he had arranged. But the moment their lips met, she knew she'd only been fooling herself. The only way she ever wanted to kiss Matthew had nothing to do with gratitude.

Boldly she swept his mouth with her tongue, holding his face between her hands so that she angled the kiss to her own satisfaction. Matt's hands went from holding her to stroking her back and hips, naked beneath her gown and robe.

Mary's kisses claimed each feature of his face, and she laved his ear until he shuddered with pleasure. And between each kiss, she was thinking, *I love you . . . I love you . . .* "I love you," she whispered, incapable of stopping herself.

Immediately he froze and pulled away.

Oh, Lord, now she'd gone and ruined everything once again. He didn't want to hear that—it put too much pressure on him.

She dared a glance at his face. His eyes reflected not anger, but surprise. "Say it again," he said.

"I'm sorry . . . it just . . . I couldn't help myself," she said woefully and on the verge of tears.

"Say it, Mary," he pressed.

"I love you," she whispered and then more strongly, "I do. I love you, Matthew, and I know it just complicates everything but—"

His eyes widened with wonder and delight. "You're serious," he said. "You really mean it, don't you?"

Mary nodded miserably. She supposed there was a way they could still make this all work . . .

Matt gave a shout of pure joy that would have knocked her off the train if he hadn't in the same moment grabbed her and lifted her high in his arms, swinging her around and around. "She loves me!" he continued to shout repeatedly to anyone in earshot up and down the river.

"Matthew, put me down!" she shouted back above the roar of the wind and the train as he stepped dangerously close to the edge without seeming to notice.

He stopped whirling but did not release her. Instead he began kissing her, and he punctuated each kiss with a declaration of his love for her.

"I love you, Mary Taylor Hubbard." Kiss. "I love your hair." Kiss. "I love the way your eyes flash and sparkle when you get your dander up." Kiss. "I love your nose." Kiss. "I love your lips." Long kiss. "I expect I'll spend the rest of my life trying to get enough of these lips," he whispered and then kissed her as if he intended to get a good start on that mission in the next several minutes.

Meanwhile Mary was trying to come to grips with what had just transpired. Instead of tragedy, she had opened the door to paradise with her unwitting declaration. Every fantasy she had ever had was coming true. All of the pain and stress and doubt of the past few days fell away with every beat of the rolling train and every kiss Matt delivered.

"This calls for a celebration," Matt whispered as he kissed the hollow of her neck.

"I thought we *were* celebrating," Mary answered with a gasp as he reached under the hem of her gown and robe and began marking a path up her bare leg.

"It's a start, but there seem to be problems."

"Such as?" Mary cupped his buttocks and urged him closer so that she could feel the power of his arousal.

"Too damned many clothes," he answered in frustration as his hand became tangled in the voluminous fabric of her gown, and he lost contact with her bare skin.

Mary laughed. "Well, Mr. Hubbard," she whispered next to his ear, loving the fact that her warm breath against his ear made his breath catch, "we could go inside."

Matt chuckled. "Maybe we'd better . . . another minute of that, Mrs. Hubbard, and I'm going to take you out here." He gave her one last hard kiss and then opened the door.

She ran ahead of him down the aisle to the bedroom, stifling a giggle of pure excitement and joy as she went.

He was right behind her, having paused only to grab a bottle of champagne, which he placed on the small table next to their bed. He pulled off his boots and then lit the lamp. "I want to see you," he said softly.

When he turned around, Mary was standing at the foot of the bed naked, surrounded by a nest of the gown and robe she had stripped off and allowed to land where they fell. "I thought you said something about too many clothes," she teased when he could utter no sound other than a sharp sucking in of his breath.

"Mary, you are so beautiful," he finally managed, but he remained standing by the bed.

Mary moved to him and began unbuttoning his shirt, kissing every inch of skin she exposed until he impatiently cast the garment aside.

He hadn't bothered with a belt, and his pants rode low on his hips. He also hadn't bothered with underwear, she realized, and suddenly lost some of her nerve. But Matt wasn't about to let her stop now. He gently grasped her hand and led her to the button on his fly. She opened the first one and then the next, trailing her nail along the hard rigid length of him as she freed each button.

When she had pushed his pants past his hips, he sat on the edge of the bed to take them off, but she was there first, easing them down his legs as he had with her clothing the first time they made love. Matt lay back on the bed and watched her. When he was naked, she stood next to the bed for a minute and looked at him.

Matt held out his arms to her, and without a word she came to him, lying down next to him, touching him lightly with the tips of her fingers. He touched her in return, preparing her body to receive him. Even when she swore she was ready for him, he did not cover her. Instead he suckled her breasts until they were heavy and swollen, then moved lower over her stomach and hipbones, bathing them with his tongue.

"Matt," she begged, "please. I need you now."

He lay back and guided her to straddle him. She protested until he had settled her astride himself, and she realized the advantage of the position. She smiled. "Like this?" she asked innocently, but at the same time moved her hips over the length of him.

Matt moaned. "Not exactly, darlin'," he said as he lifted her enough so that he could enter her. "Like this."

She felt him slide deep inside her, deeper even than he had been when he was lying on top of her. She gasped in surprise and clasped her knees to his sides. He arched, and she reacted, riding him, thrilling to the force of each thrust, to his hands massaging her breasts, to the building sensation of that feeling of eruption she now understood was the destination.

By the time it came, both she and Matt were covered with sweat from the effort of making it all last for every possible second. Finally she collapsed against him, and the only sound beyond the train was the one of them each trying to bring their own breathing back to normal. Without withdrawing, Matt pushed himself into a half-sitting position, making it clear that he wanted Mary to stay right where she was.

"Here," he said after he had opened the bottle with an explosion of the cork that had Mary giggling with excitement.

He handed her the bottle of champagne.

"You forgot the glasses," she teased.

"I had other things on my mind," he said wryly and tilted the bottle up to her lips.

Some of the liquid spilled down her cheek and dripped off her chin to land between her breasts.

Matt grinned devilishly and licked the champagne away from her cleavage.

"Stop that," Mary said with mock distress.

"I'm thirsty," Matt protested.

"Then drink," she answered and turned the bottle up to his mouth. This time the liquid ran freely down his cheeks and chin. "Oh, dear," Mary said, "let me clean that up for you." She leaned in and began kissing his jaw and cheeks and mouth.

"Stop that," he whispered, and she felt him swelling inside her.

Mary grinned. "I thought you liked that," she said as she

kissed him again. "And this as well." She tugged at his earlobe with her teeth.

He set the bottle back on the table. "So, you think you've got me all figured out," he said lazily.

Mary gave him a smug smile. "I think I've made a start," she replied saucily, raking her nails lightly down his chest.

Suddenly she was on her back, and he was kneeling over her, grinning. "Well, I happen to have a few tricks of my own, lady."

"Such as?" she challenged.

He eased his hand between her legs and probed until he found the one place he knew could have her crying out for him to take her in a matter of minutes.

"Matt," she warned and gasped as the now familiar but always mysterious torment began to build.

"I love you, Mary," he whispered just before he entered her.

CHAPTER
16

The sun was high by the time they woke the following morning. Mary winced with soreness when she tried to get up, so Matt insisted she remain in bed while he ordered some food for them. He returned with a feast of coffee and rolls and hot oatmeal, which they devoured in a matter of minutes.

When they finished eating, Matt brought a basin and bathed Mary, loving washing every inch of her, resisting the desire to take her yet again. When she wanted to return the favor by bathing him, Matt smiled.

"That would never work," he told her.

"Why not?"

"Because if you were touching me . . . all over . . . there's no way I could keep from spending the day in bed with you."

"And is that so terrible an idea?" Mary asked with a twinkle in her eye.

"It's a wonderful idea, but I think you need some . . . time to adjust to . . ." He was actually blushing.

Mary laughed. "All right. But I'm not spending the day in bed alone like some invalid. Let's go see what's happening in the observation room."

They spent the day with other passengers, visiting, playing parlor games, eating. When the train made stops along the way, they got off and took short walks on the banks of the huge river before reboarding.

That afternoon as they stood together on the platform of their private car watching the passing scenery, Matt announced that he wanted to take her shopping at the next stop. Mary protested that she didn't need anything. "Well, I need a hat," Matt admitted as they came back into the car and passed through the bedroom on their way to the parlor.

"I thought you were going to wear mine," Mary teased, glancing toward the hatbox on top of her trunk.

"I did, didn't I? Well, let me see here. I just hope the color matches what I'm wearing today," he said with a grin. He opened the box and paused.

"Do you like it?" Mary asked anxiously.

He lifted the hat from the box and admired it. "It's a beauty," he said.

"Try it on." Mary held her breath as he moved to the mirror and put on the hat. Just as she had hoped, it fit perfectly and was the perfect match for his coloring.

"How did you know the size?" he asked as he turned from side to side admiring the fit and style of it.

Mary shrugged and smiled happily.

"I love it. Thank you, darlin'," Matt said and planted a kiss on her cheek.

Mary pretended to sulk.

"What is it?" Matt asked.

"Well, Jake and Joe told me that when a man buys a woman a present during their courtship, he hopes it'll earn him more than just a peck on the cheek. So I thought . . ."

Matt started to grin. "Are you courting me, Mary?"

"Well, it was part of my plan. Of course, thanks to Byron and after yesterday it probably isn't necessary. Still, I thought a new hat would be worth at least an actual kiss."

Matt glanced in the mirror once more and then back at her. "Oh, I'd say this hat is worth more than just a kiss. After all, you went to all that trouble and nearly missed the train and all."

He tossed the hat on the chair and pulled her into his arms. "Now that I don't have to go looking for a hat at the next stop, we've got plenty of time for me to show you just how appreciative I am," he said huskily.

The next night the other passengers, having realized Mary and Matt were newlyweds, insisted on a party in the dining car. The cook decorated a small cake, and one young man played the piano. Mary and Matt danced every waltz and endured the toasts and teasing of their newfound friends. Matt even sang, and Mary felt a burst of pride at how handsome and talented and well-liked her husband was.

It was well past midnight when they returned to their car. As soon as they were inside, Matt pulled Mary into his arms and hummed a waltz as he danced with her around the parlor. Mary laughed happily.

"Oh, Matthew, I do love you so very much!" she exclaimed.

Matt slowed the dance until they were simply standing in one spot, swaying to the rhythm of the moving train and holding one another.

"I'm glad we had tonight," he said. "I'm sorry it couldn't have been like this when we were married. It would have been nice to have your family and our friends all there to see how happy we are."

Mary nodded. "They'll have a lifetime to observe how happy we are, Matt."

Matt grinned. "True. And when the little Hubbards begin arriving, they'll have no doubt at all of the depths . . . not to mention the frequency . . . of our love."

"Matthew!" Mary chastised, and her cheeks turned a deep pink.

"I wonder if the first heir might not be in there right now,"

Matt continued as he placed one hand across Mary's flat stomach.

"Matthew, you're embarrassing me," Mary protested, but she was laughing.

"No, really. Let's see what you might look like in six months." He grabbed a pillow from the sofa and held it up to her, then turned her sideways so he could look at her. "Hmmm. Hard to say."

Mary took the pillow from his hand and threw it playfully at his head. "Stop that. I doubt seriously that I'm with child."

Matt frowned. "Really?" He paced the room as if deep in thought, occasionally glancing over his shoulder to study her.

Concerned that she had upset him unnecessarily, Mary hastened to make amends. "Well, I could be . . . I mean, who's to say? We'll know in a few weeks. And if I'm not, well, then—"

Matt turned and scooped her up in his arms and carried her to the bedroom. "Then I haven't been a proper husband, have I? No, Mary, I think you may be right, and we need to work on this right now." He grinned down at her as he started to remove his clothes.

"Matt!" Mary managed between giggles. "Aren't you tired? It's so late and—" She stopped because he was naked, and he clearly was not the least bit tired.

"We have our whole lives to get enough sleep, Mary," he said with a devilish grin. "Here, let me help you with those fastenings." He knelt on the side of the bed and began undressing her, tossing the clothing onto the floor as he removed each piece.

When she was naked, Matt took his time studying every inch of her. His fingers followed the path of his heated gaze, caressing her face, the arch of her throat, the swell of her breasts with nipples hard and erect, begging for the moist comfort of his mouth. But his gaze traveled on, and the light stroking continued . . . down across her stomach to her inner thighs, pausing there as his eyes met hers.

"Touch me, Matt," she whispered.

His eyes still watching hers, he granted her wish, finding unerringly the one spot that both of them knew would send her into ecstasy. She arched, and his gaze moved to her breasts. He groaned, and without breaking the rhythm of his stroking fingers, he bent to one nipple, stroking it with his tongue, surrounding it with the humid moisture of his mouth until it blossomed.

Mary clutched handfuls of his thick soft hair as her hips arched and bucked in response to his hand. She felt Matt's mouth burning a searing trail from her breast down across one hipbone and lower until he was kissing her there between her thighs . . . his mouth and tongue replacing the erotic action of his fingers.

Mary stiffened. Surely there was something wrong with this. No one had ever even hinted . . . But her body arched, responding, demanding, wanting, needing. A passion roared through her with the force of a Kansas tornado, and she didn't care if what he was doing was wrong. She only wanted to see it through . . . to know where this feeling could take her.

When she was practically insane with need, he left her and lay back on the bedding. "Touch me, Mary," he rasped, taking her hand and guiding it to his penis.

"Teach me," she whispered, unsure what to do.

He smiled and moved her hand slowly over the length of himself. As usual she was a quick study. And as usual she added elements of her own invention . . . moving the massage beyond the length of him to rake her nails along his inner thigh, cupping him before returning her attention to stroking him.

"Taste me," he urged.

Mary hesitated, then bent and kissed the tip of him, tasting the sticky sweetness of his seed as she did. He groaned and arched, and Mary understood what he must feel when he made love to her. Now she was the one making love. Now she could arouse in him that same storm of need he created in her.

She knelt over him and took him in her mouth in the same way he suckled her breasts. He reached to pull her away, but she resisted, thrilling to the frenzy of need she was creating in him.

"Mary." It was a warning, given on a breath sucked in hard to maintain control.

He gathered his strength and lifted her until she was lying on her back. "That's for another time," he said with an unsteady chuckle. "We can't get a baby that way."

"How do we get a baby, then?" she asked coyly, still enjoying the power of making love to him.

Without a word he spread her legs and moved over her. "Wrap your legs around me," he whispered as he slid slowly inside her.

Mary did as she was told and immediately saw the advantage of it. In this position it seemed that Matt filled her more deeply, more completely. In this position she could meet his every thrust. She ran her palms the length of his back, feeling the muscles tense and release, hearing his gasps, knowing that he was near that point of explosion she had become so familiar with in his arms.

"I love you, Matthew," she whispered.

He answered with a cry of release as she felt him pour himself into her. She thought of how he was part of her now . . . every time they made love he gave a part of himself to her. Out of that would come the future . . . children and grandchildren and on, until generations of their heirs had made their place in this land. The idea was so awesome, so glorious, that she felt tears well and spill over.

Matt was immediately attentive. "Did I hurt you, darlin'?" He levered his weight off of her and tenderly touched her face.

Mary shook her head and pulled him back to her embrace. "I'm just so happy," she sobbed.

Matthew laughed and kissed away her tears. "Lord help me, darlin', if I ever make you miserable," he teased. He settled her against the hard length of his body and rocked her gently, until she fell asleep with him talking to her of the child he was now certain grew inside of her, and the plans he had for all their futures.

GETTING HITCHED

* * *

"This afternoon we'll be in Memphis," Matt said the following morning as they dressed and prepared for breakfast.

She paused in her own dressing and looked at him. "It will be all right, Matt," she said softly. She touched his cheek, and he held her hand there, bending to her touch as if it were a lifeline.

"It doesn't matter, Mary," he answered as he kissed the palm of her hand. "Now that I have you, nothing else matters."

But it did matter, whether Matt admitted it or not. Mary saw it the moment they stepped off the train in Memphis.

Matt had wired the attorney of their arrival from Topeka. The chubby and balding lawyer met them himself.

"Mr. Hubbard? I'm Franklin Dover." He offered his hand to Matt and nodded to Mary.

"This is my wife—Mary," Matt said.

Mr. Dover nodded politely, but Mary noticed how he looked at her with skepticism.

"I've made a reservation for you at a hotel near the station here." Dover said as he signaled a young boy to collect their luggage.

"That won't be necessary," Matt said.

"Oh, you have friends you're staying with?" Dover asked pleasantly.

"We're staying at my house," Matt answered firmly.

Clearly this announcement unnerved the lawyer. "Well, that is—"

"Mr. Dover, I told you I was arriving with my wife. It was my understanding those were the terms of my father's will. I assumed you would make certain all was in order."

Mary looked up at Matt. He was a different man in these surroundings . . . a man used to a position of power and influence, a man used to other people following his instructions. She felt a little sorry for Mr. Dover.

"Oh, everything is quite in order as far as it goes, Mr. Hubbard, however . . ."

"However?"

"There is the matter of Mrs.—that is, the other Mrs. Hubbard." He smiled wanly at Mary.

"And what might that be?" Matt asked, his fingers clenching and unclenching at his sides.

"She refuses to leave the house."

A scowl marred the smooth line of Matt's forehead. "We'll see about that," he muttered, and started forward toward a line of carriages for hire.

"She's quite grief-stricken," Dover hastened to add, trying in vain to keep pace with Matt's long strides. "Hasn't left the place since the accident, by all accounts."

"I'm touched," Matt responded, then stopped suddenly and wheeled around to look at the lawyer. "There must be papers I need to sign."

"Well, yes, but I wondered if—that is—did you and Mrs. Hubbard intend to live here?"

Mary was as interested in Matt's response as Dover was. Not that it mattered anymore. Oh, she would miss Harmony and her family, but being where Matthew was was all that mattered.

"Our home and family are both in Kansas," Matt replied firmly, "and the sooner we can return there, the better. Now, where are those papers?" He started walking again, and Dover trailed behind.

"In my office. However . . ."

Once again Matt stopped short and turned to the man. "Mr. Dover, I have to tell you, if you don't stop answering everything I ask you with a *however,* I may be forced to resort to some form of violence. What is the issue here? Have I or have I not lived up to the terms of my father's will?"

"You have," Dover agreed, and Mary could see the man was fighting hard not to add a disclaimer to that statement.

"Does that not mean that once the papers are signed, everything in my father's estate reverts to me as his sole heir?"

"It does."

"And does that estate not include the house where my stepmother is currently in residence?"

"It does." The lawyer was becoming more miserable with each question and answer.

Matt took a step closer to the man. "Then I would strongly suggest that you find a way to remove Louisa from that house before my wife and I arrive there this afternoon," he said in a calm but deadly voice.

"Perhaps she could use the room at the hotel," Mary suggested, unable to be quiet a moment longer.

Both men glanced at her as if they had completely forgotten she was there. She shrugged. "It's a thought," she said shyly.

"And a good one," Matt agreed. "Mr. Dover, let's go sign those papers. Then while Mrs. Hubbard and I refresh ourselves, you can make arrangements for my stepmother."

"Of course," Dover said, and nervously directed them to his own carriage. "I can loan you my carriage and driver for the afternoon if you like."

"That's very generous of you," Matt replied, "but I wouldn't want to impose. Perhaps once we've finished our business you could direct me to a good livery stable where I might rent a small rig for the afternoon. After all, my father kept any number of carriages and teams, and Mrs. Hubbard and I will be using those beginning tomorrow."

The signing of the papers took only a few minutes, though Dover was clearly trying to draw things out. Mary wondered what hold Louisa had over him, for he seemed to be searching for ways to protect her interests.

"Perhaps you could recommend a good place for Mrs. Hubbard and me to have our lunch, Mr. Dover," Matt said when he had signed the last document.

"Of course. There's a wonderful dining room just down the street here. I'll take you there and then . . . call on Mrs. Hubbard. What time do you think you'll be arriving at the house?"

Matt grinned. "You want to know how much time she's got? Just get her out of there, Mr. Dover. I'll be there when I get there, and she'd better be gone."

Dover nodded nervously as he collected his bowler and gloves. "Yes, of course. However, the packing may—"

Matt placed one hand on the lawyer's arm to gain his full attention. "There will be no packing, Mr. Dover. She is to leave the house with what's on her back. Anything that rightfully belongs to her will follow shortly."

"But surely—"

"Those are *my* terms, Mr. Dover," Matt said quietly.

Mary was fascinated by this aspect of Matt's personality. In Harmony he had been so agreeable and easygoing, to the point where she had entertained some concern about his ability to manage a business or a farm effectively. But she saw now that Matthew Hubbard was more like her father than she had imagined. Her father had that same mild manner under most circumstances, but he allowed no quarter when either his family or their security was threatened.

During lunch Matt was unusually quiet, and Mary was content to let him work out his feelings and thoughts in his own time and manner. Occasionally she would reach across the table and touch his hand or cheek to let him know she understood.

He talked sporadically about the extent of the estate. It had surprised him even though Byron had hinted at its vastness. His father had continued to add assets following Matt's departure until there was real estate and other holdings in addition to the house and farm to be disposed of.

"Are you sure you don't want to hold on to the home for a while?" Mary asked. "In time you may wish you had."

"We'll see how you feel once you see it. If you want us to keep it, Mary, then we will."

"It's a part of you," Mary said softly.

"It's a part of the past," Matt added.

"The past is important."

"Yes, it is. But it's only represented by material things and places. The real past is inside a man, and nobody can take that away."

Mary couldn't argue with that. Still, she did not want him to take actions he would regret in his zeal to be rid of Louisa.

"Did Byron tell you what happened when you talked to him that night on the way to St. Louis?"

Matt shook his head. "I didn't ask. He wanted to talk about you and Harmony. The man seems quite taken with you. I think I'm going to have to watch my step."

Mary smiled, pleased to have made such a good impression on someone so obviously important to Matthew. "Byron is a very important part of your past."

"Hey," he said tenderly, "it's the future I'm interested in, and I once answered an advertisement where part of the deal was to live in Harmony, Kansas, with a black-haired beauty who promised in return to give me a houseful of children and her undying love for the rest of my life. Seems to me that beats a big ol' empty Memphis mansion any day of the week."

"You never signed that deal," Mary teased.

"Sure did," Matt argued. "I've got it right here." He pulled out his wallet and handed her the folded copy of their marriage certificate. "Signed and sealed," he said, showing her the paper, "so don't be trying to back out of this, darlin'."

"I'm not interested in backing out," Mary answered, covering his hand with hers. "Ever."

They sat that way for a long moment, holding hands, their eyes sending messages of love and longing back and forth across the lunch table.

"I wish we hadn't been so quick to turn down that offer of a hotel room," Matt whispered with a grin and a wink.

"*We* didn't turn it down," she reminded him. "You did."

Suddenly he was laughing like his old self again. "Why, Mrs. Hubbard, you never cease to surprise me."

Mary smiled back at him. "Good. At least that way I know you'll stay around if for no other reason than to see what I might do next."

Mary admired the countryside as they rode out to the estate. It was so different from anything she had ever seen. Green and lush even now when it was nearly November, and so warm she didn't need even a light wrap. As she rode she tried to imagine Matt here. Pictured him climbing trees and fishing in the river. Imagined him riding hard and fast down this road with news to share with his father. She thought of the day he'd left home to fight in the war.

Since they'd stepped off the train his Southern accent had become stronger and more defined. She recalled how in Mr. Dover's office the tone had been a sort of drawled civility, while the atmosphere was something far more dangerous.

"Well, there it is, darlin'," Matt said as he slowed the horse to a walk and indicated the tops of two chimneys visible above the crest of a hill.

"Welcome home, Matthew," Mary said and hugged him.

They stopped first at the small family cemetery and placed flowers on the graves of his parents and his two brothers. They sat there for a while, talking about his parents.

"It's strange," Matt told her, "but even though I know they're both dead, I still feel them as a part of my life. Does that make any sense?"

"I think it means you loved them very much, as they loved you," Mary replied. "It comforts me to hear you say that. I don't know what I'll do when my parents die. I can't imagine them not being a part of my life."

Matt gazed out over the land toward the house in the distance. "It's all changed, Mary," he said wistfully. "Before the war there was so much activity and life here. Now it seems almost haunted."

"Because of the war?"

Matt shrugged. "Partly. But more, I think, because the love is gone. The love of the land. The love between my parents that sustained the land in hard times."

"We could stay and bring it all back," Mary suggested. "We could live here and raise our children, and it would sparkle with life again, just as it did before."

Matt turned his full attention to her. "You would do that for me, wouldn't you?"

"If that's what you want," Mary said.

"You love me that much?" Matt put his arm around her, holding her so that their faces were very near.

Mary smiled. "Oh, Matthew, I don't think there's any way of measuring how much I love you."

"Well, I thank you for the offer, darlin', but our future is in Harmony."

"You're sure?"

"Positive," Matt assured her. "Now shut up and kiss me," he ordered with a grin.

"Matthew! Mary!"

They hadn't noticed the arrival of anyone else, but Byron Hill was climbing down from a small carriage and making his way across the cemetery toward Matt.

"Byron!" Matt squinted against the late-afternoon sun as he watched the man approach. Then he smiled. "This is good timing. I thought you'd still be in St. Louis," he called as he moved quickly to cover the distance between them.

The two men shook hands and then hugged as if a simple handshake would not suffice. "I decided family was more important. I thought you and Mary might like to see a friendly face."

"Hello, Byron," Mary said when the two men reached her. "It's good to see you again."

"Welcome home," he said as he bent and kissed her hand.

Matt stood to one side, just next to the freshly erected tombstone marking his father's grave. "I appreciate your coming, Byron."

"I miss Jack and I like bringing your mother some flowers to brighten things a bit. Now that you're home, I expect my visits will be a bit less frequent."

"We'll talk about that," Matt said. "First, before I go up there, I need you to tell me exactly what happened. All I got was the letter, and after meeting Dover this afternoon I'm pretty sure I'll never get a straight story from him."

Byron smiled wryly and waited for Mary to sit on the low stone bench under the willow tree before joining her. Matt sat on the grass next to Mary. "You always did have your father's talent for sizing people up, Matt," he said. "Jack could take the measure of a man quicker than anybody I ever met."

"Too bad his skills failed him when it came to Louisa," Matt muttered.

"Now, Matthew, perhaps in the passing years Louisa has changed," Mary said, glancing at Byron.

"I'm afraid not, my dear." He sighed heavily and looked toward Jack Hubbard's grave. "Within a year after you left Jack realized the mistake he had made in choosing to believe Louisa over you. Louisa continued to . . . uh . . . shall we say, she continued in her restless ways."

"Mary knows the whole story," Matt said quietly. "There's no reason to sugarcoat things."

"Your father continued to indulge her shamelessly for a time. You know how he hated to be proved wrong."

Matt smiled. "The man was stubborn," he agreed.

"Well, his stubborness in this case was a tragedy. You see, he wanted very much to be in touch with you, but he was too proud to admit his error."

Matt gave the older man his full attention now. "But I wrote him . . . many times. I told him—"

"You wrote?" This was clearly news to Byron. "Matthew, he never received a single letter!"

Both of them glanced in the general direction of the house. "That witch," Matt murmured and stood up. "Mary, why don't you wait here with Byron? I just want to be sure she's gone before I bring you there."

Mary stood as well. "No," she said firmly. "You are not going to do this alone. If she's there, we'll face her together."

Byron smiled. "I do like this young lady, Matthew," he said. "Tell me, are all our Western women so loyal and strong-willed?"

"I don't know, but this one is," Matt muttered, shaking his head as Mary led the way back to their carriage.

CHAPTER
17

The trip to the house was carried out in silence. Matt stared straight ahead, his eyes fixed on the house as he drew closer and closer. Byron followed in his own carriage and gave an encouraging wave whenever Mary glanced back in his direction. For Mary's part, she appreciated the time to gather her thoughts. She hoped Louisa would be gone, but something told her the woman would not leave without a fight.

Matt reached over and covered her hand with his. "It'll be all right, darlin'," he said as he patted her hand, but he sounded as if he were trying to convince himself as much as Mary.

There was one bright spot, and that was that the moment Matthew's carriage was spotted by the house, servants gathered outside the front entrance to welcome him and to meet Mary.

"Lord, chile, you are a pretty one!" the housekeeper, Lucy, exclaimed when Matt introduced her to Mary. "Mr. Matthew, you always did have an eye for the ladies," she teased. "'Course, like most, this one could use some meat on her bones, but ol' Lucy will fix that. Got some sweet potato pie that I made fresh this morning. It's like I knew there was something special gonna happen today."

"Now, Lucy, you know that sweet potato pie of yours is my favorite," Matt teased. "My guess is that somebody in town might have mentioned we were on our way."

Lucy giggled. "Well, mebbe so. Awful glad to see you," she added more seriously and hugged Matthew hard.

Matthew hugged her back and frowned up at the second story window where a curtain moved slightly. "I take it Louisa is still here?"

"Oh, she's here all right," Lucy muttered. "Mooning around like she's all broke up over Mr. Jack's passing. But it's starting to wear on her, it is. She don't like being cooped up here all alone . . . makes her ornery as that ol' mule your daddy used to own, and twice as mean."

"Well, then, let's see if we can brighten her day," Matthew said with a wink at Lucy as he moved on to shake hands with her husband.

"Mary, this is Obediah, my father's driver and manservant."

"It's a pleasure to meet you, sir," Mary said with a smile.

"It's just Obie, ma'am, and we're all mighty pleased to meet you and to have Mr. Matthew home."

Matt let Obie and Lucy introduce the rest of the house servants, all new since he'd left. Mary liked the way Matt greeted each of them individually, taking a moment to ask about them in some personal way before moving on to the next.

"Well, Mary, shall we take a look inside?" Matt offered his arm and led Mary up the stairs to the large veranda where Franklin Dover hovered nervously by the front door. "Mr. Dover, I trust my wishes have been carried out," Matt commented as he brushed past the attorney without pausing for an answer.

Franklin Dover followed him into the house, babbling on about how distraught Louisa was and how he must understand that this was her loss as well as Matthew's.

"What I understand, Mr. Dover, is that that woman never loved my father, that my father gave her everything she ever wanted before she could even ask for it, and that in return she gave him nothing but betrayal and pain."

"But—" Dover sputtered a protest.

"And if you don't get her out of this house now, I shall be forced to take matters into my own hands—and believe me, Mr. Dover, you will not like the results."

Somehow Dover discovered a little backbone and for the first time all afternoon stood his ground with Matthew. "Mr. Hubbard, I believe I must make you aware that were it not for me, your father's estate would have gone in its entirety to Louisa, and furthermore—"

"Ha!" Byron scoffed, unable to hold his peace a moment longer. "What you are trying to say, Mr. Dover, is that Jack refused to agree to the deal you and Louisa cooked up. He had enough love for his boy here to try to make his peace with him, and the only will he would sign is one in which Matthew at least had the opportunity to return and claim his birthright."

Matthew simply raised his eyebrows in question and waited for Dover's response.

"Well, that is partially true. Jack could be a bit stubborn, and he—"

Matt grabbed the lapels of the lawyer's suit and hauled him up on his toes so that they were eye-to-eye. "My father is *Mr. Hubbard* to you, Dover, and I doubt seriously if you were ever on good enough terms for you to feel free to cast judgment on his character traits." He released the man as if he'd suddenly discovered that touching him in any way was completely disgusting.

Dover straightened his clothing and tried to rescue a modicum of his dignity. He looked at Matthew with barely concealed loathing. "I represented your father in this matter, and there are expenses," he whined.

"When you've finished the job, I trust you'll submit your bill," Matthew replied evenly. "But right now, unless you see to it that that woman is gone from this house by sundown, you are not going to see one red cent. Now, I would suggest that you get yourself upstairs to talk to your *real* client. Perhaps you can explain to her how you never thought I'd actually come forward to claim my heritage."

Dover started to retort, thought better of it, and headed for the stairs. Matthew followed him. "Oh, and Dover?"

The attorney glanced back.

"There's one consolation that should be a comfort to you . . . at least you had the honesty to follow my father's directions and attempt to make contact with me. Louisa would never have even tried."

Dover continued up the stairs without a look back.

"Let's get some air in here," Matt said brusquely.

Every drape in the house was drawn, and the air was cloying with the residue of perfume. Matt strode through the downstairs, ripping open every curtain and opening every door and window he could until the house was flooded with light and fresh air.

Mary could not believe her eyes as she followed him from room to room. It was clear that at one time the house had been a showplace, but no longer. Every room was crammed with furniture and artifacts. And while Mary was no expert, in her eyes most of what occupied every possible corner and surface of each room was downright tacky. She began to form a mental picture of Louisa based on the surroundings and found herself imagining someone who might pass for one of Lottie's girls in Harmony.

They could not help but hear the argument that raged above them. At one point something large, heavy, and breakable was hurled at the door. Seconds later Dover appeared at the top of the stairs and hurried down them, not even glancing at Matthew as he made a beeline for the front door. "I'll be on the veranda," he said as he rushed past them.

"Hello, Matthew."

Louisa stood at the top of the broad curved staircase and watched him. At least, Mary surmised this was Louisa. If so, she had been dead wrong in her expectations. The woman was spectacularly beautiful, slim and petite, but with a voluptuous figure that strained against the high-necked black taffeta gown she wore. The gown itself was something Samantha Spencer might have ordered from Paris or New York. Every detail spoke of high fashion and fine workmanship. Her hair was arranged conservatively in rolled curls and twists, but nothing could disguise the lush beauty of its sheen and flaming highlights.

She started down the stairs, one hand trailing lightly along the polished banister as she came. She moved with a grace that Mary envied, and she could not help thinking that Louisa must be a wonderful dance partner. Her expression was one of calm serenity, belying the scene that had just been played out behind her closed bedroom door.

Matthew stood at the foot of the steps and watched her come, his face registering no emotion. Byron stood near Mary and waited. Dover lurked within earshot just outside the front door, prepared to make his escape at the first sign of trouble.

"I'm so glad you came," Louisa continued in the hushed, breathless voice she had used earlier with a nod toward Mary. She smiled at Matt as if they shared a secret. "I always thought you would choose someone more . . . like us," she said and smiled at Matt as if they shared a secret. "I'll be happy to help you adjust, dear," she added, and this time she did look at Mary, her eyes sweeping over Mary's homemade gown and un-made-up face with slight amusement. Then she turned her full attention back to Matt.

A single tear rolled down her cheek, and she dabbed at it with the lace handkerchief she carried in one hand. "It's been very hard . . ." she began, choking on a sob, before making an obvious effort to compose herself and then continue. "Can you ever forgive me, Matthew? I was such a silly girl when you left, and I never forgave myself for what happened between Jack and you."

Mary saw Matt's fist clench at the mention of his father's name, but he remained standing there, impassively listening to her.

Louisa stood on the bottom step, making her eye-level with

Matt. She reached out and touched his cheek tenderly. "Dear Matthew," she whispered. "Jack loved you so."

Matt endured the touch without flinching. Mary, on the other hand, made a step forward, but was restrained by Byron's gentle hand at her shoulder.

"Where are my letters to my father, Louisa?" Matt asked, his voice low and dangerously quiet.

She blinked. Clearly this was not the question she had expected as an opener, and she was momentarily thrown off track. She smiled uncertainly. "I don't know what you mean." She crammed one small fist against her mouth with a horrified exclamation. "Oh, no. You wrote? And we never received . . . Jack never knew? Oh, Matthew . . . Matthew . . ."

She fell against him, sobbing against his chest.

Matt never lifted a finger. He simply stepped away from her, leaving her tottering there on the bottom step trying to regain her balance and her dignity. "Get out, Louisa," he ordered in the same low distant voice.

"Matthew!" she cried, reaching for him yet again.

Mary could not take another minute of this. She stepped forward. "If you touch my husband one more time, I'm going to show you just how people where I come from handle that sort of thing. Now, I believe you were asked to leave." She placed herself squarely between Louisa and Matt.

Louisa's carefully crafted performance completely disintegrated in the face of Mary's interference. "Why, you little hick," she began, but Matt's hand shot out and seized Louisa by the upper arm.

"Mr. Dover, I believe Louisa was on her way out," he said as he led a wincing Louisa to the door and handed her over to Dover with a look of such complete disgust that Mary wanted to shout with joy.

"I haven't finished packing," she protested. "Surely, you wouldn't deny me—"

Matt whirled back to face her. "Wouldn't I? This is not Jack Hubbard you are dealing with here, Louisa. You denied me the love of my father for years. I think you can wait a few hours for your property to be delivered. Believe me, the sooner it is out of my house, the happier I will be."

"Matthew!" she wailed hysterically and reached for him. "I love you—it was always you. We can work this out. Jack would want us to be together . . . he loved both of us so much."

Matthew came closer than he ever had or ever would again to striking a woman in that moment. If she said one more word, he would probably kill her with his bare hands.

Dover had the good sense to attempt to restrain Louisa. "Come along, my dear. Give him some time. I'm sure with time . . ." The lawyer could be heard consoling a sniveling Louisa as as they climbed into his waiting carriage and left.

Matt's attention now focused on Mary. He was still scowling. "If she had touched your husband one more time, you were going to what?" he asked, and then howled with laughter.

Mary started to laugh as well, and Byron joined in.

"I'm telling you, Matthew, you have found a rare diamond in this one," Byron said happily as he hugged Mary hard.

"Yessir, Mr. Matthew, you got yourself a good one here," Lucy agreed, coming from where she had been standing just under the stairway to witness the whole scene. "Why, she reminds me of your mama."

"Thank you, Lucy." Mary knew a compliment when she heard one.

"Well, come on and eat now," Lucy ordered. "I got it all ready and lots of it, so go sit yourselves down and let me feed you."

After supper Matthew, Byron, and Mary went into Jack Hubbard's study. It was the only room in the house that held no sign of Louisa. The three of them sifted through the piles of ledgers and papers. None of them was certain what their purpose was. Matt was reacquainting himself with his father. Byron was looking for documents that would be important to the future running of the multiple businesses. Mary was just trying to be helpful.

"When I was a boy," Matt recalled as the three of them took a break several hours later, "I used to come in here and play while my father conducted his business or worked on the ledgers. He'd take me over to the desk and show me how to enter the figures and add them, how to write receipts. Sometimes he would get down on the rug there with me, and we would play for hours."

"In the last years it became his refuge," Byron said sadly. "I always knew where to find him, and Louisa was happy enough to have him out of the way of her parties and . . . uh . . . other entertaining."

"Tell me about the day he died," Matt said.

Byron sighed. "He'd gone for a ride . . . some trouble at the sawmill. He was returning late at night. It had rained for several days, and the roads were mucky and slippery. The horse slipped and threw him. He hit his head. They found him the next day."

Matt's eyes widened at that. "The next day? You mean he didn't come home, and that . . . that woman did nothing?"

Byron looked at Matt for a long moment as if trying to decide whether or not to say more.

"I have to have all of it," Matt said.

Byron nodded. "I cannot say for certain, but when I was called here the following day, Mrs.—that is, Louisa—was in evening clothes. According to the servants, she had just arrived home from a ball of the night before."

Matt raked his hands through his hair and leaned back in the worn leather chair from which his father had built his empire. He swore softly, and Mary saw the tears start to pool on his lower lids. In an instant she was next to him.

"It's over, Matt," she said soothingly, pulling him against her, feeling his arms circling her as he cried against her skirt. She stroked Matt's hair and crooned words of comfort and sympathy to him.

Byron cleared his throat and picked up a pile of documents. "I'll be going now. I'll take these down to the office and file them with the rest."

Matt got up, and with Mary at his side followed Byron out to the veranda.

"I'll be back tomorrow," Byron called as he climbed into his buggy and snapped the reins.

"Yes, we need to talk," Matt agreed. "Good night, Byron."

"Good night, Matthew. Mary."

They stood on the porch watching the carriage roll down the long drive. Matthew hugged Mary with one arm wrapped protectively around her as he waved good-bye to Byron.

"Let's go to bed," Mary said. "You're exhausted, and there's still so much to be done. Let's start again in the morning."

Matt nodded and turned toward the lighted hallway. "We'll use my father's room. I'm quite sure it's untainted by Louisa's presence," he said bitterly.

They did not make love. They simply held each other through the long night and waited for the morning.

"Mary, come up here," Matt called from the attic the following morning. He'd become so agitated with having to deal with all of Louisa's changes in what had been a beautiful house that Mary had sent him off to go through the items stored in the attic. From what she had seen of Louisa, she was quite sure the woman wouldn't know how to find the attic, much less spend a single second up there.

"Mary!" Matt called again, louder and more excited than the first time.

"Coming," she called back, and gave Lucy an exasperated smile. "I'll be right back," she promised. "Don't try to move those heavy boxes yourself. You wait for me."

"I'll wait for the menfolk," Lucy answered firmly. "Lady like you got no business totin' and carryin'."

"Mary!" Matthew bellowed impatiently.

"I'm coming."

She climbed the steep attic stairs and paused a moment at the top to allow her eyes to adjust to the musky dimness. Matt was taking things out of a trunk, pausing after each item to examine it before placing it carefully aside and pulling out something else. Around him were five other trunks with the lids open and the contents strewn about.

"These are my mother's things," he said excitedly. "Her china and silver and linens and . . . even her personal things." He held up a silver locket from a velvet-lined jewel box.

"It's beautiful," she said softly.

"It's yours now," Matt answered, and placed the locket around her neck. When he had fastened it, he turned her so he could admire the necklace at her throat.

"It's so beautiful," Mary whispered, fingering the engraved locket. "It matches my wedding ring." She held up her finger to show him.

"Mother would have liked seeing you wear it," he said softly as he hugged her and kissed the top of her head. "She would like knowing everything she used will now be yours."

"Ours . . . and in years to come our children's," Mary replied as she glanced around at the treasures contained in the trunks.

"And our grandchildren's," Matt teased.

Mary laughed happily. "Oh, Matthew, we'll have a whole Hubbard dynasty running around."

"In our house in Harmony," he whispered as he caught her in his arms and lifted her to his kiss.

"Don't you want to stay here now that you've uncovered all this? We could make this house a home again, Matt."

Matt shook his head and kissed her again. "I want to go home to Harmony, Mrs. Hubbard—the sooner the better,"

It took nearly a month to settle the estate. Byron was a tremendous help, and Mary was delighted to meet his son Harvey, who was an old school friend of Matt's and who had married Matt's cousin Caroline.

At Byron's urging, the two couples often spent afternoons and evenings together. Harvey and Caroline had three children and a fourth on the way and were quickly outgrowing the house they had built on Byron's large plantation.

GETTING HITCHED

"Why don't you live at our house?" Matt asked one night.

"Oh, Matthew," Caroline said with a laugh, "we love spending time with you and Mary, but I really don't think you'd like to live with us and our four kids."

Matt smiled. "No. Mary and I will be going home to Kansas in a week or so. The house will have to be sold. I'd just as soon see you have it."

Harvey frowned. "Not every family made it through the war years as successfully as yours, Matt," he said. "Caroline and I are comfortable where we are."

"What if you and your father became my partners?" Matt asked.

"I'm not moving to Kansas," Caroline announced. "No offense, Mary."

"None taken," Mary assured her and wondered what on earth Matt was planning.

"Look, I'm going to need someone to manage everything. The estate is much bigger than I ever thought. Mary and I want to make our home in Harmony, but we also want to travel some. At least for the time being, it seems as if it would be foolish to just sell everything off. On the other hand, I don't want to leave the house unoccupied . . . and there's Lucy and Obediah and the others to consider. You'd be helping me out if you'd agree to help Byron manage the business and live here at the farm and run things for me."

Harvey considered the concept. "You're saying living in the house would be part of the bargain—part of the payment?"

"You'd be doing me a great favor, Harvey," Matt said.

Caroline could barely contain her excitement. "It is a beautiful house," she said. "It would be a shame to just—you know—let it sit here or sell it to someone who didn't appreciate it."

"There'd be a lot of room for the children to spread out," Mary suggested.

"Come on, Harve. You're the best farm manager around, and you know it. Say yes," Matt urged.

Harvey frowned. Caroline looked nervously from her husband to Matt and back again.

"I don't know," Harvey mused, stroking his bearded chin. "I always thought Bo Longworth was the best manager in these parts."

"Well, he's not," Matt said.

Harvey shrugged. "Then I guess I'm your man."

The four of them celebrated by going into town for an elegant dinner and a night at the theater. Mary wore a gown that had belonged to Matt's mother and had been carefully stored with all the other treasures in the attic. The way Matt looked at her and touched her possessively throughout the evening told her that in his eyes she was the most beautiful woman in the theater.

She and Lucy had worked miracles packing up all the gaudy things that Louisa had spread throughout the house, and rehanging family portraits and paintings that had been in the house when Matt was growing up. With each passing day the house came closer and closer to being the showplace it had been when Matt's parents had first built it.

Now Mary worked to make the house a home for Caroline and Harvey and their children. Meanwhile Matt and Obediah packed boxes and trunks and hauled them to the train station for shipment back to Harmony.

"You must take some of the furniture as well," Caroline insisted one afternoon when they were walking through the house so that Caroline could plan the placement of her own pieces when she moved in. "Harvey and I have so much furniture of our own . . . pieces from his mother and mine, plus our own. Please, Mary, you must need things for your new home."

Truthfully Mary had been fantasizing about some of the beautiful pieces from Matt's home occupying the rooms of the house on the hill in Harmony.

"Take the harpsichord," Caroline urged. "If you have girls, they'll learn to play. If you have boys . . . trust me . . . you'll learn to play in order to have a little solace. Nothing empties a room of wriggly little boys faster than the suggestion they might learn to play the harpsichord," Caroline assured her.

So the harpsichord was crated and shipped, followed by Jack's desk and three sets of bedroom furniture and the dining-room furniture and the rosewood love seat and side chairs Matt told her his mother had ordered from England.

"My father almost went through the roof when it came and he saw the bill," Matt told her. "But then Mama just smiled and went over to her desk and produced an envelope fat with money she had saved from her household accounts to pay for the set."

Mary laughed. She wished she had had the opportunity to know her mother-in-law. "Could I take the desk, too?" she asked shyly.

"Darlin', we'll ship the whole damned house if that pleases you," Matt announced and swung her up into his arms. "Because I love you, and whatever makes you happy pleases me."

"The desk will be the last piece," Mary said.

"And the chair that matches," Matt insisted.

"Well, all right."

"And the side table . . . it matches the love seat."

"Matthew," Mary said warningly, but his happiness was infectious. Since the day he had unpacked his mother's things, Matt had relaxed and enjoyed being back in this place where he had known so much happiness.

"And the cradle!" Matt declared. "How could we forget the cradle? Sorry, little fella," he crooned as he patted Mary's stomach. "Your old man sometimes forgets you're in there."

"Matthew, there is no sign that—"

"Shhh," Matt instructed. "The little guy is sleeping," he whispered.

"You are impossible." Mary laughed. "Now, put me down."

"And you are beautiful," Matt answered, serious now as he bent to kiss her. "I love you, Mary." He kissed her again. "You know, you're looking a bit tired. Why don't we go upstairs and lie down for a while?"

"What will people think?" Mary protested as he carried her up the stairs.

"The men will be green with envy, and the women will wonder what sort of spell you've cast over me. Next question."

"But, Matthew, it's the middle of the morning."

"Good, that still leaves the afternoon and the evening to get tired and do the whole thing all over again." He strode into their room and shut the door firmly by kicking it with his foot. As he kissed her he allowed her to slide the length of him until she was standing, then he started to undress her.

"I could use a little help here," he muttered as his fingers fumbled with the tiny row of pearl buttons on her dress.

"Of course, allow me," she said with an impish grin, but instead of opening the buttons on her dress, she started opening the ones on his shirt. "I'll race you to see who can get who undressed faster," she whispered as she stood on tiptoe and traced the circle of his ear with her tongue.

"You play dirty," he argued as a shiver of desire raced through him.

"I had a good teacher," Mary replied as she spread the front of his shirt and pressed her palms over his bare chest.

"Ma! Ma!!!" Harry screamed as he burst through the back door of the store and raced to the front counter where his mother was filling an order for Maisie and Minnie. All three women scowled at his outburst and waited.

"Well?" Minnie demanded.

"Let the lad catch his breath, Minnie," Maisie argued.

Harry waved a telegram at this mother. "Mary," he managed with a wide grin.

Lillie snatched the telegram from her son's hand and read it quickly. Then she let out her own squeal of delight to the astonishment of Maisie and Minnie. "They're coming home," she announced. "Harry, go tell your father. Mary's coming home." Lillie snatched off her apron and nervously fingered her hair.

"Well, it's not likely they'll be here till tomorrow," Maisie noted wryly. "We still only have one westbound train a week as far as I know."

"I know, but heavens, there's so much to do. I have to go out to their house and see to its finishing. I have to get the boys to move Mary's bedroom set over there. And, heavens, we need to stock the larder and—"

"With all that fancy furniture Matthew had shipped from Memphis, I can't imagine what Mary would want with that old bedroom set," Maisie said.

"She'll want something from her family as well," Lillie replied somewhat huffily. "She'll want her own things mixed in with his, you know. Now, I have to see that everything is in order. Oh, dear, the dusting and the cleaning. Oh, dear."

"We could help," Minnie said.

Maisie looked at her sister, as startled as Minnie that for once they were in agreement. "Well, of course, we can help, Minnie. What did you think we were going to do? Come along, and let's alert the others."

Minnie smiled happily. "You go along, Lillie. Maisie and I will handle everything here."

By nightfall, what seemed like the entire town had assembled at Mary and Matt's new house. Carefully the women unpacked the trunks Mary had sent from Memphis with the note that these contained Matt's mother's household and personal items.

"Oh my," Samantha Spencer said in an awestruck voice as she unearthed a beautiful hand-painted fan. The other women quickly gathered round her to see what else the trunk might hold.

"Look at this," Faith cried as she carefully unwrapped the beautiful silver dresser set.

Libby grinned. "Oh, this is such fun. Leave it to Mary to give us the pleasure of opening all these wonderful treasures."

"Ladies, at this rate it's going to take you all night, and the trunks downstairs still need unpacking," Kincaid teased.

"But, Papa, look," Amanda squealed as she held up a pair of white satin slippers.

Kincaid rolled his eyes and headed back downstairs. "I'd say they'll be a while, Miz Taylor. Maybe you and Miz Arnold had better start unpacking those dishes. I'll go see if I can give Jake and Joseph a hand uncrating that harpsichord."

Later that night James Taylor held Lillie in his arms as they lay together in the bed where Lillie had given birth to each of their children.

"It'll be good to have Mary home," he said.

"You've missed her." Lillie acknowledged his special love for this daughter.

"And Matt," James added. "He's a fine man and he'll make her a good husband."

Lillie frowned. "So, you think we did the right thing . . . ? I mean, making them go ahead and get married?"

"Of course." But James's hearty reply did not fool Lillie.

"You're just as worried as I am," she accused him gently. "I just wish I could tell something from her letters. But they've been so . . . dry."

James chuckled. "You mean you didn't like the way every paragraph ended with 'I'll tell you all about it when we get home'?"

"There were times I thought they might not be coming home at all," Lillie admitted. "I mean, they've been gone over a month now, and every time I asked when to expect them, Mary never answered . . . just kept going on about how much there was to do there . . . operas and parties and riverboats."

"But they are coming home," James whispered. "They'll be here tomorrow, and you have that big welcome party to put on. So why don't you close those beautiful eyes and get some rest?"

Lillie nodded and snuggled more firmly against James. "I hope Fred Winchester doesn't forget the cider. The man has a mind like a sieve sometimes."

"I'm sure you can count on Fred," James said soothingly. "He does love a good party, and my Lillie throws the best parties in the country."

* * *

GETTING HITCHED

"Can you see it, Harry?" Joe stood on the depot platform with most of the rest of the population of Harmony and looked up at the boy perched high in the cottonwood tree.

"Maybe," Harry called back, and then added excitedly, "Yeah! I see the train. I see it!"

A communal whoop went up, and Zeke tried a few notes on his fiddle.

"Oh dear, perhaps they would have preferred something more subdued," Lillie fretted.

"From this town?" Cord Spencer laughed.

"Mary will be touched," Abby Lee said comfortingly and patted Lillie's arm.

Then they could hear the train clearly, coming closer and closer.

When it finally chugged into the station, everyone squinted at the windows of the passenger car, hoping for the first glimpse of Mary and Matt.

"They're back here!" Harry called excitedly. "Kissing and stuff." He gave a rueful glance at the sky.

They were "kissing and stuff" all right.

"They do seem quite oblivious to their surroundings, don't they?" Fred Winchester noticed as he joined everyone in crowding around the passenger car and staring through the window.

"Mary Taylor!" Maisie shouted and banged her fist on the window.

"Hubbard," Minnie corrected.

Mary and Matt broke apart and gazed dreamily out at the crowd. Then they realized what they were seeing and started to laugh. The townspeople saw Matt stand up and offer his hand to Mary as the two of them walked toward the exit.

As a unit the crowd changed positions to gather around the exit. When Mary and Matt emerged, Zeke struck up a jig, and everyone began to applaud and shout their welcomes.

The minute they stepped off the train, Matt and Mary were surrounded. It seemed as if everyone wanted to hug them and tell them the latest news and ask questions.

Finally Mary saw her parents waiting quietly on the edge of the crowd. She took Matt's hand and pulled him in that direction. When he realized her destination, Matt moved he through the crowd as if he were parting water.

"Welcome home, daughter," James said in a choked voice and then grabbed Mary in a loving embrace.

Then Lillie was hugging Matt and Matt was hugging James and Mary was crying and laughing with her mother, and there wasn't a dry eye in the crowd.

"Well, heavens, let's don't stand around here all day," Lillie ordered in something more like her usual manner. "Let's get these newlyweds home."

"And in bed," Travis teased, and the crowd roared it delight.

A procession was formed, led by Matt and Mary riding in a carriage decorated by Harry and pulled by Traveler. The other followed in a bizarre parade of buckboards and carriages and horses.

The minute she saw the house Mary could not sit a minute longer. She stood up in the carriage, depending on Matt to hold on to her so she wouldn't lose her balance as Jake maneuvered the carriage up to the house.

"Oh, it's so beautiful!" she cried. "Matthew, look. It's the most beautiful house!"

Inside, the younger women excitedly led Mary and Matt on a tour. "We tried to arrange things the way we thought you might like," Abby Lee reported shyly. "Of course, you can change it all around if you want to."

"I wouldn't change a thing," Mary said and hugged her friend. "And you must come often—all of you. Matt and I want the house to be filled with people all the time."

"Well, maybe not *all* the time," Matt said wryly, and everybody laughed as Mary blushed scarlet.

Lillie noticed how Mary and Matt could not seem to stop touching each other. Everything was shared. When Matt was drawn into a conversation that did not for the moment include Mary, he would listen with a polite smile, but his eyes would follow Mary. And she sought the haven of Matt's eyes from across the room where she was surrounded by all her new things and her old friends.

"See? We did the right thing, Lil," James said softly as he, too, watched Matt and Mary.

"Shall we dine?" Fred Winchester announced from the entrance to the dining room.

"I don't know about dining, but I sure could eat," Harry clamored, and made a beeline for the table laden with food.

The evening passed quickly with food and cider and dancing and catching up.

"Matthew sold his home," Maisie reported to Bea and Minnie as the three women gathered on the veranda to watch the dancing. "Mary told Lillie that they considered this their home now . . . always would."

"What about his father's business down there?" Minnie asked.

"Some friend of his father's is running it. I think he was a partner or something. Anyway, he'll send Matthew his share."

The three women looked at Matt and Mary as they whirled happily around the yard to the lively beat of Zeke's waltz.

"And to think she ordered him through the mail," Bea said almost to herself.

Maisie grinned. "Maybe we old biddies should take a lesson, huh?"

"Maisie!" Minnie frowned severely at the very idea of such nonsense.

"Still, if a woman could get hitched on her own terms . . ." Bea mused.

All three women watched as Matthew Hubbard bent to kiss Mary while they were still dancing. "Like Mary," they whispered in unison.

If you enjoyed this book, take advantage of this special offer. Subscribe now and...

Get a Historical

No Obligation

If you enjoy reading the very best in historical romantic fiction...romances that set back the hands of time to those bygone days with strong virile heros and passionate heroines ...then you'll want to subscribe to the True Value Historical Romance Home Subscription Service. Now that you have read one of the best historical romances around today, we're sure you'll want more of the same fiery passion, intimate romance and historical settings that set these books apart from all others.

Each month the editors of True Value select the four *very best* novels from America's leading publishers of romantic fiction. We have made arrangements for you to preview them in your home *Free* for 10 days. And with the first four books you receive, we'll send you a FREE book as our introductory gift. No Obligation!

FREE HOME DELIVERY

We will send you the four best and newest historical romances as soon as they are published to preview FREE for 10 days (in many cases you may even get them before they arrive in the book stores). If for any reason you decide not to keep them, just return them and owe nothing. But if you like them as much as we think you will, you'll pay just $4.00 each and save at *least* $.50 each off the cover price. (Your savings are *guaranteed* to be at least $2.00 each month.) There is NO postage and handling—or other hidden charges. There are no minimum number of books to buy and you may cancel at any time.

FREE
Romance
(a $4.50 value)

**Send in the Coupon
Below**

To get your FREE historical
romance and start saving, fill out
the coupon below and mail it today.
As soon as we receive it we'll send
you your FREE Book along with
your first month's selections.
